Chapter 1

The sorrel horse slowly navigated the moonlit trail along the Verde River, the lights of Clarkdale to the right and dark desert to the left. Gently pulling the lead rope attached to the pack horse, the rider urged him along. "C'mon Wesley, we'll be done in a bit."

A hill swelled to their left, lights glowing in the deserted National Park Service (NPS) residential buildings. Farther ahead and slightly higher, nightlights glowed in the Tuzigoot National Monument visitor center windows. Beyond that, a darkened hill rose where ancient ruins had been excavated, an outcropping in the desert above the river that had been inhabited by ancient Native tribes who had deserted the ruins more than a millennium before.

The trail continued along the Verde River, but the rider tapped his reins against the horse's neck. "We're taking the Marsh Trail here, Jess." The horse hesitated until a gentle nudge from the rider's spurs signaled that he was serious about going off the familiar trail and turning away from the river. They continued on, the trail narrowing to a muddy path through cattails and marsh grass until it ended overlooking a small pond.

Easing off his horse, the cowboy wrapped the reins on the saddle horn and patted the horse's neck. "Steady Jess, I'll be back in a minute." A frog chorus croaked around them and something snuck past, rustling the dried cattails.

The cowboy walked to the pack horse and repeated the reassuring pat and words, then untied the body draped across the saddle. Pressing himself against the horse, he shifted the man's body onto his shoulder. Then he stepped back, pulling the man's hips and legs off the pack horse. Staggering under the literal dead weight, he turned and took a few steps to the edge of the cattails where he leaned forward and dumped the body into the weeds. He took off his Stetson and wiped his brow with a bandana. "I should've shot you here instead of at the ranch."

Blood on the saddle reflected the moonlight and the cowboy stared at it with disgust. "Shit. You're dead. Why are you still bleeding?" He went back to the corpse, unsnapped the victim's shirt and used it to wipe off the horse and saddle. Then he looked at his own shirt and vest, sweaty from the exertion of moving the body, and realized they too, were bloody.

Dead End Trail

Fletcher book 11

Dean L. Hovey

Print ISBNs
Amazon Print 9780228622383
LSI Print 9780228622390
B&N Print 9780228622406
Ingram Spark 9780228627371

This book is a work of fiction, a product of the author's imagination. Any resemblance to actual events, people, or locations is coincidental and unintended. Some actual locations are used fictionally.

Acknowledgements

I owe much to my legion of subject matter experts, beta readers, proofreaders, an editor, a cover designer, and my publisher who all collaborate with me to make these books a reality. Julie puts up with my hours on the computer and my distant stare as the characters reveal themselves and the plot to me. Because of the horse-related storyline, Deanna Wilson dove into the expanded role of early proofreader, often reading and critiquing a few out-of-context pages at a time to correct the equine jargon and suggesting a key clue. US Park Service Ranger Owen Clark helped with the park geography. Fran Brozo, Mike Westfall, Clem MacIlravie, and Brian Johnson offer plot critique and are my muses when I've written myself into a corner. Anne Flagge and Natalie Lund proofread and correct my typos and grammatical errors. Jude Pittman, of BWL Publishing, has been marvelously supportive in getting my books into the hands of my readers. Most of all, thanks to you, the readers who provide me with feedback, plot ideas, and the energy to write.

Dedication

To Deanna and Kinsley Wilson, the horse whisperers

"Lord if we should stumble, my horse and I, lift him up first because he's carried me through heaven and hell."
-Author unknown

"It has been said, and truly, that everything in the desert either stings, stabs, stinks, or sticks."
-Edward Abbey, "The Journey Home.

The horse snorted, reacting to the smell of blood and leaking body fluids. Wesley shifted his feet and edged away from the body, his unease affecting Jess, who also shifted nervously. "Easy, boy," the cowboy reached out and patted the horse's neck, "the hard part is over. We're going home."

Chapter 2

I sat staring at my laptop, trying to draft a succinct recap of the events in Big Cypress National Preserve in the NPS database. The investigation into the disappearance of two surveyors had been an unpleasant diversion from what my wife, Jill, had planned as a brief vacation on the Florida Gulf Coast. Our plans had been interrupted by a call asking for our assistance with the investigation. It turned into a messy mix of friction between local residents and activities on the preserve. The ending had been the unpleasant fodder of nightmares.

A knock on my door frame startled me back to reality. Matt Mattson, the superintendent of Padre Island National Seashore and my administrative boss, stepped into the office and dropped into my guest chair. "Am I interrupting the contemplation of your navel?"

"No," I answered, pushing the laptop aside. "I was trying to put the mess in Florida into polite NPS lingo for my closing report."

"That's easy enough. You found the missing surveyors and came home."

Blowing out a breath, I glanced at the computer. "That would gloss over them being dead, the reason they were killed, then Jill and me digging our own graves."

Matt wrinkled his nose. "Leave the details to the local sheriff and newspapers. Our bosses know what happened—they don't need the details in a report that might sound...messy. They like reports that are clean and brief."

"But..."

"Doug, you're not a cop anymore. You're an NPS investigator. You investigated a disappearance and found the missing people. Write a synopsis and leave it at that."

"Fine. I'll write up a couple paragraphs and submit it." I pulled the laptop in front of myself, expecting Matt to leave. "Is there something else?"

"Jill told Mandy she wanted to go back to Arizona to see your godson."

"Yeah, I think they're planning a christening ceremony at Liz and Jamie's church. There's no date set."

"See if they can set it up for next week while you're at Tuzigoot National Monument."

"Huh?"

"If you'd read your email rather than daydreaming, you would've seen the request for your assistance with an Arizona murder investigation."

I opened my Park Service email. "A hiker found a dead guy in a swamp? I didn't think Arizona had swamps."

Matt leaned back. "They'll fill you in when you get there. I got a follow-up call from Superintendent Goins. It appears the victim was shot elsewhere and dumped on Park Service property. You and Jill will be coordinating with the Yavapai County Sheriff's Department."

"We won't be able to leave until Jill completes her report."

Pointing at the computer, Mattson responded, "Her report was submitted the day after you returned. You could cut and paste her words into your report."

I went back to the NPS reporting site and searched for Jill Fletcher. "Assisted county and state authorities with investigation and apprehension of suspects in a kidnapping from Big Cypress National Preserve." I looked at Matt. "That's it? Nothing about the Cuban asylum seekers or the shooting?"

"That's all you need. The NPS people who need to know were briefed on the details. They know what you and Jill did. The details are in your files, along with the letter of thanks from the sheriff."

"When are you going to tell Jill we're going to Arizona?"

"She and Mandy are buying shrimp and margaritas for a bon voyage party." Matt stood. "You and Jill should come over about five. I'll have beer for us."

"When are we leaving and who's making the reservations?"

"You're booked on Phoenix flights tomorrow morning."

Matt pulled a Post-it note out of his pocket and handed it to me. "Here are the phone numbers for the superintendent in charge of Tuzigoot and Montezuma's Castle, and for the Yavapai cop assigned to the investigation. They're expecting your call."

"Where exactly is Tuzigoot National Monument?"

"The superintendent said it's about two hours from the Phoenix airport. Go north on I-17 and take the Cottonwood exit west."

"Is there a decent hotel in the area?"

Matt stopped at the door and looked back with a grin. "You're staying in on-site housing. They've got guest rooms that used to be the rangers' residence."

"I don't suppose they've got a pool and room service."

Matt snorted. "You may have to buy your own bedding in town. I heard mice have been a problem."

"You're joking," I said to the empty doorway.

After cutting and pasting Jill's report and hitting send, I shut down my laptop, locked it in the file cabinet, and entered the phone numbers from the Post-it note into my phone. Then I called the Yavapai County cop.

"Henderson."

"This is Doug Fletcher, an investigator from the Park Service. I've been assigned to assist with your investigation of the Tuzigoot murder victim."

"Hang on, Fletcher. Give me a second to park." A moment later he was back. "I heard the Park Service was sending two investigators, you and your partner."

"We're flying out of Texas tomorrow morning. I assume we'll be in the area sometime tomorrow night. Tell me about the murder."

"A hiker found the victim on an obscure trail. The coroner says the guy had a single gunshot wound to the chest and had probably been dead three or four days before he was found, not that the vultures left a lot to find. There's no evidence the crime was committed where the body was found, so we're assuming he was killed somewhere else and dumped in Tuzigoot."

"You said an obscure trail. How obscure?"

"It's not out of sight, but it's unused. There are human footprints and hoof prints, but they could've been left any time in the past thirteen days since our last rain."

"Damn inconsiderate of the killers not to timestamp their prints for us."

Henderson chuckled. "If you haven't made hotel reservations, I'd suggest the casino hotel on I-17. It's a few miles out of town, but the food's good and the rooms are nice. There are a couple places in Cottonwood, but the town is pretty quiet. They roll up the streets at nine o'clock."

"Um, the Park Service has us staying in the residential quarters at Tuzigoot National Monument."

"You're shitting me. They lock the gates at 4:45. If you're bedding down there, you'd better bring a kerosene lantern, a deck of cards, and a cribbage board."

"I assumed they'd have electricity."

Henderson chuckled. "Yeah, there are lights. I don't recall anyone staying there. There are offices used by the archaeologists and naturalists, but nobody lives there anymore. If it was me, I'd tell the Park Service to stuff it, and I'd book a hotel even if I had to pay for it out of my own pocket." He paused. "There's a quaint hotel over a tavern in old Cottonwood. I've heard it's nice and inexpensive. I don't know what the Park Service rules are for room sharing, but I doubt the tavern has rooms with two beds."

"That's not an issue. My partner is my wife."

There was a pause. "I'm sure the tavern hears that often, from Mr. and Mrs. Smith."

"Seriously, I'm married to my partner. We're Doug and Jill Fletcher."

"Huh. That's a first."

"A room over a bar doesn't sound particularly restful."

"I did mention the part about the streets rolling up at nine o'clock, right? I don't think there's been a police call to any of the Cottonwood wine tasting rooms or bars in as long as I can remember."

"I think you've solved our motel problem. We won't arrive until after the park closes and the gates are locked. Once our suitcases get unpacked, we may not want to relocate." I scribbled a note about the casino and tavern hotels.

Henderson paused. "Hey, I've got to interview combatants in a domestic dispute in a couple minutes. Give me a call when you arrive in town."

After making a one-night reservation at the casino hotel, I locked my office and drove to our rental townhouse in Port Aransas. Jill's pickup was parked across from the townhouse, and the lights were on.

"Honey, I'm home!" I called from the entryway as I removed my holster from my belt and set it on the closet shelf.

Jill emerged from the kitchen wearing khaki shorts, a loose-fitting golf shirt, and sandals. "Who do you think you are, Ward Cleaver? She rolled her eyes and shook her head. "'Honey, I'm home.' You make it sound like I should've been cooking all day and ironing your shirts."

I pecked her on the cheek. "What do you know about Tuzigoot?"

"I've been to the visitor center and seen the artifacts on display, but that's the limit of my exposure there. Have you spoken to the superintendent?"

I started up the stairs. "I spoke with the Yavapai County Investigator. He said the victim was found on a remote trail. He'd been shot three or four days before a hiker found his body."

"That's about all I got from reading the request for assistance."

I changed into a pair of shorts. "The cop I spoke with suggested we come up with a reason not to stay in the park residence. They lock the gates at 4:45 and he said it was rustic and unused."

Digging in the closet, Jill pulled out a Hawaiian shirt. "Most of the Park Service residences aren't rustic. They're more utilitarian—not fancy, but functional."

"Since we're probably arriving after the gates are locked, I made a reservation at the casino hotel on I-17. It's only a half hour from the park."

"I'm sure someone would be happy to unlock the gates for us and provide us with a key."

"Matt suggested we buy bedding in town because there may be a vermin problem."

"We won't need bedding. I'm sure they've kept the bedding in mouse-proof containers. The Park Service is accustomed to dealing with mice in the residences."

"Mice carry diseases and shit all over the place. Let's just plan to stay outside the park at some nice hotel with a pool and restaurant."

Jill smiled. "You're going to wuss out because of a couple mice?"

"It's not the mice. I prefer staying in a place with a few more amenities than a former ranger's house inside an uninhabited park. Besides, you learn things from hanging around the restaurants and bars in town that we won't hear if we're hiding inside a deserted park building."

"It's the rattlesnakes and scorpions, isn't it?"

My head snapped around. "What snakes and scorpions?"

"The park is set in the desert. There'll be the usual assortment of critters living there. It'll be like when we were sleeping under the stars in Wupatki after the flash flood."

"The Arizona cop mentioned one other thing that wasn't in the Park Service email. A horse had been on the trail where they found the body. They haven't had rain in a couple weeks, so it's impossible to say when the prints were made, but it's a consideration." I slipped on the bright-colored shirt and buttoned it. "Matt said we should be there at five. We should leave."

Jill continued to sit on the bed. "Mandy won't put the shrimp on until we get there, and the margaritas won't go bad."

"Uh oh. What's the matter?"

"I spoke with Liz, and she's really excited about us coming for the baptism. I'm feeling…uneasy about being a godmother. I mean, I'm excited, but I'm not sure what role we're supposed to play in this child's life."

I put out my hands and pulled her up. "It'll all be defined as we go along. My godparents visited a couple times a year and sent me birthday and Christmas presents. My godfather took me to a few Minnesota Twins games after my dad died, and he showed me how to tie a hook on a fishing line. It wasn't a big deal, but I knew he was there for me."

"But we're here. Liz, Jamie, and baby Noah are in Arizona. We won't be around more than a couple times a year. I'm worried."

Pulling her into a hug, I kissed the top of her head. "It'll be fine. We'll play it by ear."

"What if something happens to Liz and Jamie? Will we have to adopt the baby?"

"I'm sure their families would step forward. Our role is symbolic."

Jill blew out a breath. "You're sure?"

I pushed her toward the door. "If you don't believe me, ask Mandy. She's the maven of all things social. I'm sure being a godparent was something covered in debutante training."

Jill went down the stairs ahead of me. "Okay, now I know you're lying. Debutante training did *not* cover being a godparent."

"Debutante training must've covered every social situation. If there isn't a rule, I'm sure Mandy will make up the correct answer."

Stopping at the door, Jill put her hands on her hips. "Mandy doesn't make up the rules."

Nudging Jill ahead, I pulled the door closed behind me. "Tell me the rule about the direction of toilet paper dispensing isn't something she made up."

"Think about it, Doug. It makes sense for the paper to come over the top instead of dangling down from the back."

"And Mandy didn't make up the saying, 'Bangs, not a mullet?'"

Jill got into my Toyota. "She might've used that to illustrate the situation. It was hard to express it in a way that an unschooled person like you could understand."

After starting the engine, I pulled out of the parking spot. "I understood what she was saying. I just don't understand the point. It's a 50:50 thing, depending on how it comes out of the package."

"You're hopeless. Let's go back to discussing our godson."

"There's no point," I replied. "You already said that Mandy would explain our godparent responsibilities"

* * *

Matt opened the door before we got to the steps. Door monitoring was something covered in debutante training. Mandy always had Matt stationed at the door minutes before our arrival so he could watch us park, then magically open the door just before we crossed the sidewalk. Matt explained it to me one night when we "menfolk" were sitting outside drinking beer while Jill and Mandy cleared the table and washed the dishes. He claimed the door opening topic was right up there with arranging silverware and knowing which fork to use for salad or dessert.

The aroma of cooking sausage, sweet corn, and potatoes engulfed us as we stepped up to the door. Jill hugged Matt, "You have the sweetest wife in the whole world."

Matt laughed as he guided me into their house. "I know. She reminds me daily."

Mandy, carefully made up and wearing a summery dress, swept past Matt and hugged me, not touching anything but our cheeks and shoulders. "Did they teach you to hug without touching each other's bodies in debutante training?" I asked.

Mandy batted her eyes at me. "You wouldn't want to give the boys ideas, would you?"

"Boys have ideas whether your bodies touch or not," I replied.

"True, but nice girls don't offer encouragement." Mandy gestured toward the dining room. "Matt, serve beverages while I put the shrimp on."

The ladies prepped supper while Matt opened beer and poured margaritas. Five minutes later, a steaming bowl of Texas shrimp boil was delivered to the table, and we took our seats. We dove into the family-style dinner with gusto. Despite this being a bon voyage party, the topic of our Arizona trip never came up. Instead, we laughed at Mandy's stories about her debutante indoctrination.

I looked at Matt as I peeled a shrimp. "Did Mandy let you kiss her on your first date?"

Matt was about to reply when Mandy held up her hand. "Gentlemen don't discuss what happens on, or after, a date."

We laughed and Jill explained, "In my rural school *everyone* talked about what happened on every date. The guys often embellished the story in the retelling, ruining reputations, and leading the nerds to believe they were the only virgins in the school."

Shaking her head, Mandy explained, "Every girl is a virgin until her wedding night, regardless of what rumors have been spread."

The three of them looked at me, suggesting it was my time to share. "I've got nothing to add."

Wiping his fingers on a paper napkin, Matt shook his head. "Uh uh, Fletcher. Fess up."

"Teenage boys are idiots. Some grow up into upright citizens, like Matt and me. Others act like stupid teenagers their whole lives."

Mandy nodded and pushed herself back from the table. "Enough philosophy! Who's got room for pecan pie á la mode?"

Chapter 3

Mandy drove us to the airport at 6:30 the next morning. Her eyes were bloodshot, but her indomitable spirit wasn't dampened by the early hour or her hangover. We got extra hugs when she dropped us outside the ticket counter.

We checked a bag each, then showed our credentials to the TSA people to bypass the metal detectors with our firearms. The coffee kiosk line near the gate was long. Standing behind me, a woman with red hair and a thick Texas twang was having a very emphatic phone discussion with a co-worker. Seeing me glaring at her as the volume of her voice rose, the woman put her hand over the phone and informed me she was having a private conversation.

"Ma'am, if you want a private discussion, I suggest you get out of line and find a quiet alcove. You are NOT having a private conversation in the Starbucks line with twenty other people."

She was about to tee off on me until I slid my nylon windbreaker back, exposing my badge. She covered the phone and made some unintelligible parting comments, then stuffed the phone into her tote. I turned away, but she wasn't through. "That was extremely rude. I'd like to have your badge number and the name of your immediate superior."

Jill's hand on my arm cut my response short. "Here's my business card," she said with a smile. "Our boss is the Secretary of the Interior. I'd give you his direct number, but his administrative assistant usually deals with complaints."

Somehow, Jill soothes many confrontations while I tend to escalate them. Fingering Jill's card, the woman read it, then looked up. "You're a U.S. Park Service investigator? I didn't even know that was a thing. What kind of things do you investigate?"

"A body was found in a remote part of Tuzigoot National Monument. We've been dispatched to assist the local law enforcement agencies with their investigation."

Nodding, the woman was about to continue the conversation when Jill and I got to the front of the line. We ordered large black coffees. I held out my debit card, but the redhead edged me aside and handed the clerk a twenty. "I'm paying for their coffee."

The young Hispanic Starbucks' clerk took the twenty, ignoring my debit card and

Jill's protest. I stepped to the end of the counter while Jill explained that federal employees were not allowed to accept gifts. The conversation continued as Jill and the woman approached me with paper cups.

I reached for one of the cups the woman was carrying, and she pulled it back. "Let's go over to the seashell display." Jill's look told me the cost of the coffee was going to be extracted from us many times over before we escaped from this woman.

Bracing her tote between her knee and the wall, the woman handed us two business cards. "I'm Geraldine Holland. I'm a tech rep for a company that creates geological software used by hydrologists to evaluate water tables. We're overwhelmed with requests across the Southwest as developers seek water sources to supply the communities they want to build. Counties and states hire us to estimate how much water is available in the aquifers, and how fast it is being used and replenished. I build a computer model with all the variables so they can see how long the water will last if they continue their current or planned use. I can adjust the assumptions based on possible changes in irrigation and urban use so they can make informed, rational decisions about balancing development and agriculture."

"Do the counties and states act on your modeling?"

Smiling, Geraldine shook her head. "Not so far, but the modeling we've done in the past few years is spot on, and some of the states are taking notice."

"We have water issues in western South Dakota," Jill said, "so I get it."

"A lot of the world is starting to catch on and they're moving to drip irrigation for high water-use crops, like grapes and fruit. But that costs money compared to what people see as 'free' water."

"Like all the golf courses in Arizona," I said.

Geraldine shrugged and leaned close. "That's very visible, but the golf course water use is a single digit percentage of the total water consumption in southern Arizona. A lot of the farmers grow flowers, cotton, berries, and other high water-use crops by flooding the fields from open ditches. The crops get some benefit from the flooding, but more than half just evaporates."

The gate agent made a pre-boarding announcement for our flight. "Very interesting," I said, "but our flight is about to leave."

Slipping her tote strap over her shoulder without spilling her coffee, Geraldine shook our hands. "The Army Corps of Engineers is walking a fine line, trying to keep enough water in the Colorado River to fill reservoirs, generate power, and provide recreational opportunities. The Park Service is one of the constituents. We can help model the water use to assist with that."

Jill held up Geraldine's card. "I'll pass this along. Maybe we can help generate some interest in your computer modeling."

Leaning close to Jill as we walked away, I asked, "Will that really happen?"

"Not unless they work for free."

* * *

After uneventful flights, we were waiting for our bags in Phoenix when a familiar voice whispered in my ear, "Need a ride, cowboy?"

I was greeted by Jamie Ballard's smiling, sunburned face. Then he pulled me into a bear hug. "Why are you in Phoenix?" I asked.

Nodding to my left he said, "Liz decided she wanted to go for a drive." Jamie's wife Liz, had a baby bundled in her arms. Jill peeled back a bit of blanket.

"Phoenix is a long joy ride from Flagstaff."

"There's nothing else going on." Glancing at the baby, then back to me he added, "I think the only time Noah sleeps is in the car. It was a peaceful ride."

The baby had Jill and Liz distracted, so Jamie helped me pull our bags off the carousel. "I've got a car rented, and we're planning to spend the night at the casino hotel on I-17."

"Change of plans. We're driving you to the casino, and there'll be a Park Service pickup there for your use. We're planning to spend a couple days at the hotel, too. Liz thought it'd be fun to have someone cook for her and be lazy."

"She doesn't like your cooking?"

Jamie tilted his head and looked at me like I should know the answer. "Do you remember how much I enjoyed the dehydrated entrees Liz prepared when we were hiking in Wupatki? Well, that's because they were better than my cooking."

"They were terrible."

With the baby now in Jill's arms, she and Liz joined us. "Yes," Liz said. "They were terrible. But they're still better than Jamie's cooking. His repertoire includes gourmet meals like canned chili, and hot dogs warmed in canned baked beans."

"Hey, I offered to make rabbit on a spit roasted over an open fire."

Rolling her eyes, Liz looked at Jill. "I've had his rabbit on a spit, and the canned chili was better. I think the rabbit hair and shot pellets in the meat put me off."

Noah started fussing and Jill handed him back to Liz like he was a hot potato. "Sorry, I don't do crying babies."

Jamie shook his head. "He either needs to eat or have his diaper changed. The rest of the time he's happy."

Giving Jamie a sly look, Jill smiled. "Takes after his daddy."

"Yup." Jamie replied. "Clean, dry underwear and a full belly. The kid knows what's important."

* * *

I rode in the front seat of the Navajo Nation Police Suburban with Jamie. Jill and Liz sat on either side of Noah's infant seat behind us. "Captain Horn lets you take the Suburban home and to Phoenix?"

"I'm on call 24/7, and a trip to Shiprock isn't on the way to anywhere when I need to pick up a vehicle."

"Have you considered applying to the Flagstaff P.D. or the Coconino County Sheriff's Department?"

"I belong on the reservation, and they need me."

"But you spend all day driving to get anywhere and you said the people on the rez don't like you because of your mixed blood."

"Driving gives me time to think." Jamie paused, as he often did before speaking. "Just because people don't like me doesn't mean they don't respect and trust me."

"It takes some cops a long time to figure that out. Some never get it."

Nodding, Jamie asked, "What have you heard about the guy they found dead in Tuzigoot?"

"Only that he was local and had been dead a couple days before they found his body. Do you know more than that?"

"I overheard a conversation in a Flagstaff restaurant. The old guys said the victim and his wife run a dude ranch outside Cottonwood. His family has owned the land for generations, eking out a living by raising cattle. He married a woman from Colorado, and she came up with the dude ranch idea. The guys said they're making pretty good money, by Cottonwood standards."

"What's good money by Cottonwood standards?"

"It probably means they're not on the verge of bankruptcy."

* * *

Elevation markers announced our ascent as we drove north from Phoenix. Driving over a ridge, the casino appeared as an oasis of light in the dark desert. Liz leaned forward and tapped me on the shoulder. "The casino is on the exit to Montezuma's Castle and Montzuma's Well National Monuments. They're under the supervision of Ginny Goins, who's also responsible for Tuzigoot."

"Have you met Ginny?" I asked Liz, as Jamie slowed for the exit.

"I've met her a couple times. She's level-headed and reasonable. She walks a fine line between the historical preservationists, the local tribes, the Park Service, and the nearby businesses. It's not an easy job, but she keeps everyone equally unhappy." Liz paused. "She's almost as good at it as Jill was."

Snorting, Jill responded. "You're a golden child until you mess up. I hope this murder doesn't stain her reputation."

Jamie pulled under the casino hotel portico, leaving the engine running. "I think she'll be okay. The victim wasn't a park visitor, unlike the hikers who drowned on Jill's watch." He glanced at Jill in the rearview mirror. "Too bad the Park Service thought you should've controlled the thunderstorm leading to the flash flood. If not for the loss of those visitors, you'd still be the Flagstaff superintendent and wouldn't be saddled with Doug."

Two uniformed valets rushed from the hotel and opened our vehicle doors.

"She's saddled with me?" I asked, nodding thanks to the smiling young woman.

Walking to the rear of the Suburban with twinkling eyes, Jamie said. "She had a responsible Park Service job, and now she travels the country hauling your luggage and cleaning up your messes."

Stepping out of the vehicle and unable to resist the urge to pile it on, Liz added, "I heard she even writes your after-action summaries."

I shook my head, feigning offense as the valets unloaded our suitcases. "I had no idea that life with me was so difficult."

Jamie handed the Suburban's keys to the valet. "Captain Horn still refers to you as *Ivanbito,* the buffalo. Bull-headed and prone to charging off without considering the consequences."

Taking my suitcase from the valet, I replied, "I consider the consequences of my actions."

Jill took her bag and shook her head. "You consider them, but you don't always act appropriately."

"When have I ever done that?" I asked, tipping the valet five dollars.

"Like when you drove past the driveway sign that said, 'Trespassers will be shot and survivors will be shot again.'"

"It was a dead-end road. I had to pull into the driveway to turn around."

"Any sane person would've backed out when the homeowner showed up carrying a shotgun."

Shushing us, Liz waved her hand. "Can you two keep it down? I'd like to check in

31

and get a couple hours of sleep before Noah wants to be fed."

Jamie leaned close as we walked into the lobby. "I think Jill's right about that one. Driving past a no trespassing sign and confronting an armed homeowner is generally unwise."

"If we'd driven away, we wouldn't have located the kidnapped surveyors."

"And wouldn't have dug your own graves…"

I handed the smiling desk clerk my ID and Park Service credit card. "Mr. Fletcher, I have a double room at the U.S. government rate." He handed me a key card in an envelope and slid a second key card across the counter toward Jill. "Are you Mrs. Fletcher?"

Jill set her Park Service ID on the counter. The young man looked at the picture, then returned the ID and a key card. "I have a set of keys and a message for Investigator Fletcher."

The desk clerk was sliding them to me when Jill put her hand out. "Thank you."

Snatching the keys and envelope from the clerk, I shook my head. "I've got this, Mrs. Fletcher."

"Excuse me. I suppose I'll carry our bags to the room, Mr. Fletcher."

As deadpan as always, Jamie watched with a hint of a smile twitching in the corner of his mouth. Liz was less reserved. "I thought you two would be role models for my son." She looked at the desk clerk and said, "We're the Ballards. We reserved a room with a crib."

Checking the computer, the desk clerk nodded. "Yes, you're on the floor below Mr. and Mrs. Fletcher. The room adjoining them is unoccupied, we could move the crib there if you'd prefer."

Liz smiled. "That would be nice."

Jamie slid his charge card to the clerk. "Is the door between the rooms soundproof?"

Scanning Jamie's card, the clerk replied, "I believe so."

Jamie nodded. "Sadly, my son's godparents won't be able to enjoy the full parenthood experience."

Unable to read Jamie's face, the clerk silently handed Jamie's charge card back and passed him a room key.

"You'll have someone move the crib?" Liz asked.

Now flustered, the clerk reached for the phone. "Housekeeping should have it there shortly." He put his hand over the ringing phone. "Breakfast is served in the restaurant from six to eleven o'clock."

Pocketing the keys as we walked to the elevator, I handed the envelope with the hotel logo to Jill. She tore it open, read the message, and announced, "Virginia Goins is meeting us in the hotel restaurant at eight."

Waiting for the elevator, I looked at Jamie and Liz. "Would you like to join us for breakfast?"

Liz shook her head. "We try not to make early morning plans on the off chance that all of us will sleep later than eight."

* * *

When we walked into the hotel's restaurant the following morning, I saw a woman dressed in Park Service green and gray seated at a table, reading a newspaper. She stood and extended her hand when we approached the table. "Doug and Jill Fletcher, I presume."

When we were all seated, a waitress poured coffee for the three of us. "Will you be having the buffet, or would you rather order off the menu?"

The aroma of bacon and maple syrup called to me from the buffet. Perusing the yogurt, fruit, and cereal options, Jill opted for the buffet, too.

"Please help yourselves to the breakfast," Goins said. "I ate at home, so I'll drink coffee and fill you in on the investigation while you eat."

After loading our plates, me with greasy meats and carbs, Jill with fruit, oatmeal, and yogurt, Goins settled back and described

34

the discovery of the rancher's body and the progress of the investigation, now in the hands of the Yavapai County Sheriff's Department. Drawing a breath, she leaned forward. "What's your role in the investigation? Are you taking it over, or just observing?"

"I've spoken with Rob Henderson from the sheriff's department and made it clear that our role is to support him," I explained. "We typically bring a slightly different perspective to the investigations, but without the forensic capabilities of the local law enforcement people, we really can't lead an investigation."

Looking uncomfortable, Goins sipped her coffee. "I'd rather hoped you two would be taking over. There's a political aspect to the investigation. I'm not sure the sheriff's department can be objective."

Jill wiped her mouth with a napkin and pushed her oatmeal bowl back. "We're unaware of any politics involved in the murder and investigation, Virginia."

Goins shook her head. "First of all, please call me Ginny, I hope I may call you Jill and Doug. Secondly, this whole case is politics. The murder victim owned one of the most profitable Yavapai County businesses. The Lazy L Ranch draws hundreds of tourists a year to the Cottonwood area for trail rides, residential stays, and their monthly barn dinner/musical jamboree. They buy groceries and supplies from the local businesses and many of their customers stay around the area after their ranch experience, eating in the restaurants, tasting local beer and wine, and visiting the other area tourist attractions. That amounts to a chunk of the local economy and jobs beyond the ranch employees."

Glancing at me, Jill said, "So, the sheriff isn't going to do anything that will impact the operation of the ranch. Does that mean he's excluding the victim's wife and family?"

We leaned back silently while the waitress topped off our coffee and cleared our dishes. "Will this be charged to your rooms?"

Jill nodded and accepted the bill, signing her name and writing in our room number. She looked at Goins as the waitress walked away. "Is the county investigator walking on eggshells when he's dealing with the wife and ranch employees?"

Pursing her lips, Goins considered the question. "I'm sure he's interviewed them, but I doubt he's asked, 'Did you kill him?'"

"Do you think the rancher's wife might be complicit in the murder?"

Goins chuckled. "I've watched enough episodes of *CSI* and *Law and Order* to know the spouse is always the most likely suspect."

"You *do* know those are fictional shows," I said. "This will not be solved in an hour, and the killer won't break into tears and admit to the crime just before the credits roll."

Ginny smiled. "I've read up on you two. It appears you've been involved in a number of successful investigations. The news reports of your involvement vary. Some mention you as supporting characters and others say you two were the key to solving the crime." Goins paused and looked at Jill. "I also know that you left Flagstaff under an undeserved dark cloud. You seem to have landed on your feet and have found a new home in the Park Service Investigative Bureau. That alone is a big plus in my book."

"Our role is always supporting the local investigators," Jill replied.

"Jill, people in supportive roles are rarely involved in gunfights or the rescue of illegal alien children from a sinking van." Her focus shifted to me. "As for you Doug, I heard you are a canny investigator who can shoot a squirrel in the eye at ten paces."

"The reports of my abilities are overrated."

Goins rested her chin on her steepled fingers. "Not according to Jamie and Liz Ballard."

Changing the subject, I asked, "Where do we start?"

"Rob Henderson is going to meet you at the Tuzigoot visitor center at 10:00. He and my interpretive ranger, Owen Clark, are going to guide you to the site where the body was recovered. I'll let you determine how to proceed from there."

Folding her napkin, Jill nodded. "We got the Park Service pickup keys you left at the desk. We'll check out of the hotel and meet them at Tuzigoot."

Ginny stood and shook our hands. "I've felt out of the information loop. I hope having you two involved will bring us back into the investigation. It's our problem, and I'd like to think the Park Service should be part of solving the murder."

I stopped Ginny before she stepped away. "Are we obligated to stay in the Tuzigoot guest quarters?"

Ginny's smile made me uncomfortable. "I thought the experience would provide Jill with fond memories of her early years with the Park Service. The rooms are spartan and the cabinets are probably filled with mouse droppings. I made sure there was fresh bedding in the closets and a pest control company put out mouse poison and sprayed the building for scorpions."

"Did they spray for rattlesnakes too?" I asked.

"Um, no. We've never had a guest who stayed on the trails bitten by a rattler."

"Did you intentionally say you'd never had a guest bitten while skipping over employee snake bites?" I asked.

"There's never been anyone bitten at Tuzigoot during my tenure."

"How long have you been here?" I asked.

Ginny smiled. "I accepted the posting last December."

Doing the math, I said, "The rattlesnake season doesn't start until May. So, no one's been bitten during all four months of this snake season."

"Are snakes a problem for you, Doug?"

"I like them a little less than horses."

"That's too bad. I think Rob Henderson was planning to ride the trails that access the park along the Verde River."

Jill's smile sparkled and brought out her dimples. "That sounds great!"

"Yeah, great."

Ginny sensed my lack of enthusiasm and offered, "You're welcome to stay at the casino hotel if you'd prefer. There's also an old Cottonwood tavern with rooms over the bar. A little birdy told me there's a reservation for Fletcher there, and it's only a couple miles from Tuzigoot."

"Doug's acquired a lot of unfiltered local information when hanging around the small-town bars."

"That's a double-edged sword in old Cottonwood. More than half the people there are tourists who don't know anything about what happens behind the scenes. The local people have a mix of opinions, second-hand gossip, and a few facts. It's sometimes hard to pull the needle of fact from the haystack of gossip."

Nodding, I said, "I've got a pretty good bullshit detector."

"I've heard it's challenging to stay sober long enough to hear that one nugget of truth, and then you have to remember it when you're hungover the next day."

We walked Ginny out of the restaurant as I explained, "I've learned to nurse one beer a long time. If desperate, sparkling water and lime look just like a gin and tonic."

Ginny waited until a foursome of gamblers walked past, then she shook our hands again. "You two are the real deal. I was skeptical about what you could contribute, but I feel like you're really going to dig into this and get results."

Jill laughed. "We'll dig, but it's important to know enough to stop digging when you hit rock bottom."

Jill's cell rang while we were waiting for the elevator. "Hi, Liz, we've finished breakfast and are going back to our room. The superintendent gave us background. We're planning to check out and drive to Tuzigoot. We've got a room reservation in the Cottonwood Inn tonight." I couldn't hear

Liz's response in the elevator. Jill nodded, then said, "Okay, we'll see you in Flagstaff. We'll plan to have supper with you Saturday evening and be at the church for the baptism Sunday at 11:00."

Jill ended the call as I opened our room. "We're not going to see Liz and Jamie again until Saturday?"

"Both Jamie and Liz have to go back to work tomorrow."

"It was nice of them to pick us up, so we had some time to talk," I said, putting my shaving kit into my suitcase. "Jamie was unusually talkative."

"Did he mention his job offer from the Flagstaff PD?"

Freezing, I turned to Jill. "No. As a matter of fact, it sounded like he was pleased to be policing the Navajo reservation."

"Liz really wants him to take it. He spends so much time away from her when he's chasing around the reservation. He'd have rotating shifts in Flag, but at least he'd be home every day…and his backup would be closer."

I carried our bags out of the room, considering the friction the Flagstaff job offer might cause while Jill swept through making sure we hadn't left anything behind. "Did Liz say when he had to decide?"

"He has to give them his decision by Friday," Jill said as we walked to the elevator. "You should give him a call."

"And say what?"

"You can be amazingly compassionate and thoughtful when you try."

"When I try?" The sharpness of my reply startled an elderly couple in the elevator when the doors opened. "Sorry."

They looked at the badges on our belts and our pistols and decided not to say anything. Jill and I checked out and walked to the Park Service pickup in the back of the parking lot. I set our suitcases in the back seat and Jill started the engine. It was early morning, but the stark Arizona sun had already heated the pickup cab.

I buckled and turned to Jill. "What did you mean by that comment?"

"You coached Rachel in Texas and molded her into a good law enforcement ranger. You've done the same for me."

"But…?"

Stifling a chuckle, Jill replied, "You can be an ass when you put your mind to it."

"Being constructive and nice takes patience. Sometimes I just want to get through…life's hurdles without smiling and carefully considering what I'm about to say."

"As Jamie once said, 'I sometimes think Doug likes the flavor of a boot in his mouth.'"

"Yeah, well, sometimes I blurt things out."

"Talk to Jamie. He needs to hear a supportive, thoughtful voice. Be his friend, mentor, and advocate. He's got a lot of people yanking him one way or the other. He might need someone to listen."

"Um…we're talking about Jamie. I've spent days with him when he hasn't said a dozen words. It's not like we have conversations. I usually engage in a monologue. He grunts or offers an occasional comment."

Jill put her hand on my leg. "I think this might be a different conversation than you've had in the past. He's at a crossroads in his life and is uncertain which path to take."

Chapter 4

Passing a sign for Cornville, I looked at the rolling countryside. It appeared greener than Phoenix until I realized I was looking across the tops of bushes and the ground under the bushes was brown, rocky, and dusty. In the distance, columns of smoke rose from fires burning hundreds of acres of dry underbrush. We crossed a bridge over the Verde River, a green ribbon of water snaked between rows of cottonwood trees. Past the river were fenced pastures with horses and longhorn steers feeding on the sparse grass. Eventually, the landscape changed from small farmsteads into city lots with houses. Jill stopped at a light with a wine tasting room on one side and a tattoo parlor on the other. Across the street were a pharmacy and a truck stop.

"There's a wine tasting room?" I asked, looking at a hand-written sign listing the nightly specials.

"Wineries were starting to pop up along the river when we lived in Flagstaff."

"I never heard about them."

Turning the corner, Jill glanced at me. "You're not really a winery kind of guy."

"I occasionally drink a glass of wine."

"You drank wine when your cousins were here. You had a glass of wine with me when we were dating. And, you had a glass of sherry with my folks. None of that qualifies you as a *winery kind of guy.*"

We drove through a residential area, then passed a sign for Dead Horse Ranch State Park. Within a mile, the road took a sharp turn, leading us into old Cottonwood, the original town, now a mecca for tourists with restaurants, more wine tasting rooms, a small brewery, bars, boutiques, coffee bars, an antique emporium, and a rock shop.

"I could do a wine tasting," I said as we passed the third wine tasting room. "Don't they give you samples of wine that you swish around your mouth and spit into a bucket?"

"I suspect you buy a flight of wines that you sample. I doubt they have a wine spittoon."

"There's our tavern with the hotel rooms. It's centrally located so we can check in and walk anywhere in town for a meal."

Chuckling, Jill smiled. "Or we can walk to several of the wine tasting rooms. I'm sure each has its own selection and specialties."

"Do you think they sell enough wine to cover the cost of the samples they give away?"

"Um, Doug, they don't give away samples. Like I said, you probably buy a flight of wines to sample."

"When you say, 'buy a flight of wine,' how much are we talking about?"

"I haven't been to a wine sampling room in years, but I think we paid ten bucks for a flight of four wines."

"Ten bucks! Do you get a pint of each wine?"

I got a withering glare. "How much did you pay for a bar drink back in the day?"

"That was different. I already knew it was something I was going to like and not spit into a bucket."

We stopped for a group of women in a crosswalk. Each had a shopping bag in hand. "Do you see those bags?"

"Yes," I replied, wondering where the conversation was going.

"This is a tourist town. People don't go to wine bars to get drunk. It's trendy to sip a few wines, maybe buy a bottle or two, then move to the next tasting room. It's what tourists do."

Considering Jill's comments, I looked down the side streets, quickly realizing that the town was only a block wide. "If we want the local gossip, we'll have to find out where the locals drink."

"I saw a couple cowboy saloons behind us."

"What makes a bar a cowboy saloon?"

"They look worn and tired, with neon signs in the windows advertising mainstream beers."

"Ah, not the microbreweries that attract yuppies."

"Really, Doug. The yuppies are history. Now the microbreweries cater to generation X and millennials."

"I don't even know what those are."

"Exactly!" Jill said as she turned at the brown sign for Tuzigoot National Monument.

The road to Tuzigoot National Monument crossed the Verde River, passed two river access points before rising to the visitor center and ruins. The land was brown and looked unforgiving as we gained elevation.

"If not for the river, I can't imagine why anyone would live here," I said as Jill parked in the upper of two lots.

We got out of the truck and Jill pointed toward the hills west of Cottonwood. "Can you see the letter J on the hillside?"

A white J stood out over a small town far up the mountainside. "Sure. What about it?"

"That's the town of Jerome. It was the richest copper mine in the United States in the early 1900's. Pretty much everything around here exists because of the jobs created in the mine or in industries supporting mining. The flats we drove across are filled with the tailings from the Jerome smelting operation. The Park Service paid to have the ground restored in the 1960's. Before that, the tailings were nothing but fine dust that wouldn't grow anything."

A cowboy was speaking with Ranger Owen Clark in the visitor center. Jill stopped at the window and said we were there to meet with a Yavapai County deputy and the ranger. I looked at a glass display case housing partially restored pottery, recovered from the site. The pots were striking, still colorful after 1,200 years. I cringed at the thought of looking through a magnifying glass for hours trying to piece together a pot from shards of pottery recovered from an excavation.

The gray-haired volunteer behind the counter sized up Jill, pointed to the ranger and cowboy. "That's Owen, talking to Deputy Henderson."

The cowboy overheard the volunteer and turned as we approached. He was middle-aged, his face deep brown and creased from years in the sun. If not for the badge pinned to his western shirt and semi-automatic pistol clipped to his belt, he could easily have passed for a cowboy who'd just stepped away from a roundup; western from his sweat-stained Stetson hat to jeans and scarred cowboy boots.

"I'm Jill Fletcher, and this is my partner, Doug."

The deputy swept off his hat with theatrical flare and extended his hand. "Rob Henderson. I'm happy to meet you, ma'am."

Jill smiled but stiffened. "Call me Jill, please. I'm not a ma'am kind of person."

Henderson nodded. "Call me Rob."

The ranger shook my hand. "I'm Owen Clark. I took the report of the body and guided Rob and the recovery team to the site."

Henderson shook my hand. "Where would you like to start?"

"I'd like to see the site where you recovered the body."

Owen reached behind the counter and pulled out a sheet of paper and pointed to a box in the middle of the page. "This is a map of the trail system. We're here, at the visitor center. The body was found here, by the camera symbol on the edge of the Tavasci Marsh. We're half a mile from the site as the crow flies, but it's nearly a two-mile hike on the looping trails."

"Can we cut straight across?" I asked.

Clark and Henderson shared a look, then they both smiled. "You don't want to do that," Clark said.

"Why not?"

Henderson smiled. "Well, there's rattlesnakes, cat's claw, Ocotillo, prickly pear and cholla cactus, Spanish dagger, and scorpions. Other than that, it's a nice walk across the desert."

Putting up my hand, I said, "You had me convinced at rattlesnakes."

Clark nodded. "The locals say everything around here will either stick, sting, bite, or burn you, including the food and people."

Glancing at me, Jill said, "Doug's from Minnesota where everything is white and bland, including the winter landscape, food and people."

Henderson started laughing, which turned into a coughing fit. "Sorry, you tickled my funny bone. Let's go outside so I can smoke."

The temperature was rising. Henderson lit a cigarette and Clark appraised our footwear. "It looks like you've got good, broken in, hiking boots. We should walk to the recovery site before it heats up. I'll grab a couple bottles of water."

Clark went back into the building, and I turned to Henderson. "What should we know about the victim?"

"Al Tedeschi was a married, successful businessman. His family has been ranching in Cottonwood since they homesteaded. There was a single gunshot wound to his chest that was the cause of death. The vultures and critters had been at him before he was found, so his carcass was not a pretty sight. The coroner figures he'd been dead at least three days before the hiker found him, and it appears he'd been shot elsewhere and brought here, probably by horse or mule."

"I saw some horses as we drove into Cottonwood," I said. "Do you think that's where he was shot?"

Shrugging, Henderson took a last drag on his cigarette and ground the butt out under the toe of his boot. "It's hard to say. There are hobby ranches, real ranches, a dude ranch, and a riding school, all within ten miles of here. I'd wager that there are a hundred or more horses in that ten-mile radius and another hundred in the next twenty miles."

Clark returned with three one-liter water bottles. Taking the bottle, I looked at Henderson. "You're not coming with us?"

"We're having some ranch burglaries. I've got to run out west and look at the mess left behind by a couple druggies. Let's meet at the 45-70 Saloon for lunch." Clark looked at the ranger. "Join us if you can, Owen. I'm buying."

"I appreciate the offer, but after hiking to the marsh with the Fletchers, I'll have to cover the ticket window so the volunteers can eat lunch."

Cocking her head, Jill asked, "It's interesting someone would name a saloon after the 45-70 rifle cartridge."

Henderson smiled. "There's no mystery to it. The saloon's address is 4570 Main Street. They've got good burgers and sandwiches."

As he walked away, I noticed that Henderson's gait was stiff, and he was bow-legged, like a cowboy who'd spent many years in the saddle. Owen gestured for us to follow him to a trail leading north from the visitor center. "Henderson looks like he just got off a horse," I said.

"He's from an old ranch family. He once told me he was riding a horse before he could walk. His older brother took over the ranch and Rob got a degree in criminal justice. He still helps his brother during spring calving and the roundup."

"Tell us about Tuzigoot," Jill said as we passed stone walls rising to a stone building.

"The pueblo consists of over 100 rooms and is one of the largest Native archaeological sites in Northern Arizona. At its peak, around one thousand years ago, we believe Tuzigoot was home to hundreds of occupants, for centuries. It was abandoned about 1,300 A.D. and stood empty until the early 1930s when it was partially excavated by a team of archaeologists. The site was designated a national monument in 1939."

"Do we know why the builders left?"

"Their departure coincides with what's called the Little Ice Age, which brought cooler temperatures and droughts to this region."

"Which tribe lived here?" I asked.

"The regional indigenous inhabitants are called the Sinagua people; Sinagua meaning lack of water. We don't know where they went. Zuni oral history says the less mobile people stayed in the area. Some groups moved northeast and joined the Hopi tribe. Other groups moved northwest with the more nomadic Yavapai people."

I looked over my shoulder at the stone structure on top of the hill. "It seems strange they'd expend so much effort to build all this, then leave."

Owen smiled. "There were residents here for nearly a thousand years. That's four times longer than the United States has been a country. How many ghost towns and cities have we built and abandoned in our two hundred years?"

Smiling, Jill nodded and said, "We think of dinosaurs as models of extinction. They were on earth 200 million years. That's a hundred times longer than humans have been walking upright."

The trail split after a hundred yards, and we followed the branch going right. Owen pointed across the valley to a pond surrounded by cattails. "That's Tavasci Marsh. It's an oxbow lake that used to be part of the Verde River before a flood cut its new, direct channel, leaving this pond. The remains were found on the right side of the marsh, where the trail ends.

I read the informational signs along the trail, identifying the plants. "This sign says cat's claw."

"It looks like an innocuous bush, but the stems are covered with long sharp thorns. If you brush against it, you'll look like you lost a cat fight. The agave ahead of us is nasty, too. The tips of the fleshy leaves are dried spikes that'll pierce your skin. The edges of the leaves are serrated and create a nasty gash if you're impaled. Ahead of us is a cousin of the yucca called Spanish dagger. I assume it got that name after horse-riding Spanish conquistadors fell into them."

"Great," I said. "All this and rattlesnakes too."

Owen laughed as he led us along the trail. "No visitor has ever been bitten by a rattlesnake while I've worked here."

"Is that because the rattlesnakes aren't here, or because people hear the rattle and back away before they're bitten?" I asked.

"There aren't a lot of snakes, so people don't encounter them often, especially up here in the desert area. There are more edible critters nearer the marsh and river. I think the rattlers are more common there." Owen glanced at me. "Did you have a rattler encounter in the past that's made you wary?"

"I'm a city kid and poisonous snakes creep me out. I was a Minnesota scout and we only encountered non-venomous snakes on our camping trips. I'm fine with garter snakes, bull snakes, and hog-nosed snakes, but rattlers, coral snakes, and cottonmouths give me nightmares."

"A rattlesnake bite is unlikely to kill you, especially here, where you have quick access to a hospital and antivenom. Same with scorpion stings; they'll hurt like hell, but you won't die."

Jill chuckled. "Doug's already experienced a scorpion sting when we were backpacking in Wupatki National Monument. He made the mistake of reaching for something under a rock."

"Jill's thing is coyotes. She had a coyote encounter while leading a bunch of Girl Scouts on a trip."

"You guys have local backcountry experience. I don't need to tell you about all the plants and animals. It's interesting that you had a bad coyote experience; they tend to be shy and reclusive."

"They're more aggressive when they're old, accustomed to people, and hungry."

Owen stopped and we all drank. "Speaking of shy and elusive, we've had a couple puma sightings on the marsh trail. It's really a thrill to see one of the big cats, even if you only get a flash of tawny brown walking through the brush."

We crossed over a dry creek and took a trail going left. Owen pointed to the right-hand trail. "That path follows the river down to Dead Horse Ranch State Park and beyond."

Looking at the dusty trail, Jill stopped. "I see a hoof print. Do people ride through here?"

Waving his hand, Owen replied. "We don't advertise horse access to the park. That trail follows the river and riders occasionally come through."

Jill looked up and down the cottonwoods and sycamores lining the riverbanks. "Any of the hundreds of local horses Rob spoke about could ride through here."

"I suppose so."

Kneeling, Jill traced the outline of a horseshoe with her fingertip. "Do many people ride through here?"

"I don't recall seeing horses on the river trail more than a handful of times. I've never seen them on one of our hiking trails."

A few feet down the marsh trail I found hoofprints. "Here are more."

Owen walked to me and looked. "Yeah, they go all the way to where we recovered the body."

"You've never seen a horse on this trail?"

"No, but we close the gates at 4:45 and lock up the visitor center at 5:00. If they rode through any time after I left or before we opened, we'd never see them."

Still kneeling, Jill looked up. "These were made in the dust. When was your last rain?"

"All of Arizona is in a drought cycle." Owen pointed to a column of smoke rising somewhere north of the park, beyond the mountains ringing the Cottonwood valley. "One of the old-timers at the hardware store said it's been so dry he could barely moisten his chewing tobacco with saliva."

"These were made after the last rain," Jill said. "When was that?"

"I'm not sure. It might've rained a little two weeks ago on my day off. I wasn't here, so I'm not sure if there was rainfall here or not."

Getting up and wiping her hands together to remove the dust, Jill shook her head. "So, these could've been made any time in the past two weeks and were probably made some time between closing and when you reopen."

Owen nodded. "Rob Henderson asked the same questions and came to the same conclusion. He said it was damned inconsiderate of the riders to not timestamp their trail, so we knew when they'd been through."

I opened my water and took a swallow. "I don't suppose you have any security cameras covering this area."

"There's one camera in the visitor center and another in the staff buildings where they're restoring artifacts. But no, there's nothing looking out here. There's never been a reason to watch this area. I mean, there's like one person on this trail a week. Some weeks no one goes out here. It's not like it overlooks the Grand Canyon. There's a swamp, pond, some cattails, and some interesting birds, but nothing to make it a tourist destination."

Jill looked at her watch. "We're still three-quarters of a mile from the spot where the victim was found. We'd better get going if we're going to meet Rob for lunch."

* * *

The trail provided little of interest. The scenery was repetitive and other than the imprint left in the dust by a passing rattlesnake, the trip was uneventful. Near the end of the trail the ground was softer and marshy. Vegetation changed from the desert succulents and creosote bush to cattails and marsh plants.

Stopping at a muddy spot in the trail, I shook my head. "How many people were back here to recover the body? It looks like the Army has marched through."

Owen's cheeks puffed and he blew the air out slowly. "There were four people on the recovery team, so that'd be four sets of footprints. In addition to them, the hiker who found the body made two round trips. I made two round trips. Rob Henderson and a couple sheriff's deputies walked out and back. I supposed there were maybe twenty trips through here."

"There are some partial hoofprints over here," Jill said, kneeling.

"I hope a hoofprint is like a fingerprint."

"Not really," said Jill. "Different farriers use different shoeing methods but they're not discernible from each other based on simple hoof prints. The only difference we can really see is the size and shape. If the transport was a large draft horse, a person could immediately see the size difference, the clip impressions from the shoes, etc. Let me look a bit closer."

"What can you tell from looking at these?" I asked.

"There were at least two horses out here because one of the shoes is wider than the other, more like a draft horse. And the smaller horse had a bar shoe." She pointed to a print. "That's unusual. Most horseshoes are open in the back but this one has a bar linking the two back edges."

"How unique is that?" I asked.

"I've seen a few, so it's far from unique. On the other hand, it's distinctive and would narrow down the number of horses we'd be looking at."

* * *

The trail ended at the marsh overlooking a pond. Cattails lined both sides of the path, and there was an area a few feet wide where the cattails had been knocked over or broken off. "The body was here. The recovery team knocked down a bigger patch of cattails than the body had," Owen pointed out.

Looking at the hundreds of footprints, I shook my head. "Whatever footprint evidence was here has been compromised."

Jill walked up and down the trail, then knelt. "The horses stood here for a while where the hoofprints end. They shifted around a bit, then turned and walked back down the trail. I only see prints from two horses."

"Owen, did you notice anything special during your first trip out here?" I asked.

"To be honest, no. I mean, there were vultures circling and we chased three vultures off the site when we approached." He paused, reflecting on the discovery.

"The smell was…terrible. And the body was a mess. His eyes were gone, and the vultures had eaten a lot of his…"

Owen turned away, and I waited for him to either start gagging or swear. Jill touched my arm. "Whoever dumped the body here wanted the vultures to leave it unidentifiable or hoped it would never be found."

"I disagree. There are thousands of acres where a body could be buried and never found. The killer was either stupid or was very canny and wanted him found."

"Why would someone go to all the trouble of dragging a body out here if they wanted the victim found?"

"That motive is often the key to finding the killer."

Owen had turned toward us to listen. He was pale but intrigued by our conversation. "The cops never said anything like that when I was out here with the recovery team. They didn't know who the victim was, but they said he was probably killed by a jealous husband or had been caught rustling cattle."

I looked at Jill. "It'll be interesting to hear Rob's theories now that he knows the victim's identity."7

Chapter 5

Jill parked the pickup a half block past the 45-70 saloon, near a weary storefront advertising five acres of antiques. A rusty car sat under the eaves and the windows were cluttered with unidentifiable dusty knick-knacks. We followed three young women who were obvious tourists. Each had a bag dangling from her arm and a cell phone in hand. We paused when they stopped in front of the 45-70 for a selfie.

The 45-70 had a saloon feel to it, with rusty old rifles hanging from the rough-cut cedar walls, and a bar cut down to the height of a lunch counter running along the left side of the room. Rob Henderson was sitting at a high-top table near the back of the room, his Stetson hung on a wooden peg behind the table. Though his face was brown, his forehead and bald head, usually hidden from the sun, were untanned. Scanning the room as we walked in, Henderson spotted us and nodded.

He pushed two laminated menus across the table as we sat and nodded to the glass of dark liquid in front of him.

"They've got a full bar, but I stick with sarsaparilla when I'm working."

Jill smiled, revealing dimples. "Sarsaparilla, really? Did you just step out of a John Wayne movie?"

Pointing at a spot in the lower corner of Jill's menu, he commented, "The tourists expect bison burgers and sarsaparilla when they come out west. The saloon caters to their expectations."

"There have never been buffalo in Arizona," Jill said.

Henderson put up his hands. "Hey, there's no explaining people's expectations. I just know that bison burgers are popular here."

"I've never had sarsaparilla," I said. "What does it taste like?"

"It's root beer with a fancy name and a price to reflect the snob value. I drink Diet Coke." Henderson scanned the room again as we read the menus. "The hamburgers are good, and the sandwiches have a generous portion of meat on bakery bread."

Continuing to read, Jill asked, "How are the salads?"

"They appear leafy and green."

"You've never eaten one here?"

Chuckling, Henderson took a sip of his soda. "Jill, I've never eaten a salad anywhere. The stuff they spray on that lettuce will kill you."

"They rinse the chemicals off before they serve it."

"So they say…"

Jill shook her head. "The greasy burgers will kill you."

"Ah, but that tastes good. I'd rather die from eating something tasty than eating…lettuce." Henderson looked at me. "Do you eat rabbit food for lunch, too?"

"I prefer something meaty with a side of unhealthy fries. Don't let Jill fool you into thinking she's a health nut; she usually eats half my fries."

"After you make your choice, you have to order at the cash register. They'll call your name when your food is ready."

The order pickup clerk called out three names, including Rob's. He sauntered to the counter, returning with a French dip sandwich basket that included a pile of fries."

Jill snatched a golden fry from his basket. "A French dip sandwich seems out of place in a saloon."

Henderson playfully swatted at Jill's hand when she reached for another fry. "It's one thing to cater to the tourist trade, but the owners are smart enough to include food to satisfy the tastes of normal people. Now, go order something before you eat all my fries."

Finishing the last of his fries as we ate, Rob asked, "What did you learn on your hike to the marsh?"

"Aside from seeing a thousand sets of footprints trampling all over the evidence?" I asked.

Henderson waved a ketchup-laden fry at me. "That all happened before I showed up. But yes, the hiker, ranger, and recovery team all walked the trail before I secured the scene."

"You ride, Rob, right?" Jill asked.

Smiling, Henderson nodded. "Yeah, I saw the two sets of hoofprints. I also noticed a few drops of blood on the trail."

I stopped mid-bite. "Were you able to follow the backtrail?"

"I walked the river for half a mile in each direction and never saw another drop."

"Did you see the bar shoe prints?" Jill asked.

"I'm impressed," Henderson said, wiping his mouth with a paper napkin. "Most Arizona cops wouldn't know what that is."

"I'm a ranch girl," Jill said. "I was riding as soon as my feet could reach the stirrups."

"Be careful," I said. "She can outshoot most cops, too."

"There were shoe hoofprints in both directions on the trail, so that doesn't really help narrow the possible pool of ranches to the north or south."

"Rob, you said the victim was married. When did his wife report him missing?"

"She didn't make a report. She thought he was 'shacked up with a floozy.'"

"Did she have a specific floozy in mind?" Jill asked.

Henderson looked around, then nodded toward the bar. "Carmen is drawing a beer. It's common knowledge that she and Tedeschi were knocking boots."

Jill watched the attractive Hispanic waitress tap a beer, then flirt with a cowboy while she rang it up. "Carmen doesn't seem too broken-hearted."

"She's got a personality that gets her a lot of tips from her male clientele. She kids and laughs, but Al Tedeschi was the only one who made it to her bed."

"Did you run a background check on her?"

Henderson took a sip of his soda, partially hiding his smile. "She was ticketed a couple times for small amounts of marijuana and has one DUI conviction, all when she was in her teens and early twenties."

"Marriages?" Jill asked.

"Two, both ending in divorce."

Noticing us watching her when she scanned her customers, Carmen winked. Henderson lifted his empty glass and pointed to it. She nodded.

"She doesn't look much past her early twenties now," I said.

"Yeah, she looks pretty good…across the room," Henderson said. "Make another guess after she brings my soda pop."

"What's the story on Tedeschi's wife?" Jill asked.

"Robyn's ten years younger than Al. She has fiery red hair that matches her personality. The story is that she married him fresh out of college. He was a bronc rider at a Colorado rodeo and she was a barrel racer/buckle bunny."

"What's a buckle bunny?" I asked, garnering an eye roll from Jill.

"It's like a badge bunny, Doug. She's a woman who chases after the winning cowboys at a rodeo—the guys who've won championship belt buckles, like the ones Chet gave me."

I chuckled, "So, my mom's a buckle bunny?"

Jill covered her face with her hands. "Really, Doug? You don't want to go there."

Carmen ended our conversation by showing up with a Diet Coke. "Here you go, Rob. Who are your friends?"

"Doug and Jill Fletcher are Park Service investigators. They're here looking into Al's murder."

The smile melted from Carmen's face," Um…"

Jill broke the ice. "When did you last see Al?"

Carmen glanced around the room. "He was here Saturday night."

"So, you haven't seen him since Sunday morning?"

Her face coloring, Carmen nodded. "He was going back to the Lazy L to help with the incoming guests. I expected him back Monday, but he never showed up. Listen, I've got tables to clear, and I've been through all this with Rob."

As Carmen left, Rob looked at me. "How old?"

"Maybe thirty-five."

Rob smiled. "Jill, what's your guess."

"It's hard to tell. She's been ridden hard and put away wet. "I'll guess twenty-eight."

Leaning back, Rob pointed at Jill. "And we have a winner."

Whispering to Henderson, Jill said, "Tedeschi was in his fifties. What in hell is he doing chasing around with someone her age?"

"I'm just talking here, but I think the Lazy L Ranch is worth a million dollars. That'd make him the most eligible bachelor in the county after a divorce."

"I assume the ranch values here are like South Dakota. On paper, the land is worth a lot of money. But the cash flow barely covers the taxes and insurance."

"Their banker confided that the ranch is paying its bills and making a little profit. He wouldn't say more than that, but I happen to know that Robyn paid off the loans they took out when they built the dude ranch outbuildings. The Ford dealer said they paid cash for their last three pickups."

"I'd like to talk to Robyn Tedeschi," I said, pushing my chair back. "It sounds like she'd benefit from killing Al before he filed for divorce."

The smile on Henderson's face told me I'd missed something. "Holster your gun, sheriff. Al's been sleeping around for a while. Carmen is the latest in a string of women he's bedded in the last couple of years. None of them got more out of Al than a, 'thank you, ma'am. That was fun.' Robyn knew about his infidelities and chose to ignore them as long as Al didn't meddle in the ranch operation or pull too much out of their bank account."

I sat down and signaled Carmen for a Diet Coke refill for both Jill and me. "Tell me what I'm missing."

"Not all of Al's conquests were single, nor were all of them happy about being shoved aside. Gloria Kramer claimed she was going to shoot him when he announced the end of their relationship in the brewery one Friday night last April. Rhonda Patterson's husband was going to shoot Al if they ever met in a dark alley.

Peggy Alberg threatened to cut Al's pecker off after he wrote a 'Dear Jane' note on her bathroom mirror in lipstick before sneaking off in the dark of the night."

We stopped talking when Carmen arrived with the sodas. "Can I get you guys anything else? Our cowboy cookies are legendary."

Jill thought for a moment, then shook her head. "None for us, thanks."

"Hey!" I protested. "Not all of us want to skip a legendary cookie. We'll split one."

Carmen shook her head, smiling. "Just the one?"

Jill patted my stomach, which had started to strain my belt. "One is more than we need."

Carmen checked the tables around us, then leaned close. "You guys are talking about Al's murder, right?"

Jill reached out and put her hand on Carmen's. "I'm sorry for your loss."

Instead of the bravado I'd expected, Carmen wiped tears from her eyes. "Gawd, I can't believe I'm crying over the old goat."

Jill stood and wrapped her arms around the waitress. "It's hard losing someone you're close to."

"No one around here gets that. Everyone laughs and tells me to find a different cowboy. They don't understand that I loved him, even if he was..."

A blonde waitress leaned close as she swept past. "He was cheating on his wife, dear."

Carmen glared at the blonde as she walked away. "Bitch." Peeling herself away from Jill, Carmen stalked past the blonde to the cash register.

"She's really sad about Al," Jill said, hoisting herself onto her high stool.

Rob nodded. "All his ex-girlfriends were seriously in love. The problem was that Al had the morals of an alley cat. He sniffed at every…"

Rob's likely inappropriate comment was cut short by Carmen's arrival. "One of the cookies was broken," she said, setting a plate with a massive plastic-wrapped chocolate-chip cookie in the center of the table. "Since you guys are sharing, I figured you wouldn't care."

Rob flipped the cookie over and picked at the corner of the Saran wrap. "Where's Buck these days?" he asked.

The question made Carmen uneasy. "He's still driving a truck."

Peeling the plastic back, Rob popped a quarter-sized piece of cookie into his mouth. "He's driving over the road, so he's only around town a few days a month?"

Carmen shrugged. "I suppose. I don't see much of him since the judge issued the protection order against him."

"Greg 'Buck' Kendrick was Carmen's ex-husband," Rob explained. "Buck has some anger issues. Between beating up Carmen and guys who flirted with her, he was arrested for a couple road rage incidents in Phoenix."

The topic obviously made Carmen uneasy. "He didn't like driving in Phoenix. The traffic made him crazy."

The cookie was fabulous, as advertised. "How did Buck and Al get along?" I asked.

"Buck showed up here drunk one night, trying to pick a fight. The manager threw him out and I expected him to be parked outside waiting for me. Al offered to make sure I got home safe and…well…one thing led to another." Carmen looked at Jill. "You know how that goes, right?"

Jill made sure she was chewing a bite of cookie, so she didn't have to answer. Having spent her adult life refusing one-night stands, Jill understood, "how that went," but she didn't want to express her disgust of casual hookups. "So, that's how your relationship with Al started?"

Carmen nodded as she checked her tables. "Yeah, he came in for a nightcap and stayed for breakfast."

"How did Buck react to that?" I asked.

"He wasn't pleased and let me know about it."

"Was he mad enough to kill Al?"

Carmen wrinkled her nose. "Buck liked to use his fists. He had to sell his guns after the domestic assault conviction and protection order, so he couldn't have shot Al." She put her hand on Rob's shoulder. "We couldn't sell that broken cookie, so it's free."

Jill licked her finger and dabbed at the cookie crumbs. "Sounds like Cottonwood is like any Midwest small town, with a bunch of tourists thrown into the mix."

Finishing his Diet Coke, Rob slid a five-dollar bill under his glass and stood. "All the locals rub against each other too often and school bullying still stings." He carefully set the Stetson on his head, checking the alignment with his fingertips.

I took out ten dollars. Jill snatched it away, swapping it in my wallet for a twenty that she put on the table. "Carmen's time with us probably cost her that much in tips from other customers."

We stood outside the saloon in the glaring Arizona sun. Jill put on a pair of sunglasses and a floppy brimmed cap. "What haven't you had time to do?" She asked.

Henderson looked down the street at the tourists walking the downtown sidewalks. "Well, I haven't had time to track down all of Tedeschi's girlfriends. There are a few I mentioned, but the local rumor mill says there are many more, some no more than one-night stands. I haven't spoken with his children. His son owns a winery, and his daughter manages the dude ranch. I've put them all as less likely suspects, but hell, I got nothing else."

"How about his business dealings?" I asked.

"Like I said, I spoke to his banker, truck salesman, carpenter who built his outbuildings, and the other suppliers. None of them admitted to having a problem with Al."

"How about the ranch employees?" Jill asked. "My dad always seemed to have one disgruntled cowboy every couple years."

"Al's daughter, Theresa, runs the dude ranch. If someone had a problem with the ranch operation, it'd be with her, not her dad."

"I thought his wife ran the ranch," Jill said.

"Robyn handles the finances, but Theresa is the ranch manager." Henderson's mouth twitched and hinted at a smile. "Robyn's not well suited to dealing with the customers. She's kind of volatile. Between you and me, I think Robyn's the reason Al spent so many nights away from the ranch. Being away was probably easier than dealing with that crazy redhead."

Opening the door for a couple entering the saloon, I said, "I'm surprised he didn't divorce her."

"Before Robyn showed up, Al was eking out a living raising cattle. Without Robyn's vision and budgetary control, he'd still be chasing steers with barely enough money to buy himself drinks on Saturday night."

"His daughter is running the dude ranch operation. I'd think the cash flow would take care of itself," I said.

Jill smiled at Henderson. "Doug's a city kid. He doesn't know how fast a cowboy can piss away money unless he's got a smart wife holding the purse strings."

"Really?"

"Robyn gave Al an allowance. Without her oversight, he'd probably be paying rent for three women and buying rounds of drinks at the bar every night of the week until the bank account was empty." Henderson tipped his hat to a pair of attractive female tourists who seemed to think he was part of the local charm. "Never underestimate the ability of an alcoholic cowboy to do stupid things and not remember where the money went. I think Al was just smart enough to know he needed Robyn to keep the ranch running."

Rob added, apparently for the benefit of some approaching tourists, "I've got to round up those cattle rustlers now. Call me tomorrow and we can compare notes over lunch again."

Jill shook her head and smiled. "We should probably check into our room."

"They'll probably hold your reservation. But, this is their busy season, and you're only paying the discounted government rate."

Chapter 6

Since we were parked next to the store advertising acres of antiques, we walked around the corner and entered what appeared to be the original storefront of an old Cottonwood business. A gray-haired woman greeted us as the bell tinkled over the door. She glanced at our badges and guns, then smiled broadly. "All our artifacts come from private land, and I have the papers to prove their provenance."

"We're just playing tourist for a few minutes over our lunch hour," Jill said.

Looking at the rows of old gold and silver coins in the showcase next to the cash register, I said, "The prices on your coins seem a little high."

"Compared to loose coins, they are. But all of these have been graded for wear and defects. Several of them are mint proofs and I've got a whole shelf of uncirculated Morgan silver dollars."

Jill was looking at a display of ceramic knick-knacks behind the counter. "My mother has Hummels like those."

Laughing, the woman extended her open hand and gestured toward them. "Make me an offer. I'd happily sell you the entire collection. I'm Mary, by the way."

"Mom would have to buy another china cabinet if she got any more."

"We have antique cabinets, too. And we ship anywhere in the U.S."

Jill smirked. "I take it that Hummels aren't as valuable as they used to be."

The clerk stepped to the counter and whispered, "Do you want to inherit a Hummel collection?"

"Geez, no."

"No one born after 1940 wants Hummels anymore. It's the same with coins from the Franklin mint, decorative plates, and Coke collectibles. They were hot; now they're not. I sell a few to people who remember their mother's collections of things, but savvy collectors are spending their money elsewhere."

"Have you bought anything from Al Tedeschi?"

"He cleaned out his barn when they set up the dude ranch operation. There's a shed out back featuring a couple of his saddles with cracked leather, some rusty kerosene lamps, and assorted trinkets and metal signs the seed companies used to give away."

"Those items don't move fast?" I asked.

The woman gestured around the room. "I've got seven acres of things that don't move fast. People bring in items and hope I'll pay top dollar for them. The reality is I pay maybe half of what I expect to get out of an item because chances are their valuable antique will sit on a shelf for years before it sells, and I have to make a profit on the sale."

Several groups of tourists passed as we spoke. One shaggy young man saw our badges, turned, and left. Jill watched him leave. "I think we just scared off a shoplifter."

"Nah, that was Kenny, our local drug addict. He brings me an item now and again. I usually refuse it unless he can prove he didn't steal it. He's gun shy around cops. He sees a badge and assumes he's going to be hassled."

"Tell me more about Al Tedeschi and the dude ranch."

Snorting, the woman shook her head. "The locals all say he was hornier than a two-peckered goat. I saw him walking around town with a different woman every few weeks. Either he got bored, or the women figured out he was just a drunk with a few bucks who wasn't going to marry them or buy them a house in Sedona."

"Cottonwood is a small town. You'd think people would get wise to him."

"You've heard that old song, *Don't The Girls All get Prettier at Closing Time*. Well, I think that was the case with Al. He'd hang around until closing time, buying some lonely woman drinks, and feeding her a line of bullshit about how pretty she was and how he was falling for her."

Jill drew a breath and blew it out slowly. "Was he that good looking and persuasive, or were the women that desperate?"

"I think there was a bit of both. It's amazing how stupid a woman can be when she's looking at a guy through the beer bottle and he's saying all the words she wants to hear."

"Who do you think killed him?" I asked.

The clerk was ready to answer but hesitated as she glanced at our badges. "Why would a pair of Park Service cops care about Al Tedeschi?"

"His body was recovered on Park Service land," I said.

"I've got my thoughts, then there are rumors. None of them amount to more than talk."

Jill leaned on the counter. "Listen, we're not going to arrest anyone based on a rumor. We'd just like to have a good starting point for our investigation instead of questioning everyone in town."

The woman studied Jill's face for a moment. "You sound like a woman who grew up in a small town. Understanding how long old wounds fester might take you to some interesting places. Before the dude ranch, Al was a bit of a con man when it came to selling livestock and horses. He burned a couple people by selling them freemartin heifers as breeding stock."

"What's a freemartin?" I asked.

"It's the female twin of a bull," Jill explained. "The shared placental hormones of male/female twin calves cause problems when they mature. The freemartin heifers are always infertile, and the bulls are less fertile. So, selling someone a freemartin heifer as breeding stock is unethical. The buyer expects the heifer to have a calf the following spring, but all she does is use up pasture and cause frustration."

"And the bull calf?"

"Nearly all bull calves are castrated and sold as steers, so it's not a big deal," Jill explained.

"Who bought the freemartin heifers?" I asked.

"Tom Pochart bought them to supplement his herd. I heard he confronted Tedeschi, but Al had no answer for why the two heifers didn't get pregnant. Tom was told they were probably shy of his bull. One of Al's neighbors helped with the spring roundup and branding. He'd seen the freemartin twins with their cows and clued Tom in on the likely problem."

"Did anything come of it?" I asked.

"Tom confronted Al and demanded compensation. Al told him to sell them as slaughter cattle and consider himself paid."

Jill shook her head. "A bred heifer is worth about fifty percent more than a steer. That's compounded because a yearling heifer weighs less than a steer if they're sent to the feedlot. Tom was probably cheated out of close to a thousand dollars."

The woman watched a young couple pass, then leaned close to us. "In a lean year, that's the difference between making your tax payment or not."

"Where is the Pochart ranch?" I asked.

"You drove past it if you drove in from Cornville. They've got a big sign that says Trail's End Ranch, just after you cross the river bridge. Jake and Hazel are mostly out of beef now, focusing on horse training and riding lessons."

We thanked the clerk and left. Jill leaned close as we walked the sidewalk. "I feel like we should've purchased something."

"Did you have something in mind, or were you just speaking in general?"

"We could've found something. There are acres of displays."

"You've already got an antique—me."

Sighing, Jill grabbed my arm and stopped. "I'm serious. We took up fifteen minutes of her time. We should buy something."

"Did you see anyone waiting to check out?"

"Well, no."

I started walking. "She was probably happy to have someone to talk with instead of standing there waiting for some browser to make a purchase. She got to gossip and may even feel like she contributed to the investigation."

Pulling out the keyring with the pickup keys, Jill stopped next to our vehicle. "Do you really think so?"

"I'm sure of it. Now unlock the door before I melt. I'm not acclimated to the intense sunlight at this altitude."

After turning around in an alley, Jill drove back through town to the Tavern Grille. "I like the bright sunshine here and the low humidity. The Corpus Christi weather sometimes gets to me. I need to bring a poncho or raincoat everywhere I go. The only time my clothes feel dry is when they come out of the dryer."

"Do you want to live somewhere other than Texas?" I asked as I pulled our bags out of the backseat.

"If Matt and Mandy weren't there, I'd want to move. It's hard to put a value on friendship and they're very special."

"We can live anywhere. And we're likeable. We'll make friends wherever we live."

Jill snorted as we entered the tavern. "You're a cynical ex-cop who looks at everyone with suspicion, and I'm an introvert. We won't make friends wherever we live, and we won't find friends like Matt and Mandy. They're caring, trustworthy, and Mandy feels like the sister I never had."

The Tavern Hotel was over the bar. Its entrance was separate from the Tavern Bar and Grille, and the lobby was surprisingly modern. A young male clerk looked up from a computer and smiled when we walked in. "You must be the Fletchers. Welcome to Cottonwood."

I set our suitcases down and Jill pulled out her credit card. "We thought we'd check in before you got worried that we wouldn't show up."

The desk clerk smiled as he ran Jill's card. "That wouldn't have been a problem. Rob Henderson assured me you'd be here, even if you were running late."

"We chose this over staying in the rangers' quarters in Tuzigoot," I said.

Returning Jill's card, the clerk smiled. "I think you'll find our accommodations superior to the Park Service buildings. We have a pool and workout room. There's no room service per se, but the tavern will deliver food and beverages to your room." He paused. "We also have cable TV and free WiFi. That alone is a step above the park quarters."

"What advantage would there be to staying in the park?" I asked as he handed us key cards. "They lock the gates at 4:45."

Deep in thought, the clerk paused. "I suppose you don't have to worry about anyone disturbing your sleep."

"Is that going to be a problem here?" I asked.

"Only if someone gets drunk and disoriented." He sensed our concern about that comment, then added. "It happened once, before we upgraded the security."

Our first-floor room was less than a two-minute walk from the lobby. Jill opened the door and stopped. "Wow. This is every bit as nice as the casino hotel."

After setting the suitcases in the closet, I looked out the window at the pool. "Do you want to swim before supper?"

"Before supper? We just ate lunch."

"I thought we'd walk around downtown and talk to some bartenders. Since you felt guilty about not buying something at the antique place, and I'm not going to drink anything but sparkling water and lime, I thought we'd get a plate of appetizers at each bar."

Jill poked my belly. "Bar appetizers are either greasy or high calorie."

"Not true," I replied. "Some appetizers are both greasy and high calorie."

"We should go to the riding school and talk to the guy who bought the freemartin calves."

"Let's leave that for tomorrow."

"Why tomorrow?"

"I think we're going to hear about some of Al Tedeschi's other shady business deals at the bars. I think the sterile heifer thing will pale in comparison to some of his other shenanigans."

"As a ranch girl, I know that selling sterile heifers as breeding stock *is* a big deal. Like the antique lady said, a thousand dollars might make the difference between paying your property taxes or not."

"Bear with me," I said, reaching for the door. "Let's see what else slithers out if we start turning over rocks."

* * *

The desk clerk was talking to one of the maids when we walked into the lobby. "There are several wine-tasting rooms on Main Street. Where would you suggest we start?"

"We have a wine and dine package that includes wine tasting at three of the wineries and a gourmet dinner at the Italian Restaurant down the block." He paused and added, "Your government rate doesn't include those options."

Jill stepped up, looking concerned. "There are a dozen wineries, but you only have relationships with three of them?"

The maid smiled. "The boss is part owner of those three wineries. Some of the others are as good, or better. Some are…"

The desk clerk nodded. "Some make fruit wines that cater to a certain segment of the tourists. The owner doesn't consider them *real* wines, but there are people who enjoy them."

"There's a winery across the street and up the block. Is it part of your wine-tasting package?"

The maid wrinkled her nose. "Start somewhere else." The clerk nodded.

"Is there a problem with their wine?"

The desk clerk exchanged a look with the maid before answering. "You might not be welcome there with your badges on. The owner has had some scrapes with the police, so the license is in his wife's name. He imports grape juice from California."

The maid nodded. "No California vineyard sells their best grapes to an Arizona crook."

"Where should we start?" Jill asked.

The desk clerk pointed across the street. "I'd either start or end at Charlie's Wine Corner."

Frowning, Jill asked, "Why would we end or start there?"

The maid covered her face, hiding her smile. The clerk drew a breath and said, "Charlie's wines aren't very good. If you start there, everything else will probably taste better."

"Why would we end there?"

"If you've had enough wine, Charlie's stuff might not taste too bad, if you've been to a lot of tasting rooms, it's easy to stagger to the hotel because we're just across the crosswalk."

"We heard Al Tedeschi's son ran one of the wineries," I said.

"He's about three blocks down on our side of the street. He grows his own grapes and makes some award-winning wines."

Jill picked up a map showing all the tasting rooms. "Is he part of your wine package?"

Pausing to compose his response, the clerk studied the desktop. "Tedeschi's don't give away anything, nor do they partner with the local businesses or offer discount coupons. Robyn Tedeschi runs a tight ship—not a penny slips through her fingers."

"Do they make good wine?" Jill asked.

"I've never tried any of their wines, but our customers have said the Tedeschi wines compare favorably with the top California vineyards."

Jill found the Tedeschi tasting room on the map and put her finger on it. "Let's start there. It's only a few blocks away."

The maid laughed. "Nothing in old Cottonwood is more than a few blocks from here."

Gesturing toward the door, I said, "Let's start at Charlie's."

Jill frowned but followed me out the door. "They said Charlie's had bad wine. Why go there at all?"

"Because we're gathering information, not tasting wine." Getting *the look*, I added. "Besides, we're on duty. We can taste, but not swallow."

"And I had such romantic plans for the evening."

"We don't have to cancel an evening of romance just because we're not drinking."

Jill grabbed my hand at the crosswalk. Unlike most places I've lived, the vehicles traveling both directions stopped for us. Nodding politely, we walked across the street and turned toward Charlie's.

Jill stopped outside the door and looked through the front window. "There's no one here. Let's move on."

"We're gathering information. It's easier to talk to the staff if they're not busy with other customers."

The interior was burgundy; the color, not the wine. Paintings and photos of wine glasses, bottles, and vineyards covered the walls in a random pattern of varied sizes. It looked chaotic to me. Under the art were wine racks made of weathered barnwood. Bottle prices were posted over each row. Considering the poor review given by the hotel clerk, the prices, starting at $32, seemed exorbitant.

Slender was overstating the physique of the tall man behind the bar. He folded the Sudoku he was solving and took off the reading glasses perched on his nose. "Good afternoon," he said with a welcoming smile. Setting a sheet of paper in front of us, he ran his finger from the top listing to the bottom. "The dry reds are at the top, whites are in the middle, and dessert wines at the bottom. I suggest starting with dry and ending with the sweet dessert wines."

I noted the ten-dollar a flight price. "How many glasses are in a flight?"

"A flight is three glasses. People often share two flights so they can sample six wines." He appraised our badges, then added. "If you two are afraid of each other's germs, I can pour half-flights for you."

"My partner doesn't drink, and I'm on duty. Can I taste a couple thimblefuls?"

The slender man drew a deep breath and let it out slowly. "Fine. Ten bucks and I'll let you taste whatever you like. If you buy a bottle, I'll knock the tasting price off the bottle you buy."

Running her finger up and down the list, Jill asked. "What's your best wine?"

"It's really a matter of taste. Do you prefer reds or whites, dry or sweet?"

"I prefer dry reds, but I enjoy a nice white too."

Reaching under the bar, he pulled out a wine glass and a bottle with a wolf logo. "Not that I'm not trusting, but I'd like the tasting fee up front."

"We're Park Service rangers investigating Al Tedeschi's murder," I said, pulling a twenty-dollar bill out of my wallet.

Taking the twenty and returning a ten, the server poured half an inch of wine into Jill's glass. "Al's never graced my establishment. You might find people who knew him best at the Howling Coyote or the 45-70." He slid the glass to Jill and stood back with his arms crossed.

Jill went through the tasting process, swirling the wine, holding the glass toward the window to inspect the color, then deeply inhaling the bouquet. She sipped, swished the wine around her mouth, then spit the remainder into a ceramic jar on the counter.

Obviously unimpressed by Jill's tasting prowess, the man waited for her response. "What do you think?"

Jill slid the glass to me. "Try this."

Not being a wine connoisseur, I hesitated. "I'm on duty."

"One sip and spit," she said, pushing the glass closer to my hand.

I sniffed the wine, caught notes of apple cider vinegar and grape jelly, then set it down. "No."

The slender man shrugged, took the glass, rinsed it, and poured a dollop of a white wine. He slid it to Jill. "This is a pinot grigio/petite Verdot blend from Napa County grapes. It's one of our best sellers."

As Jill repeated her tasting drill, I asked, "What do you know about Al Tedeschi?"

"He was an alley cat who screwed anything that moved."

Jill was sipping as the man made his pronouncement. She started coughing and the server quickly handed her a bar towel to cover her mouth. I watched, wondering if she was reacting to the wine or the description of Tedeschi. Catching her breath, she said, "You didn't think much of him."

"I've got no time for any of that family. He slept around. His wife is a mean cheapskate. His son is an arrogant, obnoxious jackass."

"What about his daughter, Theresa?"

Shaking his head, the server leaned forward. "Theresa is a piece of work. She'll smile at you while she slips a knife in your back. I think she got the worst of her mother and father's traits, then taught arrogance to Carlton, her brother."

Jill pushed the white wine across the bar, apparently done with it. "I thought she ran the dude ranch. You've got to be personable to be in that business."

Dumping the rest of Jill's wine, the server rinsed the glass. "She's a damn chameleon. She turns whatever color suits her environment. I hear the customers like her well enough, but the people around town know her and what she's capable of." He pulled out an amber-colored bottle of wine and poured a sample, then pushed it to Jill.

"What's this?" Jill asked, holding the glass up to the light.

"It's a mead made from cactus honey. A bit of the prickly pear fruit comes through."

Skipping the tasting routine, Jill sipped the mead, spit, and smiled. "It's not bad." She pushed the glass to me, smiling with her mouth, but not her eyes.

Without properly reading Jill's tepid reaction, I took a sip. There was no hint of prickly pear, only a sweet yeasty flavor. Stifling my gag reflex, I spit it back into the glass. "Can I have a glass of water?"

"Yeah, that might need a little more age," the server said as he handed me a glass and a pitcher of water. I drank deeply before realizing the water tasted like algae. I hoped the flavors would cancel each other but somehow, they had synergy, each making the other worse.

Jill watched with amusement, knowing how terrible the mead was and reveling in my discomfort.

"Would you like to try our strawberry wine?" the server asked, setting a rose'-colored bottle on the counter.

Jill stood. "I think we're good, thanks."

Hesitating, I asked, "Who would be the best person to ask about Al Tedeschi?"

"Any of his conquests, I suppose."

"Is there anyone he hasn't spurned who might give us an honest opinion of him and who might've hated him enough to kill him?"

Putting the wine back under the counter, the server cocked his head in thought. "You should talk to Anna Weise. She's the Lazy L cook. She's worked for Al about twenty years."

"She's not another of Al's conquests?" Jill asked.

"Nah, Anna's a salty woman who's immune to Al's lines of bullshit. I think that's why she's lasted so long with the ranch. Carlton, Theresa, and Robyn all trust her."

"Is there somewhere we could contact her away from the ranch?" I asked.

"She sometimes hangs out at the Riverside Bar."

"Ah, a heavy drinker, like Al."

"She doesn't touch a drop of liquor. She just likes to hang out with the cowboys."

"Thanks," I said, putting a five-dollar bill into the tip jar.

"One thing about Anna," the server said as we reached the door. "She could teach a mule skinner new cuss words."

Laughing, Jill stood at the door. "I've known some characters like her."

About three storefronts away from Charlie's, Jill stopped me. "I have never tasted anything as bad as his white wine."

"It was worse than the mead?" I asked

"I really dislike bourbon, but a shot might take the flavor of those two out of my mouth."

Chapter 7

"The 20/20 Wine Room is just ahead. Maybe they'll have something better than Charlie's mead."

Jill hooked my arm in hers. "The hotel clerk was right. Charlie's was definitely the place to start or end."

"It's all downhill from here," I said, holding the door.

Charlie's had been dark and imposing. In contrast, the 20/20 had big windows and bright lights. The walls were white plaster and the chairs, wine racks, and bar were all made of light-colored pine finished with urethane to bring out the natural wood grain. There were half a dozen tables, two with people seated around them. Six young women were lined up at the bar, joking with a cute brunette who was pouring for them.

Jill pulled my arm. "I have a good feeling about this place."

We chose two stools at the end of the bar, away from the laughing sixsome tasting a white wine. One of the six had a white lace veil on top of her head. "I think it's a bachelorette party," Jill whispered.

The server stepped away from the happy women and slid wine glasses in front of us, then handed us sheets of wine selections. "The dry reds are first. The sweet whites are last. I suggest you sample in that order," she said, smiling. "A sampling flight of four wines is ten dollars or a single glass is six."

Sliding my glass back to her, I asked, "Can I get sparkling water?"

"Certainly!" She turned to Jill, "and what would you like, ma'am?"

"I'd like a flight of reds."

"Are there any particular wines you'd like to try?"

"Give me whatever you'd choose," Jill said, handing the server the wine menu.

One of the party women called, "Paulette, we're ready for the Pinot Grigio blend."

Paulette took a bottle of wine from the back counter and poured an inch of wine into Jill's glass. "This is my favorite. It's a Syrah/Grenache blend." She reached under the counter, then set a bottle of sparkling water in front of me. "We've got a sandwich and appetizer menu on the wall. I'll be back in a moment."

"There's nothing fried on their appetizer menu," Jill said, swirling the wine in her glass. She inhaled through her nose over the glass, then smiled. "I think this will cover the taste of the yeasty mead."

Twisting open the sparkling water, I studied the chalkboard menu. "I think a cheese and olive plate would taste good."

Jill's eyes were closed for a moment, then she swallowed. "We've definitely taken a step up from Charlie's."

Paulette was back a moment later. "What do you think of the syrah/grenache blend?"

Jill nodded, taking a second sip of wine which finished the glass. She swallowed and said, "It's very nice."

"That won a silver ribbon at the Arizona State Fair last year." Paulette rinsed her glass and poured wine from a second bottle. "Our GSM won the gold. It's a grenache/syrah/merlot blend."

"Do you have any greasy deep-fried appetizers?" I asked as Jill inhaled the aroma of the second wine.

With a laugh, Paulette said, "No. We only have a sandwich bar and a pizza oven. You'll have to hit one of the bars to get fried appetizers. Our Margherita pizza is outstanding."

"Please bring us a cheese and olive plate."

The increasingly boisterous women hailed Paulette again. Turning to a young man wearing a hairnet and slicing a pizza, she relayed our order. With the pizza in one hand and a stack of plates and napkins in the other, she returned to the women who hooted and laughed when their order arrived. One of the bridesmaids slipped money to Paulette, and she took a bottle from the back counter, uncapped it, and poured white wine into the six glasses, emptying the bottle.

The dark-haired cook, presumably the owner, brought our cheese and olive plate, along with a basket of seasoned flatbreads. "My wife is being monopolized by the bridal party. Can I get anything for you before she gets free?"

Jill finished her second sample and slid the glass away. "Your GSM is heavenly. Paulette said it won a gold medal."

"Thank you," he said, wiping his hands, then offering his right hand to Jill. "I'm Jerry Hansmann, cook, winemaker, and CEO of the 20/20 winery. What brings two cops here on a Wednesday afternoon?"

"I'm Jill Fletcher and this is my partner, Doug. We're investigating Al Tedeschi's murder."

The smile melted from the cook's face. "That's a sad situation."

"You're from the area, Jerry?" I asked, popping an olive into my mouth.

"The grapes we're harvesting today were planted by my family in the 1920s."

Laughter broke out among the women and Paulette leaned close to them, apparently sharing a joke or story.

"So, you probably know the Tedeschis."

Nodding, Jerry leaned on the counter to be heard over the increasingly boisterous women. "I went to school with Theresa and Carlton. I used to buy their grapes until Carlton started their winery."

"You're friends?" Jill asked.

After a moment of hesitation, Hansmann said, "We're not exactly friends. We know each other well, but Carlton and Theresa aren't people we'd invite over for supper."

"What do you know about Al and his death?" I asked.

Jerry reached under the counter and uncapped a bottle with a gold medallion on the label. "Try this zin blend. It won the gold medal at the Arizona vintner's convention two years ago."

Checking the wine list as he poured, Jill frowned. "There's no zinfandel on the wine list."

"We only have a few cases left, so we keep it under the counter for people we judge to be connoisseurs."

I looked at Jill, then at Jerry. "We're hardly wine aficionados, and that isn't a tasting sample. You poured a full glass."

Hansmann put the bottle away and nodded. "It's included with the cheese and olive plate."

Jill sipped the wine, then closed her eyes. She slid the glass to me. "You *have to* taste this."

Taking a sip, I paused. Hansmann was staring at me. "That's nice, even for someone who's not much into wine."

He took out an empty glass and filled it with a red wine from the shelf behind him. I put up my hand. "I'm only drinking sparkling water."

Our host picked up the plate of cheese and olives, and the fresh glass of wine, then nodded toward an empty table in the back corner. He set the wine and plate on the table, then pulled out a chair for Jill. I sat in the back corner facing the door. Jerry sat across from me and took a sip of wine.

"I can best describe the Tedeschis as an enigma. At first glance, they seem like businesspeople and concerned citizens. They belong to the chamber of commerce and donate to the local charities. On the other hand, they're canny businesspeople who negotiate carefully and squeeze every penny out of their suppliers. Carlton smiles and shakes my hand at all the vintners' meetings, but he tells people in his tasting room that our wines are swill."

Frowning, Jill leaned forward. "That's harsh. I thought you helped him get into the business."

"I did. I helped him set up his operation, showed him how to make wine, and gave him hints on how to get the most from the grapes they grow. In return, he tells people

I don't know anything about cultivating grapes or operating a winery."

"Are either Theresa or Carlton married?"

"Neither will marry while Robyn's alive."

"Why not?" Jill asked.

"Because there's no one good enough for Robyn's children. They dated in high school, but whenever Carlton or Theresa brought someone home to meet Mom and Dad, they'd get browbeaten, and the date would flee as if they'd been scalded with boiling water."

"That's harsh."

Jerry made sure no one was close enough to hear, then said, "I dated Theresa a couple times. Then I went over for Sunday dinner with the family. Robyn was all smiles until after the table was cleared, then she took me to the back step and berated me like a dog. The things she said to me made the high school bullies sound like amateurs. She recited the missteps of all my family members and made up a few on top of those. Her final words were, 'If you ever come near my daughter again, I'll castrate you like a steer and feed your nuts to the dogs.'"

"Ouch," I said.

"That pretty much ended my interest in Theresa."

"Do you think Theresa knows that's why you stopped dating her?" Jill asked.

"I have no idea. I never called her again."

Paulette motioned the increasingly boisterous women to the door. A white limo double-parked outside the wine bar.

"I'd hoped they weren't going to drive," I said.

"We know them, and part of the package was a limo that's taking them to dinner."

Pulling out the fourth chair, Paulette collapsed. "They're finally gone." She looked at Jerry, then his glass. "Be a sweetheart, bring us a round of the GSM and toss a pizza in the oven."

Jerry got up and looked at me. "Are you sticking with bubbly water?"

"I'm the designated driver." Looking at Jill, I said, "And you're on duty."

Jill considered her wine glass for a moment, then pulled the badge off her belt and slipped it into her back pocket. "I just went off duty."

Paulette laughed. "I like your style."

"Jerry was just filling us in on the Tedeschi clan," I said.

Her smile disappeared and Paulette reached for Jerry's wine glass. "I prefer not to discuss them, and I certainly won't talk about them when I'm sober."

"They're that bad?" Jill asked.

"I think of them as being slightly lower on the food chain than the green algae scum that forms on the river."

"Ouch," Jill said. "Is there some event that makes you say that?"

Paulette glanced at Jerry, who was assembling a pizza in the kitchen. "This is not public knowledge, but Al, Carlton, and Theresa have all hit on me at some point in my life."

I looked at Paulette, who was cute, but not Hollywood beautiful. She had a pleasant personality that was engaging. "Even Theresa?"

"She was circumspect, but I thought I knew where she was going when she asked me out to the ranch one weekend when they didn't have customers." Paulette paused. "Other people have had the same proposition, and some have accepted. She throws a party, not looking for anything permanent, just enjoying the company of whomever is attractive and available that evening. I've heard she swings from both sides of the saddle."

"That sounds like a lot of small-town rumors," Jill said. I reflected on her life, being labeled a lesbian in high school because she was a tomboy and refused the affection of a boy she didn't like.

Jerry came back with the wine and another bottle of water. "The pizza will be a minute more." He went back to the kitchen.

The wine bar was empty at 4:00, but Jill looked around to confirm no one was close. "Why would someone want to kill Al?"

Snorting, Paulette took a drink of the generous wine portion Jerry had poured. "How much time do you have? First of all, there are the women he's screwed. Second, are the jealous husbands and boyfriends. Third, are the suppliers who got partial payment for their goods and services, then were told they weren't getting more because whatever they'd supplied was sub-par, at least in Al's book."

The aroma of garlic preceded the arrival of our food. Jerry used a rolling cutter to slice the pizza into wedges. The cheese was melted and browned with red sauce and pepperoni peeking through gaps in the cheese. It was early for supper, but the aroma pushed aside all memories of our large lunch with Rob and the mega-sized cookie.

We sat back and watched Jerry place slices on the four plates. Expecting Jill to comment on the lack of vegetables, I watched as she used a fork and knife to cut through the oozing mozzarella. The wine was hitting her, and the siren's song of the pizza put all thoughts of "rabbit food" out of her brain.

After blowing on the pizza for a moment, Jill put a piece in her mouth. She closed her eyes as she chewed, then moaned. "If I wasn't old enough to be your mother, and if Doug wasn't sitting here, I'd ask you to marry me, Jerry."

Paulette laughed with her mouth full, choking on the pizza. After catching her breath, she wiped her mouth. "I haven't heard that one before."

Jerry smiled. "That's because women tell me that when you're not around."

The pizza was excellent, even better than my favorite Red's Savoy Pizza in St. Paul. "I'd ask you to marry me too, but that would be weird."

"Are you sure I can't talk you into a glass of wine, Doug? The Grenache/Syrah/Merlot goes really well with the red sauce." When I didn't immediately respond, Jerry added, "Jill already declared you off duty for the day."

"What the hell. Sure."

Jerry got up and walked to the door. He turned the bolt and flipped the sign over, so it displayed CLOSED to anyone passing by. Paulette smiled and nodded to me. "I guess we're off duty, too."

Jerry brought a fresh glass and a bottle. After pouring for me, he topped off the other three glasses. "I'm not sad Al's dead," he said, taking a bite of pizza. "On the other hand, he was part of the town's color, a throwback to the old cowboy and mining days. Men outnumbered the women ten to one, and every miner was looking for…romance the evening after payday."

"As much as things change, they remain the same," Paulette said, sipping her wine. "I get propositioned by half the drunks who come through here."

Jill shook her head. "You're wearing a wedding ring, and people know that Jerry's in the back."

"They know that, but married men, single men, even a few I swore were gay, have hit on me when their inhibitions are down."

"That's because you're a hot momma," Jerry said while chewing pizza. "You smile, are polite, and fill out your jeans nicely. That's an invitation in some men's minds."

Jill looked at me, expecting a comment. "Guys start drinking and their testosterone overwhelms their brains."

Paulette glanced at my badge. "Is that a problem for the Park Service?"

"Not as much as when I was a St. Paul cop."

"I saw you coming out of the 45-70 with Rob Henderson. Are you taking over the murder investigation?" Paulette asked, wiping her fingers, then setting her napkin on the empty plate.

"Because Al was found inside the Tuzigoot Monument, we've been asked to assist Rob. He seems like a competent investigator, and we'll help him however we can."

Paulette smiled. "I guess that includes plying the locals with alcohol to get inside information about the victim and potential murderers."

"Hey!" I said, putting up my left hand, my right hand still holding a slice of pizza. "I was drinking sparkling water until you plied me with wine, trying to get inside information on the investigation."

Having consumed more wine than the rest of us and being half my weight, Jill was feeling no pain. Her barriers were down. "Rob is too close to the people in town. We look at things through a different lens, one not clouded by history."

Paulette shrugged. "I bet you'll hear much the same things Rob has heard."

"But we listen with a different ear," Jill said, sipping more wine. "I bet Rob doesn't know that Theresa is throwing parties for her pals when the dude ranch is between guests."

Paulette's eyes went wide. "I'd never tell Rob that, but Jill gets me talking girl talk, and suddenly I'm spilling stories I've never told any customer." Pointing her finger at Jill she said, "You're good."

Waving off the compliment, Jill took another bite of pizza. "I'm invisible to most people. I'm a tomboy who grew up around horses. I don't wear makeup. I don't flaunt my figure. Women don't feel threatened, and they talk to me."

Jerry leaned back and wiped the grease from his fingers. "You two are such an unlikely pair. How did you end up together in the Park Service?"

"I was a retired cop running away from my past, and Jill was my boss. We both needed a friend, and our friendship became more than that." I stared at the last piece of pizza and the napkins on everyone else's plates. "Okay, I'm not letting this go to waste. Tell me about you two. How'd you end up in the wine business?"

Paulette smiled at Jerry. "We were high school sweethearts. He got me pregnant senior year and there was a shotgun wedding. We moved into the bunkhouse on Jerry's family ranch, and we helped make wine from the grapes they grew. Then, we'd go to my dad's ranch and do the same thing. After a couple years, Jerry started experimenting with blends of wines from the two ranches and he won a prize at the state fair. Jerry took some courses, and we planted some new varietals. The old guy who owned this building was a friend of my dad's. He'd been sampling our wines for years, and he offered to fix up the space and lease it to us as a tasting room. I started offering people crackers with their wine, and that led to cheese and crackers, then came pizza and sandwiches. All those things sold more wine and added to our cash flow."

"Were you the first tasting room in Cottonwood?"

"We were."

"How do you feel about all the others popping up?"

Jerry drew a breath. "At first, we were pissed. Then we realized that more people were coming to town, and they didn't stop at just one tasting room. As Cottonwood became a wine destination, business grew, and we had to start buying grapes from other local farmers to keep up with the demand."

"I assume you must've expanded your own vineyards too," I said.

"As much as we could," Paulette said. "The problem became the limited amount of water we could tap into for irrigation. Once we were consuming all the water rights associated with our ranches, we couldn't add any more vines."

"I'm from Minnesota and there's water everywhere," I explained. "Can't you just drill another well?"

"It's not that simple," Jerry explained. "Water rights are associated with the land and were allocated decades ago. If anything, we're going to get less water as Lake Mead goes down and water that's been diverted from the Colorado River is no longer available. It's a regional problem that's starting to affect ranches and all varieties of farming across the whole Southwest."

"But there's still development in Phoenix and the whole I-17 corridor."

"The developers are buying water rights from the ranchers and the tribes. That'll end at some point when no one is willing to sell."

Jill put her hand on my arm. "I think we've taken enough of Jerry and Paulette's time. We should let them reopen."

Paulette looked at the clock and got up. "I've got to get the kids from daycare."

"Can you handle the cooking and wine tasting alone tonight, Jerry?"

"Colleen Little will be here in half an hour. She'll handle the tasting while I make sandwiches and do the books."

Paulette's smile was warm and genuine. "You're good folks. It's been a pleasure to meet you."

Jerry picked up the wine glasses and I grabbed the plates and dirty napkins. "Thanks for your time and the information."

I followed him to a hidden dishwasher in the back corner of their space. "Doug, it's been a pleasure being able to step away from the business for an hour and talk to someone who wants to talk about something other than the smoky blackberry notes in the GSM."

"I appreciate your insights into the Tedeschis."

"I wish I could tell you I knew who the murderer was, but I really don't know."

I laughed. "That's what everyone says right before we connect their DNA to the crime scene."

"I have an alibi," he said, putting up his hands. "Remind me which night Al was murdered."

We emerged from the kitchen laughing. Paulette and Jill were having a more heated discussion. "No, Jill. You will NOT pay for the pizza or the bottle of wine we drank. They're our treat."

"But you're running a business…"

"Not this afternoon. We had a pleasant conversation with our new friends. Let it be."

I pulled out a credit card and waved it at Paulette. "We want a case of the GSM."

"Seriously?"

"Seriously. We want to buy a case of that wine."

Jerry went in the back and returned with a 12-bottle case. "I assume you don't want to carry this down the street to your car or hotel. Where can I deliver it?"

"I'll take two bottles with us. You can drop the rest off at the Tavern Hotel at your leisure."

Paulette took my VISA card to the cash register and ran the charge. Jill, who'd had a little too much wine watched. "Please put half the pizza on Doug's card."

Paulette smiled and patted Jill's arm. "We'll make enough profit on this case of wine to cover the pizza."

Jerry removed two bottles from the case and put them in paper sacks. He held out his hand. "Thanks for coming by. I appreciate your purchase, but the time with you was a special treat for us."

Jill looped her arm through mine and leaned her head against my shoulder as we walked down the sidewalk. "They are very nice people."

"They are."

Stopping abruptly, Jill turned to me. "What are we going to do with a case of wine? We're only here a couple more nights."

"We'll bring it to Jamie and Liz as a housewarming present."

Satisfied with that answer, we continued toward the hotel. "You bought that wine because I was being insensitive."

"It's good wine, and it's my way of saying thanks and doing it in a way that doesn't deny the gift of pizza and their time."

"When did you get so smart, Fletcher?"

"I've learned a lot of things through the school of hard knocks."

"The Spearfish South Dakota school of hard knocks never taught me about things like that."

"You learned to shoot, ride horses, and rope cattle. Those are important ranching skills."

Jill stopped and turned to me again. "I'm lucky I met you."

"We balance each other nicely."

After kissing me in the middle of the sidewalk, Jill said, "I got the better part of the deal."

"Um, dear. People are staring at the two cops kissing and blocking the sidewalk."

Jill looped her arm through mine again and started walking. "Let's go back to the hotel and put out the do not disturb sign."

"You'll fall asleep and wake up at three in the morning."

We stepped into the crosswalk and the traffic stopped. Halfway across the street, Jill whispered. "I'll probably wake you at three for the second act of the performance."

"We have to work tomorrow."

"Don't you think making love to your wife is a higher priority?"

"They're on different scales. Both are important, but different."

"Listen, Fletcher, you caused the problem."

"What problem is that?"

"You awakened my libido after fifty years of celibacy. Now, I expect you to perform your marital duty."

I laughed as we crossed the lobby. The desk clerk waved me over. "Mr. Fletcher, there's a message for you."

Jill ripped the envelope open as we walked down the hall. "It's from Matt. It says, 'why is your damned phone off again?'"

Patting my pocket, I realized the phone was still on the charger in the hotel room. "I'll have to call him."

"Like hell you will. He can wait until morning. It's not like there's anything we're going to do tonight."

I laughed as Jill opened the door. "The lifelong Park Service employee is telling me not to call my boss after he left an urgent message?"

As soon as the door closed, Jill started unbuttoning my shirt. "We're off duty, remember? I took off my badge, and you drank wine. We're in no condition to answer his call or deal with whatever issue has come up."

"But…"

"This is *Jill* time. Shut off your phone, your other thoughts, and set aside the investigation. There is only one thing on your mind right now."

"There was a time in my life when that was about the only thing I thought about."

"Great, I'm taking you back in time. You're young and your only thought is…" She pressed her hips against me. "I think you're already on that thought."

"That's my pistol."

"Your pistol is on your hip. That is *not* what I'm leaning against."

Chapter 8

The next morning, Jill was on the bed, staring at the ceiling when I got out of the shower. "How much wine did you force me to drink last night?"

"It was you who forced me to drink half a bottle of wine last night, not the other way around."

"It was a poor choice."

"After breakfast, we need to talk to the people who bought the sterile heifers. Take a shower."

Sighing, Jill rolled off the bed. "Breakfast seems like a bad idea right now. Go down without me and I'll join you for a cup of tea after my shower."

I was reading the newspaper when Jill arrived. She looked at the remnants of my sausage and scrambled eggs, then quickly turned away. "I saw tea and coffee in the lobby. Let's grab a couple to-go cups and drive to the riding school."

Folding the paper, I got up. "A bowl of oatmeal might be good."

Already walking away, Jill waved over her shoulder. "Not right now."

We had to backtrack through old Cottonwood on Highway 89A to the new part of town. Waiting at the first stoplight, we idled across from a tattoo parlor. Jill frowned. "They're not open yet."

"I think of people who get tattoos as the afternoon and evening crowd."

"What makes you think that?"

The turn arrow changed to green, and I followed the flow of cars. "I suspect a lot of people are more amenable to a tattoo after a couple drinks and some peer pressure."

"Have you ever considered getting a tattoo?"

"A few guys got them after our Iraq deployment. When I was a cop, there was a department policy against visible tattoos."

"Your ex-wife had a rose tattoo on her ankle."

"All her artsy buddies had tattoos. In my mind, that was another argument against a tattoo."

After a moment of silence, Jill turned to me. "Water rights are a big issue in dry country like this. Our discussion last night about not having enough water to add more grape vines got me thinking about our conversation with Geraldine Holland. Her company specializes in water management. You'd think the counties here would be using her to model sustainable water supplies for the ranchers and farmers."

"The counties probably don't have the budget to pay for her services. On the other hand, if the fruit growers' water supplies are cut off, I expect they'd form a cooperative to spread the cost of water modeling among all the members."

Jill pulled out her phone and found the number for Jerry and Paulette Hansmann's tasting room. Surprisingly, Jerry answered on the first ring. After thanking him for the wine and pizza, Jill told him about Geraldine Holland's company and their modeling capability. "Perhaps you can form a wine producers' cooperative and use her to find more water for your grapes."

Turning on the speaker, Jill held out the phone. "We've viewed the other winemakers as competition rather than cooperative members. Given the recent cuts in Colorado River water allocations, we might do well to get a plan together ahead of the developers and farmers. Do you have a phone number for that woman?"

After pulling out her credentials, Jill found Geraldine Holland's card behind her Park Service ID. "Here's her number. Give her a call."

Within a block, we were out of the Cottonwood business district. After two blocks of houses came a hobby farm, followed by a rough-sawn board fence. At the driveway were tall gate posts topped with a wrought-iron sign for Trail's End Ranch. Mounted on the post was a smaller hand-painted sign that read, horse training. The pasture inside the fence was brown. The half dozen horses inside the enclosure were clustered under an open-sided pole structure with a corrugated steel roof, shielding them from the oppressive Arizona sun.

I parked next to a single-story house in need of paint. Across the driveway was a relatively new barn. Inside, bales of hay were stacked neatly in front of a John Deere tractor. Attached to the barn was a smaller building with windows. A hand-written sign on the door said, "C'mon in."

Jill stepped out of the pickup and walked to what was apparently an office. Her stride told me she was feeling better, or that this felt like home territory. I followed behind, scanning the house and barn for signs of activity. Although I didn't expect a horse trainer to meet us with a gun, I was paranoid after our most recent Florida experience.

A bell jangled inside the office when Jill opened the door, and cool air met me as I stepped inside. The woman sitting behind the desk looked up from her paperwork. "I heard the park cops might stop by. I'll have to thank Charlie for putting us on the suspect list."

The woman's face was freckled, her once naturally red hair was now mostly white and pulled into a ponytail. She didn't get up, just gestured to two rickety wooden desk chairs that creaked when we sat. "Your horses look well cared for," Jill said. "Some riding schools have strings of malnourished sway-backed nags."

A smile flickered on the woman's lips. "You've been around horses." It was a comment, not a question.

"I grew up on a South Dakota ranch." Jill paused. "The grass in your paddock is brown. Do you have grazing land near the river?"

"We feed hay most of the year here. It'll rain some in the upcoming monsoon season, but we have to buy hay."

"We heard that Al Tedeschi sold you a couple freemartin heifers."

The woman cocked her head. "You must be a ranch girl. No city slicker knows what a freemartin is."

"We never had many freemartin twins, but we sold them as feed cattle and told the buyers the heifers were sterile so there was no confusion or expectations of them calving."

The smile left the woman's face and she set her pen down. "That old bastard had the nerve to sell us sterile heifers when he knew we were trying to buy breeding stock."

After a second, she added, "It's not like we didn't sell them at a profit, but when hay is expensive, you don't want to waste it on heifers who aren't going to give you calves. We raise a steer for our own use, but we sell off the rest of the steers to people up north who have good grass or forest service leases."

"How angry were you with Al?" I asked.

"Jake gave him a piece of his mind and demanded a refund for the price difference between breeding stock and feeders. Al laughed in his face. We were mad, but we didn't kill him."

Jill shook her head in sympathy. "That might've been the difference between making a few dollars or taking a loss for the season."

"We do okay because of the riding school and training horses. There's no way we'd make a living here otherwise. We're close to the river and the town figures our land is worth more than ranch land farther from downtown, so we're taxed accordingly."

"I suppose you've had developers who'd like to build here."

"We've got water rights and there's always someone who's trying to buy us out, pretending they're doing us a favor. They want the water rights more than the land. One of these days, someone's going to come along and offer us what this place is worth. Until then, we'll stay and raise riding stock."

"A good cattle horse is valuable," Jill said.

"Ranching is changing. More people are working their cattle with ATV's that burn gas instead of hay." The woman got a far away look, then a smile. "No ATV has a personality like a horse. They're better friends than most of the folks around town."

I leaned forward. "Someone killed Al and dumped him at Tuzigoot. Who disliked him enough to kill him?"

The door swung open and a man wearing a western shirt, a brimmed hat, boots, and dusty leather chaps walked in. He hesitated when he saw us. "Um, sorry, Hazel. I didn't know anyone was here."

I stood and offered my hand. "I'm Doug Fletcher. We're with the Park Service and we're investigating Al Tedeschi's murder."

After wiping his hand on his shirt, he shook. "I'm Jake Pochart. You've got your work cut out for you if you're looking for someone who wanted Al dead. Hell, half of Cottonwood wouldn't have pissed on his head if Al's hair was on fire."

"Jake! Don't go speaking ill of the dead."

"Oh hell, Hazel, it's no secret that Al was a cheap, cheating sonofabitch."

"Can you think of anyone who held a particular grudge against him?" Jill asked.

"Al was an equal opportunity bastard," Jake said. "I can't think of a person who liked him."

Eyes darting between us, Hazel shifted in her chair. "Well, there were a few women who liked Al…but that never lasted long."

Jake opened the door and spat a stream of tobacco juice onto the driveway. "Only long enough for them to sober up or realize Al's wallet only came out of his pocket when he thought he could get into their pants."

"I imagine some of those women were pretty bitter," I said, hoping Jake would add some names to the suspect list.

"Nah, most knew what they were getting into. Now, there are some husbands who might've taken a dim view of Al poking their wives."

"Jake, stop right now. You don't know anything except rumors."

Looking at me, Jake raised his eyebrows. "Where there's smoke, there's fire. I've heard enough talk about Al's escapades to know there's more than rumor to them."

"You were pretty upset with the freemartin sale," Jill said.

Jake shook his head. "I put that on myself. I should've known better than to trust Al. The deal was too good, and I should've been suspicious."

Hazel coughed. "The deal wasn't that good. It was the same price everyone was getting for heifers."

"But knowing it was Al selling at the going price should've tipped me off. He always tried to make an extra buck on everything. I should've known."

"So, why did you buy from Al," Jill asked.

"Everyone else had already sold their young stock. Al had these two heifers, and we were looking for breeding stock when no one else had any."

Jill stood. "We shouldn't take up any more of your time. Thanks for talking to us."

Shaking hands, we said goodbye. Jill hesitated while I held the door for her. "Say, do you have any horses with bar shoes?"

Jake shook his head. "We haven't had a horse that needed a bar shoe in maybe twenty years. Why do you ask?"

Jill shrugged. "Just curious. Thanks."

In the truck, Jill turned the air-conditioning control to maximum. "I think we need to talk to the local farriers. They'll know which horses use bar shoes."

"Do you think they'd have an office in Cottonwood?"

Pulling out her cell phone, Jill started a search. "Most farriers work out of their trucks. It's a mobile service and they travel to the barns to shoe the horses."

"Are there any farrier listings?"

"There's one in Prescott and another near Tucson. They both have websites."

"That's it?" I asked. "There are only two people in all of Arizona who shoe horses?"

Jill typed in a new search. "Those are operations big enough to have a web presence. There are probably dozens of others who have a string of regular customers and don't want or need any additional business. Most probably find business by word-of-mouth or with business cards posted on store bulletin boards."

Glancing at her phone, I asked, "What are you searching for?"

"Tack stores."

"Tacks for horseshoes?"

Sighing, Jill shook her head. "Horseshoes are nailed on, dear. Tack is a generic term for horse and riding supplies."

"Are there tack stores here?"

Jill snorted. "I found one called The Naughty Cowgirl. Here's another called J.J.'s Saddle Shop."

"Give me directions to the cowgirl shop."

"Um, it's in Sedona. I'm on their website and…" Jill sighed.

"What?"

"It's a tourist place, not a tack shop."

Stopping for a red light, I tipped her phone so I could see the pouting model displayed on the cell phone screen. "We should go there. You don't have a black leather camisole."

"Nor do I need one."

I tried to page down. "What else do they have?"

Jill pulled the phone away. "The light's green. Go straight and we'll pass J.J.'s Saddle Shop."

"How far away is the cowgirl shop?"

"Give it a rest, Doug. There's nothing there I'm interested in buying,"

"I could buy something for you."

Shaking her head, Jill slipped her phone into her pocket. "Anything you bought there would be a gift for *you*. It's like a guy shopping for his girlfriend at Victoria's Secret. Anything he buys is for his enjoyment." Jill pointed. "The saddle shop is ahead on the right."

"You're just trying to end the conversation," I said, steering into a parking spot on the street.

Jill stepped out of the pickup without answering.

The store smelled of leather. The displays featured horse gear from saddles to spurs. A mannequin inside the door wore a complete western cut outfit including heavy leather chaps. I wandered around while Jill walked to the cash register.

A man who belonged in a Marlboro ad looked up from a display of beautifully embossed leather handbags. "Can I help you, ma'am?"

A display case of spurs, a mixture of new and antique, caught my eye. "Holy shit!" I said a little too loudly when I saw the $500 price.

The clerk looked from Jill to me. "They're made by E. Garcia."

"They're western fashion accessories, Doug. Each is a piece of art made to be worn."

"I thought you'd be able to buy a pair of spurs for $25."

The clerk laughed. "That's what basic working spurs cost. Like the lady said, these are accessories."

"You have to excuse him. My partner is a city kid."

Chuckling, the clerk waved off the apology. "How can I help you?"

"We're looking for local farriers."

"There's a cork board next to the back door with business cards from local businesses tacked on it. Lacy Jackson owns the Bonanza Blacksmith shop. While her primary business is wrought iron railings and branding irons, she also shoes horses."

"There's a business in branding irons?"

"The ranches are changing over to cattle ear tags, but every business with a western theme wants a couple branding irons hanging on the wall."

"Is Lacy the only farrier in town?"

"Chuck Painter shoes horses too, but he works out of his truck and doesn't advertise. I think he has more work than he can handle."

"How can we contact them?" Jill asked.

"Lacy's probably got a card on the board. You'll have to look Chuck's number up." The clerk hesitated. "Hang on, I've got a phone book under here somewhere. Chuck's probably in the white pages."

The thin phone directory, dogeared and yellow, was buried under a stack of wholesale catalogs and magazines featuring horses. The clerk flipped through the pages. He stopped in the P section and ran his finger down the column. "Yep, here he is."

Jill took out her cell phone, ready to punch in the number.

The clerk hesitated. "You'd best let me call him. Chuck's a bit prickly around strangers, and if your number isn't local, he's likely to assume it's spam and ignore the call." Pulling a pair of reading glasses from under the counter, our helper punched the number into the desktop phone.

"Hey, Chuck. This is Pete, from the saddle shop. I've got a couple cops here who want to talk to you." Pete listened, then put his hand over the phone. "He's in Prescott Valley and wants to know who you are and what you want."

"We're Park Service rangers investigating Al Tedeschi's murder."

Pete relayed the message. Nodding, he listened to the response, then put his hand over the phone. "Chuck says you should find the killer and give him a medal." More conversation followed, then Pete hung up.

"Is he coming this way?"

"I'm not entirely sure. He did make it clear he didn't want word getting around that he was helping the cops find Al's murderer." Pete smiled and said, "Chuck thought that might hurt his business."

"Really?" Jill asked. "People dislike Al Tedeschi that much?"

"To be honest with you, I probably wouldn't have given you either Chuck or Lacy's name if I'd known you were looking for Al's killer. You're not going to make any friends around here if you arrest someone local." Pete paused, then his eyes sparkled. "Well, unless you arrest the bitch he's married to."

"You don't like Robyn Tedeschi?"

"I closed her account and asked her to take her business elsewhere."

"That's tough in a small town like Cottonwood," Jill said.

"Not really. She didn't pay on time, tried to get a discount months after she'd bought the equipment, and her screaming arguments were driving away other customers. I do just fine without the Lazy L business."

"Where does she buy her tack?" Jill asked.

"Frankly my dear, I don't give a damn." Pete smiled, imitating Rhett Butler.

"We heard that Anna Weise, the Lazy L cook, sometimes hangs out at the Riverside Bar," I said. "Do you think it's too early to find her there?"

Pete looked at a clock mounted near the door. "She cooks breakfast and lunch, then heads out after cleaning up the lunch dishes. It's still a bit early for her. Grab yourselves a bite, then head over there."

Jill thanked him while I searched for Lacy's business card on the corkboard. I found it buried under dozens of other cards offering anything from car insurance to horse training and stud service.

I tossed the pickup keys to Jill after we walked outside. "I think the 45-70 should be opening about now. Let's get a table and wait for Rob."

"Are you calling the blacksmith shop?" Jill asked as she started the engine.

"Based on the response we got from Pete, I think Lacy might be more receptive to us in person. The shop's address is in Cornville. Maybe we'll go there before going to the bar to meet Anna."

Obviously looking for something, Pete walked out of the saddle shop. Seeing the

Park Service pickup, he waved and walked over. I rolled down the window and smiled. "You thought of who else might've killed Al?"

Pete knelt next to my window. "I won't give Tedeschi's murder another thought. But I thought I'd warn you about Anna."

"What about her?" Jill asked.

"Well, you seem nice, maybe churchgoing folks." Pete paused. "You might want to be prepared to have your ears singed."

Laughing, Jill shook her head. "We've been warned she's a bit…salty."

"Ma'am, the ocean is salty. Anna can cuss up a storm if she gets mad. And she might not be entirely happy that you're trying to solve Al's murder. She's not an Al Tedeschi fan."

"She worked for him," Jill said.

"No, she works for Robyn and Theresa. In Anna's book, Al was…" Pete looked at Jill, then considered his words. "I won't say what Anna thought about Al in front of a lady."

"I guess I'm flattered," Jill said, smiling.

Looking at me, Pete said, "Your partner is a lady. I hope you appreciate her."

"I'm married to her."

Pete looked at Jill to see if I was kidding. "I'll be darned. You, sir, are a lucky man."

"Thanks."

* * *

Checking traffic, Jill made a U-turn in the quiet street. She drove silently.

"What's with you?"

"What?" she asked.

"You rarely pass up an opportunity to rub my nose in a compliment like that."

"You already know how lucky you are to be married to me. I don't need to remind you."

Frowning, I looked at her. "You always tell me you're the lucky one."

"The broom sweeps both ways."

At the traffic light, Jill stopped behind a trailer loaded with round bales of hay. "That load has to weigh twelve tons."

"Is that a lot?" I asked.

"It's probably twice what his trailer is rated for."

The pickup pulling the hay moved ahead when the arrow turned green and we followed, turning toward old Cottonwood. "How's your hangover?"

"I'm thirsty, but ready to eat. I have a strange craving for a cheeseburger and fries."

"You're going to order a cheeseburger?"

She glanced at me. "I'm going to order a salad, but I'll eat a bite of your burger and half your fries."

133

"I'm having a pulled pork sandwich. Order your own cheeseburger."

"I'll change your order when you're in the bathroom."

"What?"

"You heard me."

I looked at her in disbelief. "Where's this coming from?"

"You had several cups of coffee with breakfast, and your bladder is probably ready to pop. I'll order a cheeseburger for you while you're gone."

"You *never* order cheeseburgers."

"Maybe it's the pizza and wine. That tasted really good and for some reason, I feel like eating a burger today."

"Maybe you're pregnant."

"That horse left the gate a few years ago." Jill paused, then glanced at me. "But I am looking forward to being a godmother."

A car backed out of a parking spot a half block from the 45-70. Feeling like karma was smiling on us, we walked in the door just moments past 11:00, the posted opening time. Rob Henderson was seated at the same high-top table we'd used the day before. His Stetson was hanging on a peg and there was a Diet Coke in front of him. With her elbows resting on the table, Carmen was seated across from him.

I sat on the stool next to Henderson with Jill next to Carmen. Being gentlemanly, Henderson stood until Jill sat down.

"Carmen is joining us for lunch today," he said.

"I'm glad you could join us," Jill said, smiling.

"It's strange coming to the place I work on my day off, but Rob offered to buy me lunch."

"Actually, the county is buying. We're having a business lunch. Order what you want at the counter. They've started a tab for me, and we've already ordered."

Jill glanced at the blackboard behind the cash register. "What do you suggest, Carmen?"

"I'm having fish tacos with extra Jalapenos. They're really good."

"I was thinking about a cheeseburger," Jill said, still studying the board.

Carmen frowned. "I'm vegetarian. I don't do burgers."

Intrigued, I cocked my head. "Most vegetarians don't eat fish."

"Fish aren't mammals, so they don't count."

Henderson was smiling. Jill looked at me, then at Carmen. "How do you feel about chicken and turkey?"

"Chickens are cute, so they're off the menu. Turkeys are stupid and taste really good, so I eat them."

Rob turned his head and made a noise that was half cough, half laugh.

"Doug's having a cheeseburger basket," Jill said, getting up from the stool. She hesitated for a second, awaiting my protest, then walked to the cash register to place our order.

Henderson's questioning look was priceless, but I didn't respond. "What have you two been up to since yesterday's lunch?"

"We visited a couple of the wine tasting shops yesterday. This morning we went to a saddle shop hoping to identify local farriers."

"Do you think a farrier killed Al?" Carmen asked.

Not wanting to share too much information, I skirted the question. "We're looking at a number of avenues."

Nodding discreetly, Rob signaled he didn't want to divulge details of the investigation. Although nothing pointed to Carmen's involvement, she wasn't off my suspects list. Deftly changing the topic he asked, "Why did Jill announce you were having a cheeseburger?"

"She wants a cheeseburger but feels like she should eat something leafy and green. She plans to eat part of my burger and half the fries."

Smiling, Rob asked, "Does that mean you have to eat half her salad?"

"Um, no. That might mean I'll be hungry enough to eat a cookie."

Carmen's mind had been elsewhere until she heard me say cookie. "Zander makes a really good chocolate malt that goes well with a cookie."

"Wow," I said. "I can't remember the last time I had a malt."

Carmen waved at a goth-looking guy behind the counter. Using hand gestures, she communicated our request. "He'll make one as soon as he's done with the sandwich he's making."

Sliding back onto her stool, Jill looked at us. "So, have you solved the murder while I've been gone?"

Turning toward Carmen, Rob said, "No, but a couple interesting things came to light overnight. Tell Doug and Jill what happened."

"Robyn Tedeschi showed up at my apartment last night and told me to pack my clothes and move out."

"What?" Jill asked.

"She said Al's name was on the lease and he'd paid for all the furniture. According to her, the only things that belonged to me were my clothes."

Jill put her hand on Carmen's arm. "What'd you do?"

"I told her that most of the furniture was mine from before I met Al, and the rest was a gift from him. As for the lease, I don't really know whose name is on it. I think Al and I signed together."

"Did she leave?" I asked.

"She tried to push her way into the apartment, but I started screaming at her. She left when one of the neighbors came over, but said I'd be hearing from her lawyer."

Zander carried a platter to the table and balanced it on one hand as he set out Carmen's fish tacos, Rob's club sandwich, then set a glass mug, topped with whipped cream and a cherry, in front of me. He set a frosty metal container alongside the malt. "Would you like a second straw?"

Raising my eyebrows, I smiled at Jill. "Would you like some of my chocolate malt?"

Without hesitation, she said, "Sure."

Zander pulled another paper-wrapped straw out of his apron and slid it to Jill. "Enjoy."

After sliding the metal can in front of her, Jill unwrapped the straw and plunged it into the creamy malt. She stirred slightly. "Looks like I'll have to spend an hour on the hotel's elliptical trainer tonight to burn these calories." She took a sip and sighed. "I'd forgotten what a malt made with real ice cream tastes like."

I sighed. "An hour in the fitness center? Really?"

"You'll probably need two hours—one for the malt and one for the cheeseburger basket."

Rob wiped a crumb from his chin. "How many hours did you exercise last night to burn off the pizza?"

Jill looked up from the malt. "Who told you about pizza?"

"Small town," Rob said, smiling. "I heard you unpinned your badge and enjoyed a couple glasses of wine, too. Doug carried a couple bottles to the hotel, so I'd guess you two had quite a hangover this morning."

Jill glanced at me over the rim of her malt container.

"He's a detective," I said.

Shaking her head, Carmen blew out a breath. "The whole town is full of snoops. I can't go out for a meal without someone asking me how my dinner was. They also know which cars were left in the bar parking lot overnight."

And who the owners are, who they left with, and where they spent the night, I thought to myself.

"Jill, your order's up," a woman wearing a hairnet called from behind the bar as she set two trays on the counter.

Because I was halfway through a swallow of malt, Jill hopped off her barstool and walked to the counter. Returning, she set a burger basket in front of me and sat down, sliding a tray with tacos in front of her. "Thanks for the tip about the fish tacos. They look wonderful," she said to Carmen.

I took a bite of burger and squeezed ketchup onto my fries from a plastic bottle. Jill dipped two fries into the ketchup and popped them into her mouth before I took a bite of my cheeseburger.

"I hope the fries are good," I said, sarcastically.

Without answering, she smiled and took a bite of her fish taco. Then she made a yummy sound. "These are really good."

My half-pound burger was excellent and after the first bite I knew I wasn't going to be able to eat it all. I cut it in half and ate some fries.

Jill eyed the half burger I'd set aside. "Can you cut that in half again? I don't want that much."

Henderson shook his head as he watched me cut the burger into quarters. "My wife does that all the time. I order something and she skewers a piece off my plate asking, 'Is this any good?'"

"If a guy did that to me," Carmen said, "I'd bury my fork in his hand."

Henderson laughed. "Putting up with things like that lead to a twentieth anniversary."

Shaking her head, Carmen ate the last bite of her taco. "I haven't met a man I like enough to let him steal food off my plate."

And that's why you've had two divorces before your thirtieth birthday, I thought.

Reading my mind, Jill gave me *the look.* Although we've only been married a little over a year, she'd become amazingly perceptive. Her quick head shakes and nudges helped me keep my foot out of my mouth.

Hoping I'd received the message, she said, "Your burger tastes much better than the boot leather you sometimes eat."

The comment went over Carmen's head, but Rob caught it and smiled.

Jill wiped her hands after finishing a quarter of my burger and half the fries. "Have you thought of anyone else we should consider a suspect in Al's murder?"

Carmen pushed her tray aside. "I don't know of anyone who'd kill Al. I mean, there are a lot of people who disliked him. This is a small town, and we tend to keep running into the same people, eventually irritating some of them." She looked around the dining room that had filled as we ate. "I'm sure there are a few people watching us who don't know it's my day off and assume I'm goofing off because I'm not clearing tables and ringing up orders. That's just the way it is."

Beating Jill to the last fry, I popped it into my mouth. "Al seemed to irritate a lot of businesspeople."

"He told me, 'You don't get rich by spending money.' He didn't get into any business deal unless he was sure he'd make a profit. Some people felt he took advantage of them, but Al viewed all his business dealings as that, just business. In Al's book, friendship wasn't a consideration if money was involved."

"Think back to your last few months with Al," Jill said. "Is there someone who was particularly irritated with some transaction?"

Nodding to a table near the windows, Carmen leaned close to Jill. "Frank Butler went bankrupt, and the sheriff auctioned off his store. Al bought it, and all the inventory, for next to nothing because everyone was Frank's friend, and they didn't want to insult him by paying so little for a hardware store that was his life's work. After the sheriff's sale, Al had a fire sale on all the hardware. He made back the auction price in an hour, and everything else was clear profit for the next week, until most everything was gone. Al cleared out the last of it and donated it to an orphanage, deducting the full retail value of the odds and ends on his taxes. He leased out the building to a woman who's running a clothing consignment shop, and getting a healthy monthly rent, after making close to a quarter million dollars on the hardware sale."

We glanced at the man at the front table. I'd guess he was in his late 50s but might be younger. He looked tired and beaten down. "He doesn't look like someone who'd shoot Al, throw him across a horse, and dump his body somewhere."

Stacking our dishes and trays together, Rob said, "I wrote Frank off early on. His wife left with his kids during the bankruptcy. He's renting an old trailer on the way to Jerome and works part-time packing bags at the grocery store. He doesn't own a horse and probably doesn't have access to one."

Carmen shrugged. "You asked if he'd screwed anyone lately. Frank's the only one I can think of." She glanced at her watch, then got off the stool. "I've got a hair appointment. Thanks for lunch, Rob."

With Carmen gone, Rob leaned close to us. "What have you heard that I've missed?"

"We talked to the saddle shop and neither of the local farriers will shoe Tedeschi's horses. They told Robyn to take her business elsewhere too," I said.

"I didn't know that, but I suspected it. The local vet doesn't answer Tedeshci's calls, either."

Jill looked around. "Robyn intimidates Theresa's boyfriends because none of them are good enough for her little girl. And Theresa Tedeschi invites her buddies out to party at the Lazy L when they're between bookings. I don't know what that would have to do with Al's death, but it's one more piece of information."

"I don't know what that'd have to do with Al, either. But it's another piece of fat to chew." Rob leaned back. "Let's talk about that a little. I'd guess it'd be more likely that Robyn would get crosswise with one of Theresa's love interests than Al."

"Unless Robyn browbeat Al into chasing off a boyfriend…or girlfriend."

The sharp pain from the toe of Jill's boot shot up from my shin. "Shut up, Doug. We're not spreading baseless rumors."

Laughing, Henderson signaled Zander for a Diet Coke refill. "I'd heard that Theresa batted for both teams but discounted it. She seems to be much more attracted to men than women. I'd also heard about the Lazy L parties, and the sense I got was that she invited pretty women out there to improve the selection of male…guests."

I lifted the leg of my jeans to see if I was bleeding. There was no blood, but a lump was rising and starting to color. "Again, I can't see how that would involve Al."

Henderson shook his head. "Maybe Al interrupted something and whoever was involved couldn't afford to have it leaked that he and Theresa were knocking boots."

Jill's eyes lit up. "Maybe Al was blackmailing someone who'd been visiting Theresa's bedroom."

Zander delivered the Diet Coke and cleared the table. "Do you guys want another malt or a cookie?"

I felt the toe of Jill's boot against my shin. "Um, I think we've had plenty. Thanks."

Jill smiled and moved her boot back under her stool. "What do you think about the blackmail scenario, Rob?"

Rob put his elbows on the table and clasped his hands. "Wow. That's not something I'd considered. Al was into making money any way he could. I guess blackmail would be a step beyond his usual shady deals. The question becomes, who would he blackmail?"

Jill leaned back. "A good-looking, married guy who had a lot to lose if the news of his indiscretion got out."

Deep in thought, Rob stared into the distance. "There are five, maybe six local businessmen who fit that description. If we think more broadly, there are a lot more possible victims in Sedona and Cornville."

"A politician?" Jill asked.

"Phew," Henderson said, blowing out a breath. "That's way beyond what I've considered. There's a congressman who lives in Page Springs. I have no idea if he's ever met Tedeschis, but he's got a reputation for extra-marital affairs. A couple years ago we ran an online prostitution sting, and he was trolling there. We didn't actually get him to bite, but he was texting with one of our deputies who was posing as an underage girl."

"I'd love to take down someone like that." Jill said.

Henderson looked down. "He's untouchable. Even asking for an interview would bring down a shitstorm of political pressure. If we get any credible evidence tying him to Al's death, I'll talk to the sheriff. For now, let's put him on a back burner."

Chapter 9

The Riverside Bar's gravel parking lot had room for thirty or more cars. At 1:30 on a weekday afternoon there were only six vehicles. Five were dusty pickups, likely belonging to working folks, and an old green Pontiac that looked worn out. Unlike the cowboy bars I'd experienced in Flagstaff, this one didn't have music drifting out of the doors. The only noise from the bar was a hearty woman's laugh.

"This is a serious drinker's bar," I said, halfway across the parking lot.

"Because of the dusty pickups?"

"Hard core drinkers shy away from the swanky bars playing music. They gravitate to silent places where they can talk to their buddies without yelling to be heard over the jukebox."

The bar's interior was dark, and it took a moment for my eyes to adjust after walking in from the blazing Arizona sun. Jill grabbed my arm. "I feel like I just walked through the looking glass."

Eight sets of eyes were locked on us. None looked pleased. After a moment, the regulars returned to their drinks, having checked out the strangers. We walked past a table where a young woman in medical scrubs had her hands wrapped around a glass of clear liquid. She sat, staring at the table while a guy, probably twenty years older, leaned close. He appeared to be selling a plan. She appeared to be listening skeptically. I judged her to be close to legally drunk, and the guy looked like a predator hoping to take advantage of her intoxication. Jill glanced at them as we passed. I saw her look of revulsion and grabbed Jill's arm before she intervened in something that was none of our business.

At the bar sat four men and a woman. They were all leaning together, and the man on the right seemed to be telling a story. I caught the last line as we neared the bar. "…and she said, 'You're so drunk you couldn't get it up if I did go home with you!'"

The five of them laughed, the woman's voice echoing throughout the bar. The bartender, who looked old enough to be retired, shook his head, probably having heard the same story at least a half dozen times. He walked down to us, moving like he had a bad back. A black eyepatch was the most distinctive feature of his craggy face. "What can I get for you?"

"Sparkling water with lime," I said, trying to not stare at the eyepatch.

Jill hesitated, then blew out a breath. "Diet Coke."

"Is a can okay?" The bartender asked.

"Yeah," Jill replied.

Jill turned her back to the bar and studied the couple at the table. The man had his arm over the woman's shoulder and was whispering in her ear. The woman sat staring at her nearly empty glass, not reacting to his words.

The bartender returned with my sparkling water, a lime wedge draped over the rim of the glass. He set the Diet Coke in front of Jill and put a glass full of ice next to it. "You two must be on duty. I don't recognize your badges, so you're not local cops or state troopers."

I pulled out my wallet and set a five-dollar bill on the bar. "Will this cover it?"

The bartender picked up the bill and smiled. "I'll get your four dollars change."

"Keep the change," I said.

He'd started to turn away from us but stopped. "Why do I get the feeling this is going to cost me?"

Jill stopped me before I could ask about the case. "Get that woman a cab."

The bartender leaned to look past Jill, then leaned back. "Viola's good. She's been nursing that same double vodka for over an hour."

Viola's partner had passed whispering and was now alternately kissing her neck and nibbling on her earlobe. Viola offered neither resistance nor encouragement.

The five-some down the bar broke into another round of laughter. Jill frowned. "Whatever's going on, she'll regret it tomorrow."

The bartender sighed. "Welcome to happy hour at the Riverside Bar."

"You're not going to stop them?" Jill asked.

The bartender looked past Jill again. "She hasn't said no."

"But look at her."

The bartender blew out a breath, then leaned on the bar. "Hey, Viola, do you want me to peel Dave off you?"

Viola looked up. Her eyes were bloodshot, and her face looked doughy. I'd seen other women like Viola in dozens of bars. They were part of the mainstay, as were the five people sitting down the bar from us. They probably showed up every afternoon, had a few drinks, or stayed until closing, then went home to sleep it off.

Dave looked up. His face was lined from years of working in the sun. His eyes looked almost feral, making me feel like I'd want to check with the dispatcher for open warrants if I'd pulled him over for a traffic violation. Dave held up his beer bottle. "Viola and I'll have another," he slurred.

Viola hesitated, then gulped down the last of her drink in one swallow before nodding her assent to the bartender.

The bartender reached into a cooler and pulled out a beer. As he uncapped it, he said, "She works half days for the dentist. Then she comes over here and drinks."

Jill grimaced. "But that guy's a slimeball."

Pouring vodka into a glass without ice, he nodded. "And she's a hardcore alcoholic who never has to buy a drink for herself."

"She's a hooker?" Jill asked.

The bartender picked up the beer and the glass, then shook his head. "Nope, just a drunk who lets guys buy her drinks until they go back to her place or his."

Jill watched the bartender deliver the drinks, then said, "Yuck."

"Like he said, welcome to happy hour at the Riverside Bar."

After checking on the other customers and drawing a couple draft beers, the bartender returned to us. "You didn't come in here to drink soda and bullshit with me. What's up?"

The hum of conversation down the bar was interrupted by a string of profanity that rivaled what I'd heard from drill instructors during boot camp. And it all came from the dark-haired woman with the four men.

"C'mon, Anna, you've got to admit..." the rest of the conversation was lost.

"Emmet, that's so much bullshit I'm glad I've got my boots on," the woman replied before breaking into laughter.

Jill looked down the bar. "I'll bet that's Anna Weise."

Smiling, the bartender said, "I take it you've heard about her."

Jill cocked her head. "We heard she was a bit salty."

Looking first at Anna, then back at Jill, the bartender said, "A pretzel is salty, Anna's a cussing sparkplug who doesn't take shit from anyone. A guy put his hand on her butt once. She grabbed his thumb, twisted it, then yanked it back against his arm so far I heard it pop. I swear he's lucky she didn't tear it clean off his hand. She pinned his thumb there while he jumped up and down howling in pain. All the while, she singed his moustache with a string of swearing. I gotta tell you, I wish I'd recorded that tirade and submitted it to the cussing hall of fame."

Jill laughed politely. "We'd like to talk to Anna about Al Tedeschi's murder."

"Hey, Anna! There are a couple cops down here who want to know if you killed Al Tedeschi!"

That brought a round of laughter from the men down the bar. The woman who hopped off the barstool didn't fit the laugh or the stream of profanity we'd heard. She was a couple inches shorter than Jill, slender, with medium brown hair and a deeply tanned face.

She ignored Jill and marched right into my personal space. Sticking her finger an inch from my nose, she stared me in the eye. "You listen here. I had nothing to do with Al's death. NOTHING. Anybody who says otherwise is a..." she hesitated, probably biting back a profanity, "liar."

I was surprised that her breath smelled of root beer, not liquor, then I remembered Henderson's comment that Anna didn't drink liquor. Not backing down, I stared past her finger into her brown eyes. "I never said that *you* killed Tedeschi. I said I wanted to talk to you about his murder."

Jill put her hand on Anna's shoulder, trying to back her out of my face. Anna spun and glared at her. "Listen, sister. You aren't part of this and if you don't take your hand off my shoulder, I'll rip it off and shove it up your..."

Jill held up her badge. "That would be assaulting a federal officer. It's a class D felony subject to penalties up to 40 years in a federal prison."

Anna was fired up, almost seething. She turned back to me. "Are you going to let Sally Sundress step into this?"

Anna froze when Jill started laughing. "What's so funny?"

"In my whole life, no one has ever called me Sally Sundress." Jill put out her hand. "I'm Jill Fletcher."

Anna took a breath, rolled her shoulders, and shook Jill's hand. "I'm Anna Weise."

"This is my partner, Doug. We're helping Rob Henderson investigate Al Tedeschi's murder."

"You said you were federal," Anna said, sliding onto the stool next to Jill.

"We're Park Service investigators involved because Al's body was found on Tuzigoot National Monument land."

The bartender had been watching the exchange with a Cheshire Cat grin. Anna turned to him. "What the hell, Rooster? You yank my freaking chain and nearly get me to punch a federal cop."

Rooster laughed. "Freaking? Are you turning over a new leaf?"

Anna flipped her hand at him. "I think there's a law against swearing at federal cops."

Jill raised her eyebrows. "Rooster?"

"It's the eyepatch. Someone said I look like John Wayne in *Rooster Cogburn*. It stuck."

Anna snorted. "My horse's ass looks more like John Wayne than you do. Get us something to drink. If we're talking about Al, we're going to get thirsty." She gestured toward a table in a corner next to a dust-covered, darkened jukebox with 45 rpm records inside. "If we're talking about Al, I'd like to be away from the drunks at the bar."

Jill sat with her back to the jukebox. "Tell us about Al."

Anna sat facing the bar. After taking a breath she leaned close. "Al wasn't as big a jerk as people in town will tell you. Yeah, he pulled a couple shady deals, but he always treated me well."

"How long have you worked for Al?" I asked.

"Since before he married the wicked witch of the west." Sensing that she'd misspoken, Anna added, "I'm not a Robyn Tedeschi fan."

Rooster brought a round of soft drinks for us and waved off my attempt to pay. "I'm putting this on Anna's tab."

"Al's got quite a reputation as a ladies' man," I said. "You're an attractive woman. Have you had to fend off his affections?"

Anna laughed. "Ooh, I'm an attractive woman." She shook her head. "Al and my late husband were school buddies. When Art died, Al paid for the funeral and offered me a job as his cook. I made it clear I wasn't interested in marrying again, and Al respected my wishes."

"Why did you stay on after he married Robyn?" I asked.

Anna snorted. "Robyn doesn't know a measuring cup from a coffee mug, and her attempt at being a mother was a freaking disaster. She spent two days crying after she and Carlton came home from the hospital. I stepped in and let her do her horsey things while I fed him and changed his diapers."

"And Al treated you fairly?"

Anna shrugged. "What's fair? I paid off my house, paid cash for used pickups, never went hungry, and had enough left to put a little in the bank. I'm not complaining."

"It sounds like Al was quite a womanizer," Jill said.

"Yeah, after the wicked witch kicked him out of his own bedroom, he moved out to the old chicken coop. After it was clear he wasn't going to get any love at home, he started drinking and shacking up. Can you blame him?"

"Why didn't he divorce her?"

"It came down to finances. Robyn's running the ranch. It's making money, the kids are employed through the ranch, and he had enough money to drink and carouse. A divorce would've split their assets up and likely killed the goose that was laying golden eggs. Besides, the bimbos Al was shacking up with were treating him better than the wicked witch ever did." Anna smiled. "As long as he was still married, he told me he had a perfect excuse for not marrying any of the bimbos and he could leave whenever they got bored with each other."

"Does Robyn have a boyfriend, too?" I asked.

Anna paused and looked around the room. "She's had her boy toys. The ranch employs a few people. Robyn hires local women as housekeepers and servers, and there are cowboys who come and go. Robyn seems more attached to some than others."

"Do you think Robyn killed Al?"

"Oh, hell no. She couldn't even wring a chicken's neck."

Jill leaned close. "We heard Theresa likes to throw parties when the ranch is between bookings."

Anna shifted in her chair and looked around the room. "I'm through after lunch is cleaned up, so I don't know what happens in the evenings."

"Have any guests stayed over for breakfast?"

"I don't engage in rumors."

Jill didn't let the topic drop. "What you've personally seen isn't a rumor."

"Sure, some of Theresa's friends have stayed over."

"Male friends or female friends?"

"Does it matter?"

Jill smiled. "I was curious about the sleeping arrangements and if some of the breakfast guests might've been uncomfortable about being seen the morning after a party."

"Listen, Jill, I don't know, nor do I care, what the sleeping arrangements were at Theresa's parties. I saw faces, but I rarely heard names. So, I'm not going to fill in any blanks for you."

Jill looked my way, handing me the reins. "We think Al might've been killed because he was blackmailing some high-profile person who didn't want his wife, or voters, to know he was partying."

Anna put up her hands. "You're skating on thin ice, Mr. Federal Cop."

"We're trying to figure out who killed your boss."

"Uh uh. I'm not naming names. Al wasn't blackmailing anyone. You've got to look at someone else. It was probably a jealous husband. He was warming Carmen's bed last. That's where I'd start."

"Carmen isn't married," Jill said.

"She has two ex-husbands and one of them still tells people they're married."

"Rob Henderson checked them out and they've both got alibis."

Jill changed direction. "Tell us about Tedeschi's water rights."

"What's to tell? There are water rights associated with the ranch. Some are used for pasture and hay, and Carlton uses some to grow grapes."

"We heard Carlton wants to expand and needs more water for his grapes."

Shrugging, Anna took another drink of root beer. "That's between Carlton, Theresa, and Robyn. I've got no horse in that race."

"How could Carlton get more water?"

"I suppose Robyn could buy hay instead of irrigating. Like I said, that's between the family members. They don't talk about that stuff around the hired help, like me."

One of the cowboys yelled down the length of the bar. "Hey, Anna, Leroy wants you to come cook for him."

"He can't afford to hire me and he's too ugly to marry, so I'll pass."

The men roared and Anna shook her head. "You get a couple beers in a cowboy, and he suddenly thinks he's smart."

"You hang out here with these guys, right?" Jill asked.

Anna smiled. "I give back as much as I take, and this bunch of old geldings is harmless. We're old friends."

"Are they ranchers?" I asked.

"Hell, no. Leroy runs a bookkeeping business, Pisser is a plumber, Knothole owns a portable sawmill, and Larry writes western stories. He's the Louis L'Amour of Yavapai County."

"Have I ever read anything by him?"

"Nah, I doubt he's sold a book south of Prescott or north of Flag." Anna leaned back and yelled, "Larry, how many books have you sold?"

"I had a good month in July. I was paid enough in royalties to buy a round for the house."

Rooster leaned on the bar. "Yeah, enough to buy a round for the five of you, but not enough to leave a tip."

"Rooster, I left you a tip last December."

"I wonder where I put that quarter?"

That brought another round of laughter from the bar.

"You two have any other questions, or can I get back to verbally abusing the drunks?"

"Have fun with your friends," Jill said, standing up.

I slapped a twenty on the counter and pushed it to Rooster. "Buy the boys a round and keep the change."

He snatched the bill off the bar and waved it. "Looks like I won't have to throw you out for not paying your bar tabs. And he left enough for a tip!"

We were walking past the table Viola and Dave had vacated during our discussion with Anna. Jill was about to comment about their sad situation when one of the guys at the bar made a wolf whistle. "Hey there lady federal cop, you put on a couple pounds and come back here some time."

I expected Jill to stick her finger into the guy's ribs or stomp his foot. Instead, she turned and smiled. "Haven't you ever heard the expression, the closer the bone, the sweeter the meat?"

That brought a round of laughter that followed us out the door. I looked at Jill, "Where did that come from?"

"It's an old ranch line I must've heard a hundred times when the cowboys started talking about skinny versus chunky women."

I shook my head and unlocked the pickup.

"What's that supposed to mean, Fletcher? Do you think I need to put on a few pounds to fill out my jeans?"

"I've got no complaints about the view or our love life."

Jill smiled. "Good answer, Cowboy."

I started the engine and sat.

"What's next?" Jill asked.

"I suppose we could visit a few more wine tasting rooms."

"I've had enough wine for a day. Let's go to Hoofbeats Ranch, that riding place, and borrow a couple horses."

Before I could protest, Jill dialed their number and explained her plan to ride the river trail past Tuzigoot. She was excited. "We won't need a trail guide. I'm an experienced rider…but my partner is a novice."

Leaning close to be heard on Jill's phone I said, "Yeah, no horses named Nitro or Tornado."

Jill shoved me away. "We'll be there in fifteen minutes."

I drove out of the parking lot to main street. "What's your plan?"

"I want to see the trails along the river."

"Why?"

"Because there may be something there that was missed."

"Can't we walk the trail?"

Jill looked at me. "It's ninety degrees and I want to ride five or six miles. We're not walking when we can ride."

"I saw a place that rents ATVs in Cornville."

"We're riding."

"I hate horses."

Jill turned toward me. "You *own* a horse."

"Yeah, but he doesn't like me."

"Quit whining and suck it up. You're going to look like a pro when we get back to South Dakota."

"Aren't the pro cowboys the ones with broken bones?"

"They're bronc and bull riders, not people taking a leisurely ride on a bridle path."

"There's no leisurely ride with you. You always gallop and I fear for my life."

Pointing through the windshield, Jill said, "Oh, go straight. Take a right at the corner and park at the saddle shop."

"Are we checking on farriers?"

"No, we're buying you a pair of riding boots."

"I like my Rocky hiking boots just fine."

"You won't like them if your horse spooks and you can't get your foot out of the stirrups."

I parked in front of the saddle shop with the engine idling.

"What?" Jill asked.

"Did I mention that I hate horses?"

Jill stepped out of the pickup. "Are you going for a basic cowhide upper, or do you want something fancier with tooling?"

"Which ones will make the horse like me?"

"The boots have nothing to do with the horse liking you. They respect you if you're in control and riding them correctly."

Jill was already through the door when I muttered, "I hate horses."

Pete was helping a customer when we walked in. Nodding, he acknowledged us, but stayed with the young woman looking at western-cut shirts. Jill led me to the boots, near the back of the store. "You don't need Tony Lamas if you're only going to ride."

Looking at snakeskin boots I said, "Your dad bought ostrich skin boots when we got married."

"He only wears them for special occasions. He's got a pair of sturdy basic leather boots for riding." Jill picked up a brown boot, undecorated except for the stitching. "Like these."

Pete rang up the woman's purchase and thanked her. He was behind me before I heard him approach. "Boot shopping?"

"Jill thinks we need to go for a horseback ride. I need a pair of boots that'll keep me in the saddle and prevent my butt from getting sore."

Pete glanced at Jill, then grinned and walked down the shelving. He picked up a boot embossed with lassos, saddles, snakes, and spurs. "I recommend these."

I accepted the boot from him, appreciating the workmanship. "How will these keep me in the saddle?"

"They won't, but you'll look like a real cowboy in the ambulance."

"I'm already depressed about the ride. I don't need smartass remarks from the boot salesman."

"The boot your partner is holding is a very basic, inexpensive boot. It's well-made and will keep you in the saddle just as well as any of the Justin boots."

"I wear size 10D."

Pete paused in thought. "I may have a deal for you. Hang on."

"What do you think he's up to?" I asked.

"I've got no clue." Jill turned and lifted a western-cut shirt off a bargain rack. You should buy this, too."

I sighed. "Are we getting a Stetson next?"

"This has long sleeves. You'll want that for sun protection."

"But it'll be hotter than my golf shirt."

"Actually, this woven cotton will be cooler than your knit shirt. And it won't snag if you rub against brush or a branch."

Pete returned with a pair of boots with a few scratches. "I had a guy buy these on the way to the Lazy L. After a week on the ranch, he decided he was never going to ride again. I gave him a $20 trade-in credit on a pair of top-end hiking boots."

I sat in a chair near the door to the back room and pulled them on. "They fit okay when they're on, but I had to pull hard to get them over my ankles."

"That's so they don't fall off while you're riding," Pete explained. "The tight fit gives you an excuse to have your partner help pull them off."

"Oh boy, cowboy bonding," I said, reaching down to pull them off.

"Leave them on, Doug. We'll be riding in a few minutes." Handing the shirt to Pete, Jill said, "We'll take this, too."

With my wallet in hand, I followed Pete to the cash register. He cut the tags off the shirt and handed it to me. "The changing room is behind you. The total is $30."

I handed Pete my Visa card. "You forgot the boots."

"They're collecting dust in the back, and I can't sell them as new. They fit, so just take them."

"You can't make any money giving away merchandise," Jill said.

Pete smiled. "Don't worry. I made a profit on the boots the first time I sold them, and I made a profit on the expensive hiking boots that replaced them. I'm not losing anything, and I'm gaining shelf space."

I changed into the western shirt and met Jill at the cash register where she and Pete were having an earnest discussion. "How do I look?"

Pete smiled. "You look just like John Travolta."

"I'm not sure that's a compliment. Wasn't he a city dude trying to look like a cowboy?"

"Like I said, you look just like Travolta."

I glared at Jill. "Does this make you happy?"

Her eyes lit up. "I'm smiling, aren't I?"

I took $20 out of my wallet and slid it across the counter. "Federal employees can't accept gifts."

Putting the bill into his shirt pocket, Pete nodded. "If I run into you in town, the first round is on me."

Jill set my hiking boots and golf shirt on the back seat. "You spent too much time preening in the mirror. We're running late."

I snorted as I drove away from the saddle shop. "This from the woman who spent an hour trying on bathing suits."

"None of them fit right."

"Whatever."

* * *

Hoofbeats was less than ten minutes away. Turning into the driveway, I saw two saddled horses tied to a hitching post next to the office. Parking alongside the barn, I turned to Jill. "I hope one of them is named Petunia and has a personality to match her name."

"You don't want Petunia."

"Why not?"

"Mares like to challenge inexperienced male riders."

Out of the truck, I sped up to catch Jill as I pulled on my Minnesota Twins cap. "Your dad always puts me on a mare when we ride on your ranch."

Jill turned her head and smiled. "Yes."

"Why?"

"Dad was testing you."

"Really? The shooting wasn't enough?"

Jill shrugged as we entered the office. A woman was hunched over a pile of invoices with her fingers poised over the computer keyboard. She looked annoyed at the interruption, then smiled when she saw us. "You're the rangers who called. I've got Weed and Lash saddled up for you. By the way, I'm Megan."

"You've got a horse named Weed?" I asked as we followed her out of the office.

"We bought Weed from a drug dealer just before he was busted by the county. We raised Lash from a colt."

"Why'd you call him Lash?"

"Tom got whiplash every time he spurred Lash when he was training him."

I looked at Jill. "You get Lash."

Megan patted the right horse's neck. "He's past that now and you're not wearing spurs."

Jill checked her cinch, then put her foot in the stirrup and mounted the horse with the grace of a gymnast. Meanwhile, Megan held Weed's reins while I struggled to lift my foot high enough to reach the stirrup. After two tries, I got a toe on the stirrup, straightened my left leg, and swung my right over the saddle. I was still trying to get my boot into the stirrup when Megan handed me the reins.

"The horses know the riverside trail from here to beyond Clarkdale. All you need to do is hold the reins and enjoy the ride."

Clucking her tongue, Jill eased Lash away from the rail. Weed followed without any prompting from me. I relaxed and found a rhythm with Weed by the time we were past the last Hoofbeats Ranch fence. Spurring Weed, I got side by side with Jill. "What are we looking for?"

"You're the detective. What should we be looking for?"

"Anomalies."

"What do you mean?"

"Look for anything that's not right— something that is somewhere it doesn't belong or something that's missing."

After a glance, Jill shook her head. "I'm so adept at noticing things missing from an unfamiliar landscape. 'Oh look, there's a rock missing over there, Doug. Do you think it's been gone long?'"

"I was unaware of your sarcastic side before I proposed to you."

"Bullshit. Half our banter in Flagstaff was playful sarcasm." We rode on for a few minutes in silence. "Seriously, what are we doing?"

"We don't know where the murderer killed Al, so we don't know which direction they rode. I hope we'll see something that'll give us a clue. We need something to narrow the field of suspects."

"It's been too long since they rode through here, with too many sets of hoof and footprints on the trail."

"I suppose the killer brought Al's body out strapped to a pack horse. Do they leave different hoofprints?"

"Pack horses are often bigger than riding horses. Their shoes are larger and because they're wider across the beam, their trail is wider."

"Did you see any pack horses at the riding stable?"

"I've seen a few mules grazing around here. I think they're a more common pack animal than a larger horse."

"So, riding stables here don't have pack horses?"

"Not usually. I mean, some stables keep a larger horse in case they have a heavy rider, but in general, no. At home, we kept a pack horse for hauling stuff around and for bringing in game from the high-country during hunting season. I don't know if that's a big deal here."

"Who would keep a pack horse around here?"

"Maybe someone who's prospecting or into elk hunting. There are outfitters in Flagstaff who specialize in backcountry camping trips, often having as many pack horses as riding horses. I've hired outfitters a couple times when we've had to search in timber or rescue someone miles off the road in rough country."

"You'd use horses rather than ATVs?"

"Horses can go places I wouldn't take an ATV."

"Why horses and not a helicopter?"

"Helicopters are expensive and they're not as effective as a horse in heavy timber."

"I suppose it's hard to follow a trail from a helicopter."

"I helped the Border Patrol rescue some stranded illegal immigrants when I worked at Big Bend. They had lots of agents who rode ATVs, and very few who could handle a horse."

"I bet that made you feel good about yourself and your skills."

Jill glanced at me and smiled. "It did. There were a few cocky SOBs who thought a skinny little girl shouldn't be sent on that trip. Some of them were so saddle-sore after five days on the trail they could hardly sit. I was just hitting my stride."

"Were you able to rescue all the migrants?"

Jill got very quiet, then said. "The ones who were still alive were dehydrated and had heat stroke. More than half of the group died."

"Were there kids?"

"None of the kids made it."

Having never heard that story before made me think it was an episode Jill wanted to forget rather than retell. A thought struck me. "The kids you swam out to save from the van…"

"Yeah, I didn't want to have another set of nightmares if I could help it."

"Don't look, but there's someone shadowing us. They're staying mostly out of sight on the other side of the cottonwoods."

"We could give them a thrill."

"What do you have in mind?" I asked.

"We'll spur our horses and see if they try to keep up."

"I'm working on plan B."

"Killjoy."

"I really don't want to know if these boots slip easily out of the stirrups if I fall off."

Jill reined her horse to a stop. "Do you think we're in danger?"

"Keep riding," I said. "If someone wants to hurt us, they'll wait until we're past Old Cottonwood where there are fewer people around."

"Gee, Doug, that makes me feel so secure. Whoever is over there probably doesn't want to shoot me until we're farther from civilization."

"Your sarcasm isn't helpful right now."

"Then come up with a plan to keep me alive that doesn't involve slowly moving to a more dangerous place."

Weed started snorting and acting squirrely, like he was dancing. Lash danced sideways, which I assumed was a response to something Jill was doing. Her struggle to get Lash back on the trail made Weed even more fidgety.

"Knock it off, Doug. You're spooking the horses."

"Knock what off?"

"Whatever you're doing is spooking the horses."

"I'm hanging onto the reins and saddle horn. How is that spooking the horses?"

"They can sense your tension."

"Bullshit. Next you're going to tell me they can understand what I'm saying."

"They react to the tone of your voice. Take a breath and relax."

"How can I relax when Weed's doing the hokey pokey? I'm just trying to stay in the saddle."

Leaning forward, Jill patted Lash's neck and spoke softly to him. He settled, although Weed wasn't getting the full message. Following Jill's model, and reasoning it was harder to fall out of the saddle if I was leaning forward, I patted Weed's neck. "Easy boy. I'm sorry I spooked you. There's something scary going on across the river and it's got me a little rattled. I'll try not to talk loudly or let my heart pound. Deal?"

Weed settled a bit, which lowered my blood pressure and heart rate. Jill moved Lash in a circle until she was next to me.

"Horse ancestors were prey animals, and they travel in herds for protection. They can sense the changing heartbeat of another herd member, or you, and they prepare to flee. If you're calm, they'll react to you and settle down."

I adjusted my cap, which had nearly fallen off during the horse hijinks. With my voice carefully modulated, I said, "I'm anxious about whatever is going on across the river. I don't know how to be worried, upset, anxious, and paranoid without ending up on my butt in the dirt because Weed senses my feelings."

"You're spooking me."

"I'm spooking you?" I said too loudly, making Weed fidget again. "Geez, recreational marijuana is legal here. Maybe we should've brought some weed to mellow out Weed."

In apparent exasperation, Jill gasped. "Were you planning to have him smoke it or were you going to bake a batch of brownies?"

"I was being facetious."

"Great! You think there's someone who might shoot us and you're being facetious."

"There's a break in the trees ahead at the Dead Horse Ranch State Park sign. We'll be able to see who's across the river. Pick up the pace. It'll make us more difficult targets."

Jill clucked her tongue and Lash trotted ahead. Having barely mastered, "whoa," I wasn't quite sure how the horse accelerator worked. Luckily, Weed decided the pack was on the move and trotted to keep up with Lash, taking the responsibility for speeding up out of my hands.

Lash turned toward the state park, which was across the river. Weed and I followed, pretending I was in control. We splashed across the ford in the river, seeing a few people and a couple cars ahead of us. I looked downstream as we crossed but saw nothing unusual. Once on top of the opposite riverbank I saw what appeared to be an orange volleyball behind the trees.

"Weed, it's like this. I think there's someone down there, to our left. We've got a couple choices. One would be to continue on with Jill into the park among the people, where we'll be safe. Or, we can take a quick left and gallop down this side of the river and maybe get a look at that orange ball before it realizes we're coming."

Lash stopped and Jill looked over her shoulder. "What's your plan?"

Against all better judgment, I was overcome with curiosity. I reined Weed left and spurred him. "Charge!"

I'd never ridden a horse who went from stopped to full gallop in two bounds. My cap flew off and I'd have been in the dust with it if not for the saddle horn. I pulled myself forward and gathered my senses enough to look ahead. There was a face in the middle of the orange ball, and I saw his eyes go wide when he realized Weed and I were galloping toward him. His horse wheeled and flew up the riverbank and across the open desert between the river and Cottonwood. Unlike me, the rider was one with his horse. He leaned forward and used his reins like a whip.

It seemed Lash was faster than Weed because Jill passed us as we ran. In retrospect, our speed difference might've been more about Jill's horsemanship, and my focus on staying in the saddle. As the rider moved out of the trees into the open desert, I could see that he was wearing an orange football helmet.

As we neared a residential area, the rider cut between two houses and Jill pulled back on Lash's reins. I tried to mimic her move, saying "Whoa," my one word of horse language. Weed, more than me, stopped next to Jill and Lash.

"Why'd we stop?"

Jill looked at me like a slow child. "I'm not playing Roy Rogers and chasing the bad guy through town."

"Why not?"

"Doug, there's traffic and innocent people. It'd be a disaster if a car ran into one of the horses, or if a horse ran into a tourist."

"Um, good thought. We don't want that pile of paperwork."

"Besides, I suspect there aren't many Cottonwood residents who ride around wearing a Denver Broncos helmet."

"Huh?"

We turned the horses and walked back to the park. Jill was deep in thought until she turned to me. "'Charge,' was the best thing you could say?"

"It's what the cavalry says when they start a chase."

"We're not in the cavalry."

"That's all that came to mind. No one gave me an English/Horse dictionary."

"Next time try, 'giddy-up.'"

I felt sheepish but wasn't ready to admit defeat. "'Giddy-up' lacks the urgency of 'Charge!'"

"I swear, that's undoubtedly the first time Weed ever heard the word charge."

"It worked. He took off like a rocket."

Jill started to laugh. "I wish I'd had a camera. You looked like a rookie cowboy on his first bronc ride. Feet in the air, arms flailing, holding onto the saddle horn like your life depended on it."

"Did you pick up my cap?"

"A fox ran out of the river bottom and picked it up. He'll probably fetch it for you, just like a Labrador Retriever."

"Smartass."

"You're the one who thought I'd stop to pick up your filthy Twins cap during a horse chase. Buy a new one. That cap was so tattered and sweat-stained I didn't want to put my coat in the closet with it."

"You could've said something."

"I was afraid it was something from your childhood, like a baby blanket you couldn't leave behind."

"No, it was just a cap. It wasn't worn out, so I kept wearing it. If I'd known it offended you, I would've bought a new one."

"It offends me. Buy a new one." Jill reined Lash over to a water trough next to the maintenance building. She threw her leg over the saddle and slipped down like a ranch girl. She looked up at me, still in the saddle. "Are you getting down?"

"I don't think so."

"Why not?"

I loosened the reins so Weed could drink from the trough. "Because I'm not sure I can get back up here again."

"Are you hurt?"

"Only my dignity."

"You've lost me."

"There was a moment back there where things were out of control."

"Yeah. So what?"

"I mean, my body was out of control."

Jill frowned, then smiled. "You peed your pants?"

"Just a bit."

"Hop down. You can rinse them off under the faucet."

"I'd rather let them air dry."

"They're not going to air dry while you're sitting in a saddle. Get down."

I'd just slid down when a mother with two little girls rushed over to Jill. "What's your horse's name? Can I pet her?"

Jill knelt down to eye level with the girls who might've been kindergarten-age. "My horse is Lash and the other one is Weed."

The girls ate up Jill's attention and Lash seemed pleased to let them touch and pet his muzzle. The mom watched, then walked over to me. "Are you two some kind of cops?"

"We're Park Service investigators."

"This is a state park."

"We're just riding through."

The mother peeked around Weed's rump to check on the girls, who were firing questions at Jill. "It looked like you were chasing Gunner."

"You know the guy wearing the helmet?"

She shrugged. "Everyone knows Gunner."

"I suppose his helmet is distinctive."

"He had a rodeo head injury. He wears the Broncos helmet to protect the plate in his head when he's riding."

"He seemed to be spying on us."

The woman shook her head. "He was probably just curious because you're strangers. He's harmless, but since his injury, he's been…simple."

"How old is Gunner?"

"Oh, I suppose he's about forty. The horse kicked him when I was about fourteen. I remember the fundraisers to pay his hospital bills. Cowboys don't often have medical insurance and he had a lot of bills."

"Thanks for letting us pet your horse," the girls said. They stepped around the trough and looked at me suspiciously. The younger one sniffed and turned to her mother. "It smells like pee here. Can we go?"

I heard laughter from the other side of the horses as the girls walked away. "It's not funny, dear."

"It's funny as hell. Strip out of your pants and rinse them, so you don't smell like 'pee.'"

"I think that'd be ill-advised with little girls hanging around."

"They're driving off. Stay behind the horses and no one will notice."

"I think there's a men's room on the other side of the building. I'll rinse my jeans and underwear in the sink." I heard snickering. "What?"

"You'd better hope no little boys wander in while your boxers are in the sink."

"Aw crap. Tie off the horses and watch the door."

Following me around the building, Jill asked, "What did the mom have to say?"

"The guy in the orange helmet is named Gunner. He's a local character who hasn't been right since being kicked in the head by a rodeo horse. She thought Gunner was watching us because we're strangers."

Chapter 10

Even after wringing them out, my pants were more than damp. I used the edge of the horse trough to step up to the stirrups. "Do we go on, or should we go back to the riding stable?" I asked.

Jill hopped onto the saddle in one easy motion. "I wiped the pee off your saddle, so it doesn't stink," Jill said, smiling. "The humidity is so low here your pants will dry in no time. Let's continue riding along the river."

Shifting uncomfortably in the saddle, I settled in. "Lead the way."

We crossed the Verde River again and climbed the riverbank to the trail. With the Tuzigoot ruins visible in the distance, we rode north. The dusty trail showed horseshoe prints mingled with those left by hikers in boots and athletic shoes. A light breeze blew in our faces and the ride was leisurely and pleasant, aside from the chafing of wet jeans on the inside of my thighs.

Jill slowed, and we rode side-by side as we neared the road leading to Tuzigoot

National Monument. "I'd like to talk to some of the locals about Gunner."

"It was strange that he followed us. If he has some sort of mental disorder, I could see how he'd be more openly curious about strangers."

"Being a country girl, I get that local people are curious about newcomers. You saw how everyone turned to check us out when we walked into the Riverside Bar. They look, ask each other if they know who we are, then go back to their conversations. Gunner spends his days riding around and checking things out. He probably noticed us and wanted to see what we were doing."

"Why wouldn't he just ride up and ask who we were?"

"Maybe his verbal skills aren't very good, or he's just shy."

"I wonder how far he followed us. I'd seen flashes of orange for maybe ten minutes before I got the feeling someone was shadowing us. He could've been watching longer than that if he was hanging back out of sight."

Twisting in the saddle, Jill looked behind us. "Gunner may have been curious, or maybe someone asked him to keep an eye on us."

"We're probably riding the trail used to bring Al's body out here. Maybe someone's afraid there are more clues along the trail."

"The killer may have noticed something missing when he dumped the body. I assume Al's hat was gone before he was loaded onto the horse. What else would he have that might've fallen off during his transport here?"

"We've been working on the theory that Al was killed somewhere else, then transported here. Maybe he and the killer were on horseback and Al was shot during the ride. We should talk to the coroner and look through Al's personal effects. I scanned the list, but I wasn't focused on what might be missing. His wallet was recovered with his body and that gave them a preliminary identification. Beyond that, I don't remember anything significant."

After a moment of thought, Jill said, "There wasn't a cell phone listed among his belongings."

"The killer may have taken that because the last call, or series of calls, may have pointed to him."

"Maybe it fell out of his pocket and is lying alongside the trail."

I pondered the cell phone, kicking myself for not considering it earlier. "We need to find out who Al's cell phone provider was. Rob Henderson can subpoena his call and text history."

"I don't remember keys or a wristwatch among Al's possessions." Jill said over her shoulder.

"Not everyone wears a watch anymore. It's kind of irrelevant when you can pull out your cell phone and get an exact time." I paused and thought. "We can ask the coroner if Al had a tan line on his wrist. His skin was deeply tanned. If he'd worn a watch, his wrist would show it."

"Owen, the ranger, said he rarely sees horses on this trail, but there are horseshoe prints all over here and they're all since the last rain. There are at least half a dozen horses who've been ridden here."

"I suppose they're riding in the evening after the park is closed."

Reining Lash to the left, Jill turned to follow the Tuzigoot entrance road. "Where are we going?"

"There are a couple of river access points down here. Let's see if there are any hoofprints by the river."

"Um, no one's going to bring a horse here in a boat."

The look told me I'd said something stupid. "Maybe someone rode in from the highway, or they might've ridden down here to give their horses a drink."

A Subaru Outback with a kayak rack on top was parked at the second river access. There were hoofprints around the landing, so we rode to the water, surprising a couple pulling kayaks onto the riverbank. The man stepped protectively between us and his female partner. He was about to say something but stopped when he saw our badges and guns. "This is a legal spot to park and launch our kayaks, right?"

Something about his posturing made me uneasy. Knowing I would struggle to get back on the horse, I threw my leg over the saddle anyway and stepped down. "Yes, this is a legal spot to park and launch. Did you kayak very far?"

The young female kayaking partner wore a bikini top and nylon shorts. Her brown hair was cut short and was sweaty at her neck. She wasn't a fit, hard-body athlete, like her male partner. The man appeared to be at least ten years older than the woman. He had dark hair and a carefully manicured two-day dark beard. His wife-beater t-shirt revealed his hairy back and chest, with well-muscled arms and torso. I assessed him as a narcissistic bodybuilder.

I heard Jill dismount behind me. Handing her the reins, I extended my hand to the man and smiled. "I'm Ranger Fletcher from the National Park Service."

Uneasy, the man shook my hand, but didn't introduce himself. "I didn't know the Park Service had mounted rangers patrolling the grounds."

"It's something we're evaluating. Tuzigoot National monument is over a thousand acres and it's easier to cover it on horseback than hiking."

"Makes sense."

"Do you two kayak here often?"

The question bothered the girl. She looked at the man like she expected him to offer an answer, which made me even more suspicious. With a quick glance over my shoulder, I asked Jill to tie up the horses.

"I try to get down here once a week or so."

"A body was found on the other side of the park last week. Did you happen to see someone riding through, leading a pack horse?"

Shaking his head, the man said, "No."

The girl wrapped her arms over her chest like she'd felt a sudden chill and she looked at the ground. My bad vibe got worse. "Can I see your driver's license?"

"Why?"

With my mind racing, I tried to formulate an excuse. "You're supposed to purchase a park permit to use the boat launch. Since there isn't an entry hut to collect the fee at Tuzigoot, you have to pay for your permit at the visitor center."

"That's bullshit. We're not even at the park gate."

I smiled. "You are on park property as soon as you cross the river. Show me your driver's license and we'll talk about going to the visitor center so you can pay your entry fee."

Patting the pockets of his nylon shorts, he smiled. "I don't carry my wallet on the water."

"Do you keep it in a dry bag tied inside your kayak?"

"I've just got a cell phone and my car keys in the kayak."

"You really shouldn't leave valuables like your wallet in the car while you're kayaking. Let's walk to the car and you can show me your license."

The man pulled a zippered rubber bag out of the kayak and started walking up the trail. Looking at Jill, I nodded toward the girl. *Talk to her.* I mouthed.

The car was parked nearly 100 feet from the river, putting us far enough from the river so the girl was out of sight. Hot air rushed from the Subaru when the man opened the door. I stood on the far side of the open driver's door with my hand on the butt of my pistol. I was far enough away to dodge a punch, but close enough to see if he was reaching for a gun or trying to hide drugs. He removed a billfold from the center console and stood up.

"Here," he said, handing me an Arizona driver's license from his wallet.

Glancing at his wallet when he handed me the driver's license, I noticed a picture I.D. with a corporate logo I didn't recognize.

"Mr. Larkin, you drive down here weekly to kayak from Prescott Valley? That's a bit of a trek." I took out my cell phone to take a photo of his license.

"Hey, what are you doing?"

"I'm taking a picture of your driver's license. Is that a problem?"

He rested his wrist on top of the driver's door, gesturing that he wanted his license back. "Why are you taking a picture?"

"It's a convenient way of keeping track of who's in the park, especially if you haven't been paying your access fee. What's the other photo ID in your wallet?"

"It's my work ID, and it's got nothing to do with anything."

"Where do you work, Mr. Larkin?"

His eyes narrowed. The vessels in his neck started to pulse. "I'd like my license back. We're going to mount the kayaks and leave."

Bells and whistles were going off in my brain. I kept the license and stepped back from the car. "Just a minute, please."

The sound of soft crying came up from the river and Larkin looked away from me. "What's your partner doing?"

I punched 911 into my phone without answering Larkin's question. "This is Park Service Inspector Doug Fletcher. Please run a driver's license for me and check for wants and warrants." I read Larkin's name and address to the dispatcher.

After a glance at me, Larkin spun and ran toward the boat launch. I ran after him, cell phone still in my hand. "Jill, he's coming!"

As I ran, I lifted the cell phone to my ear. "Dispatch, I need backup at the Tuzigoot National Monument boat launch." I left the phone on but jammed it in my pocket.

I rounded a clump of green brush, twenty steps behind Larkin. He was at the launch and had a vise-like grip on the girl's arm. Jill had one hand on the girl and was pulling her Glock with the other hand.

"What did you tell her?" Larkin yelled at the girl as he tried to pull her out of Jill's grasp.

I suddenly viewed the scene in slow motion, my body seemingly moving through molasses as I ran to intervene. "He's unarmed!" I yelled to Jill, whose gun was out of her holster and rising.

Larkin yanked the girl's arm, pulling her free from Jill's grip and throwing her to the ground. "What did you tell the bitch cop?" he yelled at the girl while squaring his shoulders toward Jill.

The girl curled into a ball, covering the back of her head. The move exposed bruises on her upper arms and scratches on her back. A siren wailed somewhere in Cottonwood. Muffled words from the dispatcher came from the phone in my pocket.

"You're too close!" I yelled. "He'll be on top of you before your bullets stop him."

Jill's arms were extended, knees bent, elbows locked, and her focus totally on Larkin. She adjusted her aim from his chest to his face. "If you take one step toward me, I'll put a bullet between your eyes," she hissed through clenched teeth as the approaching siren neared. Something the girl told her had Jill's self-control on the brink.

"Larkin!" I yelled, trying to divert his attention from Jill. I stopped a few yards away from the confrontation and pulled the phone out of my pocket, hoping whatever happened would be captured by the dispatcher's recording of my call.

Larkin refused to look away from Jill as he clenched and unclenched his fists. "Whatever the kid told you is a lie."

Switching the phone to my left hand, I drew my gun. Because he was unarmed, I wasn't going to shoot unless Jill or the girl's life was in immediate danger.

The dispatcher's voice caught my attention. "Inspector Fletcher, are you there? Your backup is less than two minutes away. What's your situation?"

I dropped the phone and reached my hand out to the girl while holding my gun on Larkin. "Are you okay? Can you stand up?"

Jill nodded, acknowledging her agreement that the girl needed to be removed from Larkin's reach. She readjusted her aim to the middle of Larkin's chest and took a breath. "Take Toni to the car."

I put out my left hand. "Toni, come to me. He's not going to hurt you."

The girl looked at me, still curled into a fetal position with her hands behind her head. I realized she was younger than I'd thought, possibly in her early teens. "I just wanted to go kayaking," she said before breaking into tears.

The siren stopped nearby, and I heard a car brake on the gravel parking lot behind me.

"Larkin, there are more cops here. Put your hands behind your head and get on your knees."

Larkin's glance was chilling. His eyes were filled with hatred and every muscle seemed to quiver. "I'm leaving. If you try to stop me, I'll wring your partner's neck like a chicken."

I heard someone running down the gravel behind me and a young female officer slid to a stop next to me with her gun drawn. "What the hell is going on?"

"Mr. Larkin was kayaking with this girl. He became agitated when I asked for his driver's license and after my partner interviewed the girl."

The officer aimed her gun at Larkin's chest but kept her finger outside the trigger guard. "The dispatcher has been trying to reach you. Larkin is a registered sex offender who's only been out of prison a few weeks. He likes to make dates with young girls over the internet."

I saw Jill's hand tighten on the Glock, although her finger also remained outside the trigger guard.

"Officer," I said, "the girl is named Toni. Please move her to safety."

In my peripheral vision, I saw the Cottonwood officer holster her gun and kneel. She put out her hand. "Toni. I'm Ellen and I'm going to take you to my car. Can you stand up?"

I moved aside so they'd be well out of my line of fire as another siren approached. Toni reached out and took Ellen's hand, then got to her knees and stood. They walked away with Larkin's eyes boring holes in the girl's back.

Larkin watched until they were out of sight, then he looked between Jill and me. "I'm not going back to prison."

I heard Ellen talking to Toni and then the dispatcher. The girl started sobbing, and I heard a car door slam.

"Take it easy," I said, easing my gun down so it was aimed at Larkin's feet. "Put your hands behind your head and kneel down. We'll talk this through. It doesn't have to end here."

A second siren stopped as it crossed the river and the car slid to a stop in the gravel parking lot. A third siren started wailing in the distance.

Footsteps pounded down the gravel behind me and Rob Henderson approached. "What the hell, Fletcher?"

Ellen stepped past me on the opposite side. Her gun was drawn, and her finger was on the trigger. Whatever Toni said, had her ready to kill Larkin.

Henderson spoke softly. "Don't, Ellen. He's a slimeball, but he's unarmed. You can't shoot him."

Ellen glared at Rob. "You don't know what he did to that girl."

Rob stepped behind me and eased next to Ellen. "Put your gun up Ellen, he's unarmed."

Sensing that we were distracted, Larkin lunged toward the kayaks. Jill holstered her gun and threw herself on Larkin's back, trying to restrain him. Larkin swept his left arm back, flipping Jill into the second kayak like a rag doll. She bounced off the covered kayak bow and splashed into the river.

Larkin pulled out a waterproof bag. "Drop it!" Rob yelled. I looked past him, trying to see Jill in the water. Her arm shot up, followed by her head. She stood in waist-deep water, grabbed a rope tied to the kayak, then slipped on something and fell back into the river. The kayak drifted into the current while Jill tried to pull herself up in the now chest-deep water.

Having been focused on Jill, I'd tuned out Rob and the Cottonwood cop who were both yelling. "Put it down! NOW!"

Ignoring them, Larkin struggled with the zipper. Using incredible strength, Larkin ripped the rubberized pouch open, a black pistol falling out and rattling into the plastic kayak's hull. When he reached for the gun, two shots rang out and Ellen's arms jumped with her pistol's recoil.

Unfazed by Ellen's shots, Larkin continued to scramble for the gun. Assuming Ellen had missed, I fired twice, each shot hitting Larkin's chest, but not stopping his desperate effort to retrieve the gun from the kayak. I was taking aim when a staccato burst of gunfire sounded to my left, some bullets hitting Larkin while others raised geysers in the river behind him. Thankfully, Jill and the second kayak drifted a few yards downstream.

My concern for Jill, the deafening sound of the nearby shots, and muzzle blast distracted me for a moment. When I put my sights on Larkin, he was wavering. With a confused look on his face, he teetered, the pistol dangling from his fingers. His hand relaxed and the gun fell from his grasp. He pitched forward, momentarily catching himself on the gunwale of the kayak, with bright red blood frothing in his mouth.

Looking at me, his earlier hatred was replaced by a look of resolution and solitude. Jill slogged through the river, towing the second kayak behind her.

Ellen holstered her gun and requested an ambulance on her shoulder-mounted radio. I knew it would only transport Larkin's body to a morgue.

Rob walked toward the kayak with his pistol extended and ready to fire. I was a step behind him when Larkin's arms buckled, his body toppling onto the kayak.

Holstering my gun, I knelt beside the kayak. Jill stepped next to me as Larkin blinked a few times, then he exhaled a rattle I'd heard too often. His last breath.

Henderson blew out a breath, reminding me he was at my side. "Suicide by cop."

With green river water dripping from her fingertips, Jill shook her hands. Her hair plastered to her head like a wet helmet, and her now green-tinted shirt clinging to her trim torso. "Someone should've prevented this." She looked at Rob. "Talk to his parole officer. Hell, talk to the parole board. He should never have been allowed out of prison."

Rob shook his head. "I imagine he'd served his sentence."

The ambulance's siren died as the vehicle pulled into the parking lot. Ellen looked up at the EMTs rushing down the trail carrying their rescue equipment. "I told the dispatcher to call the coroner."

Rob looked at the spent cartridge cases on the ground around us. "There'll be a shooting review board," he sighed. "It'll be a formality. No one's going to accuse us of doing anything wrong."

"Damned straight," Ellen said. "All we did was put down a rabid skunk. Not a person around here will disagree with that after they hear what that girl has to say."

"Do you need my weapon for testing?" I asked.

Rob considered my question while staring at Larkin's body. "Nah, we all hit him. I doubt the coroner will be able to identify the kill shot. His lungs will look like Swiss cheese. Your biggest problem will be filling out the Park Service paperwork. Copy me on the report when you send it in. I'll attach it to Ellen's and my reports."

I looked at Jill. "I'll copy and paste your report."

"This one's all yours, Fletcher. I was in the water and never fired my weapon."

We stepped back and let an EMT confirm the death by putting a stethoscope on Larkin's chest.

Jill leaned against a Cottonwood tree. With considerable effort, she pulled off her boots and emptied the water out of them. "Leather shrinks when it dries. I'll have to wear these until they dry out or we'll have to buy me a new pair at the saddle shop."

I nodded. "We'll throw them in the hotel trash. You don't want a remembrance of today."

The leather squished as Jill pulled the boots back on. "Sadly, I'm going to have nightmares about today whether I keep the boots or not."

* * *

Sensing our glum moods, the horses plodded with their heads down on the ride back to the riding stable. Jill looked over at me. "We'll have to finish the ride tomorrow if the horses are available."

I exhaled. "I suppose so."

"You'll have to call Matt and let him know what happened before he hears it from his boss."

I shook my head. "You call. I don't want to discuss it."

Jill reached in her back pocket and pulled out her phone. "My phone went swimming and there's no amount of rice that's going to save it."

"Shit."

After jamming the phone in her back pocket, she moved Lash over until our legs were nearly touching. Then she held out her hand. "Are you okay?"

198

"I was afraid you were going to drown. Then, I was afraid you were in the line of fire."

Squeezing my hand, we rode on. "I'm very much alive, and very much in need of a hot shower. I smell like algae and dead fish."

"Gee, you make that sound so romantic."

"Yeah, we've had quite a day. The horse scared the piss out of you, and a sex offender threw me into the river. It'll be hard to top that."

We chatted idly about Gunner and the incidents at Dead Horse Ranch State Park.

"I wonder why they named it Dead Horse Ranch State Park?" I asked. "That seems…morbid."

"I read about it when I was stationed in Flagstaff. There was a Minnesota family relocating to Arizona in the 1940s, and they looked at several ranches. This ranch had a dead horse lying next to the road. When it came time to decide about the purchase, the family's kids said, 'Let's buy the ranch with the dead horse.' The name stuck, and one of the conditions of the sale was that the park retain the name."

"Why would a Minnesota farmer buy a ranch in Arizona?"

"Gee, Doug, why would someone from Minnesota move to Arizona? Don't you have personal experience with that?"

"I was running away from a divorce and starting a new life."

"I suppose WWII had just ended and they were doing much the same thing."

Looking up, I spotted a figure leaning on a gatepost ahead of us. "Someone is expecting us."

Megan opened the gate, then followed us to the barn. Jill dismounted gracefully. I slid down from the saddle without falling on my butt.

"What the hell happened out there? I heard sirens and fireworks. Were you involved in that?"

With a flourish, Jill tied off Lash. "Yeah, that was us."

Megan took Weed's reins from me and looked at Jill. "You look like you went swimming with your clothes on."

"I fell out of a kayak."

Tying up Weed, Megan nodded to the office. "Let's go inside, where it's cool. I want to hear this story."

We followed Megan into the office but before telling her what happened, Jill asked, "Can we ride Lash and Weed again tomorrow, or do you already have them booked?"

Megan sat down at the computer. "I'll check, but I'm reasonably certain you can have them again." Then she froze. "The fireworks were gunshots. Are you and the horses okay?"

"All the good guys and the horses are fine."

"There was a bad guy?"

Jill looked around the office. "Do you have a bottle of water or a soft drink? I'm parched and I'd like to rinse the taste of the Verde River out of my mouth."

Megan turned her chair and opened a small refrigerator behind her desk. "Oh, Geez. I was so interested in hearing what happened that I forgot my manners." She handed each of us a half-liter bottle of water.

After taking a few swallows, Jill took a deep breath. "We stumbled across a sex offender at the Tuzigoot boat launch." Jill told the story about talking with the girl, the revelation that she'd been "recruited" on the internet, her kayak trip leading to her rape, and us saving the girl and shooting the rapist.

Megan frowned. "You said you fell out of a kayak?"

"She was thrown into a kayak that tipped over," I said. "Jill thought she could single-handedly handcuff a bodybuilder rapist. He swept her off his back like he was swatting a mosquito. She flew into the kayak that tipped and dumped her into the river."

Focusing on Jill, Megan asked. "Are you okay? You must be bruised."

"To tell the truth, I was so full of adrenaline I didn't notice the injuries. I'm getting sore now, and I imagine tomorrow will be worse."

"There was all that gunfire and neither of you were hit?" Megan froze. "I heard sirens. There were other cops there, too. Are they okay?"

"The rapist never got a shot off and all our shots hit him or went into the river."

"But Jill was in the river!"

"I'd drifted downstream with the kayak. They missed me."

Megan leaned back. "Well, thank the Lord for that!"

Jill glanced at me. "Yeah, He's been watching over me for a while."

Megan stood and shooed us toward the door. "You guys smell like horses and river water. Go take a shower and I'll take care of Lash and Weed."

"We can help you unsaddle them."

"Git! I'll take care of the horses."

"We need to pay..."

Megan waved us off. "We'll settle up tomorrow."

Patting her pockets, Jill looked at me. "I hope you've got the pickup keys. If not, they're on the bottom of the river."

I pulled out the keys and dangled them from my fingers. "I've got them, and I'll drive."

Jill opened the rear door while I started the engine. "What are you doing?"

She held up my golf shirt before spreading it on the pickup's seat. "I didn't want to stink up the upholstery, so I'm sitting on your shirt."

"Oh, good. I'll have a golf shirt that stinks of algae and fish."

"We'll wash it in a heavy-duty cycle with our jeans and shirts."

"I didn't see a laundromat in town."

"There's got to be a laundromat in a town the size of Cottonwood." Jill's eyes lit up. "Laundromats, hair salons, and barbershops are great places to pick up gossip. There are people trapped there and everyone seems chatty."

After driving out of the parking lot, I glanced at Jill's hair. "A trip to a hair salon might be a good option for you. They might be able to get the algae out of your hair without leaving it looking like straw."

Jill flipped down the visor and looked at herself in the mirror. Running her fingers through her hair, she sighed. "I hate to admit it, but it might take a beautician to restore this mess. I'll see if I can get an appointment yet this afternoon while you do the laundry."

"I thought..."

"Yeah, you thought I'd do the laundry while you cruised the bars. I've got news for you, Fletcher. I just delegated laundry duty."

The desk clerk gave me the laundromat address and exchanged a roll of quarters for cash. She was calling hair salons when Jill and I left the lobby to shower and change.

Jill took khaki shorts, a t-shirt, and underwear out of the suitcase and disappeared into the shower. I wiped Jill's Glock dry, then I field stripped, cleaned, oiled, and reassembled my Sig pistol. As I put it into the holster, Jill emerged from the bathroom with her hair wrapped in a towel. She was dressed but looked tired.

"The shower is yours," she said, taking off the towel and shaking her head.

The room phone rang just as I closed the bathroom door. I heard a muffled conversation, then Jill knocked on the door. "I'm going to a salon around the corner. I'll see you back here in an hour or so."

Letting the hot water pound on my shoulders, took some of the stress out of my shoulder muscles and let me rerun the afternoon events through my mind. Serendipity had put us at the boat launch. A half hour earlier or later, we wouldn't have ever seen Larkin and the girl. The truth was that law enforcement was often like that; you happened upon a bad person breaking the law. Dozens of other illegal events happened out of sight, but on that one occasion, you happened to be at the right place at the right time.

After the shower, I gathered our jeans and shirts from the day, as well as our other sweaty clothing and put them into a plastic laundry bag hanging in the closet. I waved at the clerk as I passed through the lobby, then drove to the laundromat. Two women were leaning on a counter chatting, their clothes tumbling in dryers. I sorted dark and light clothing into two washers and started the cycles, then went to the wall-mounted dispenser to purchase tiny packets of detergent and dryer sheets at exorbitant prices.

"Don't let them rip you off," one of the women said, carrying an orange container to me. "Take a couple of my pods."

"Thanks," I said. After dropping the detergent pods into the washer, I walked over to the women. "How much do I owe you for the pods?"

"Nothing. I buy them at Costco by the box. I don't even know what a single pod costs. I do know that it's a hell of a lot less than you were about to pay for detergent out of the machine." She put out her hand. "I'm McKenzie Smith."

Both of the women were young, probably just past their teens. Because they were at the laundromat, I assumed they lived in nearby apartments. I introduced myself, shaking hands with both McKenzie and her friend, Christina.

McKenzie was outgoing and friendly. Christina was reserved, choosing to listen to McKenzie grill me about who I was, what I was doing in town, where my wife was, and how long I planned to be in town. After giving my life story, I asked, "Did you both grow up in Cottonwood?"

McKenzie, who was heavyset, wore jeans shorts, an oversized t-shirt, and sandals, shook her head. "I grew up north of Sedona. I couldn't afford the rent there on a waitresses' salary, so I moved down here. I live above the rock shop."

"What's your story Christina?"

"I…um…moved here with my…um…boyfriend. We're from Colorado." Christina was short and slender. She looked undernourished and her demeanor made me think she was the meek, submissive half of the couple. "How do you get to be a ranger? I mean, I'd like to apply. It seems like a good job. You get health insurance and everything, Right?"

"Yes, healthcare insurance and a pension."

"How do I apply?"

I didn't actually know, so I said, "Do a computer search for National Park Service jobs. I think you can fill out the application online."

"Thanks, I'll check it out on the library computer tomorrow."

A buzzer went off and Christina took her laundry basket to a dryer and removed the dry clothes. McKenzie glanced at her, then leaned close. "Her boyfriend is a shit. He's a loan officer at one of the big national banks and they moved him down here from Denver. Christina doesn't know anyone here and she can't find a job."

"Do you work in town?"

"I commute into Sedona. There's more tourist trade there and the restaurants are more upscale, so the tips are better. I hate the traffic and parking, but I can't afford to live there." She paused and studied me for a second. "You're older than the rangers who work around here. Are you like a supervisor or something?"

"I'm investigating the death of the guy whose body was found at Tuzigoot National Monument."

"Oh, so you're a cop?"

"I'm a Park Service investigator based in Texas. I travel all over the country."

McKenzie wrinkled her nose. "You're chasing all over looking at dead bodies?"

"I don't spend much time with dead bodies. I interview witnesses and try to figure out what happened and why."

Christina dumped her basket of white clothes on the counter and started folding them into piles of men's and women's underwear and t-shirts. "So, you're investigating that old guy who was dumped by the swamp?"

"That's why I'm here."

Shaking out a man's t-shirt, she asked, "You weren't at Dead Horse Ranch State Park when there was all that shooting, were you?"

"I heard about that," I said, wanting to get their input rather than giving a witness statement.

Christina loaded the folded clothes back into her plastic laundry basket. "I heard the cops shot an unarmed guy and arrested his girlfriend."

"He was pulling a gun," I said. "And they took the girl into protective custody until they contacted her parents."

Christina shook her head. "I heard the cops planted a gun and drugs on them."

I looked at McKenzie. "What did you hear?"

After a shrug, she said, "I heard the guy was a pervert who'd been hooking up with escort services on the internet. Somebody said the girl was like twelve and the cops saved the world a lot of problems by taking out another sex predator."

Apparently unhappy about being corrected, Christina walked to another dryer and stopped it. She unloaded the colored clothing into the basket. I waited for her to say something, but she just took her clothes to the counter and folded them without comment.

McKenzie watched her for a bit, then whispered, "She told me they moved here after her boyfriend was busted for marijuana in Colorado. They don't like cops."

Searching my mind, I said, "Recreational marijuana is legal in Colorado. Nobody busted them for having or smoking marijuana."

McKenzie raised her eyebrows, acting surprised, but she obviously had the same information. Christina's excuse was a convenient lie.

"How do you feel about cops?"

"I like to have them around the restaurant. Things are quieter and there aren't walkouts who stiff me on their bills." She glanced at my wedding ring. "Married, huh?"

I smiled. "I'm old enough to be your father."

"Guys my age are only interested in beer and hookups. I'd like to find someone more mature."

Unsure if McKenzie was just stating fact or flirting, I felt it would be best to change the subject. "Do you know who Al Tedeschi was?"

"Yeah, he was a man-whore. My landlord warned me about him when we saw him chatting up a cute Mexican girl the week I moved to Cottonwood. Alexis pointed him out and said Tedeschi was on a mission to give every woman in town HPV and herpes."

That news left me speechless.

When I didn't respond, McKenzie feigned concern. "Did I shock you?"

"That's not a line I've heard before."

"That's the problem with casual hookups. You just don't know what gifts you might receive when you spend a night with a stranger."

I flashed back to a conversation I'd had when I was drinking. A drunk woman was flirting with me in a St. Paul bar. After a couple drinks, she leaned over and said, "You know, casual sex is like spring snow—you don't know how many inches you're going to get or how long it'll last." I brushed her off and she left later with another guy, but that line stuck in my head.

Christina stacked her baskets and walked out, not offering any thoughts about casual sex, Al Tedeschi, or STDs. She hesitated at the door. "You probably won't shoot anyone else today. I heard it looks bad if you kill two people in the same day."

We watched Christina wrestle her laundry into an aging Prius, its hatchback secured by a bungee cord. With one hand balancing the laundry, she struggled to release the bungee cord. When she got the hook free from the bumper, the rubber slipped out of her grasp and snapped her shoulder. She stumbled back, dropping the laundry baskets, strewing items on the pavement. She glared at me through the window as if I was somehow responsible for the mess.

McKenzie stopped folding clothes and watched. "I don't suppose there's much point in helping her. She's already mad at you."

"Yup."

"Why didn't you argue with her about shooting people?"

"Nothing I could say would change her mind."

McKenzie leaned back against the folding counter. "See, that's what I like about men who are more mature. Guys like you know when an argument is a lost cause and throw in the towel. Do you ever argue with your wife?"

"We're pretty much on the same wavelength on most issues."

"But not everything; you're individuals, not clones."

"We don't agree on everything, but I respect her opinion on most things, even if we disagree."

"Give me an example of something you disagree on, but don't fight about."

"She likes creamy peanut butter and I like crunchy. We've compromised by having a jar of each."

"Get serious. What's something big, like politics? Do you both vote for the same candidate?"

"Probably not, but we don't make it an issue."

"I don't know if I could live with a left-wing commie nut."

"Neither of us have extreme political views. I'd struggle being married to someone at either political extreme."

McKenzie studied me. "Do you have an unmarried younger brother?"

"I'm an only child." I tried to steer the conversation back to the investigation. "What else did you hear about Tedeschi?"

"I guess he was a rich rancher and several of the girls thought they could lure him away from his wife and become the next Mrs. Tedeschi, living on the big ranch."

"What's the rumor mill saying about his wife?"

"I've never heard about his wife. Folks only talk about Al and how he wasn't too concerned about his marriage vows. It makes me think things weren't great back at the ranch."

"How about his kids, Carlton and Theresa?"

McKenzie frowned, deep in thought. "Isn't his son the one who runs their winery tasting room? I didn't know he had a daughter."

A dryer buzzer went off and McKenzie grabbed her basket. "Nice to meet you," she said. Then she paused and pulled a couple dryer sheets out of a box in her laundry basket. "You don't want to buy any of these either."

I had the laundromat to myself when I moved our clothes from the washers to the dryers. I pondered McKenzie's comments about Tedeschi and his rumored STD situation. *Does that have anything to do with Al's murder? Was someone very upset because Al infected them with herpes? Was someone's spouse or boyfriend unhappy that Al had infected their partner?*

Chapter 11

I was placing clean, folded clothes in our suitcases when I heard a keycard slide in the door. Reflexively, I put my hand on the pistol I'd set on the bed when I'd changed back into my jeans.

Jill stepped in smiling. "What do you think of the makeover?"

Her hair was shorter, curled, and bouncy. She wore subdued pink lipstick and subtle eyeshadow. "Wow." I looked at the bag in her hand. "Did you buy some shampoo or something?"

Emptying the bag onto the bed, she pulled a cell phone from a few boxes and plastic clamshell cases. "Nope. I found a cell phone store with a government contract. They replaced the wet phone and programmed my number and contacts into this one while I had my hair done." She snapped the phone into a blue case that looked like it would survive a gunshot. "The clerk sold me a waterproof case."

"It's thicker than your old phone. People will stare at your butt if you carry it in your back pocket like usual."

She made a dismissive sound, walked to me, and wrapped her arms around my neck. "Take me out for supper."

"I'll be the envy of every guy in Cottonwood. I'll change into my western shirt and boots. I'll look like one of the locals."

"Um, putting on a western shirt won't make you look like a local. You haven't spent enough years in the sun, and you don't look like you just got off a horse."

"Good. Then I'm going to wear comfortable shoes and a golf shirt."

Jill never primped and preened, but she brushed her hair in front of the bathroom mirror while I changed. She hesitated at the bathroom door, thinking. "Take a photo of me with my cell phone and I'll text it to our moms."

I grabbed her hand. "Let's get a selfie of us together in front of one of the old shops."

* * *

The desk clerk made a reservation at an upscale Italian restaurant and told us to turn left and go down three blocks. With our hands clasped, we walked down the sidewalk looking like newlyweds.

Jill leaned against my shoulder when we stopped at a street corner. "I'm sorry I stuck you with the laundry, but the beauty shop was the perfect tonic for my gloomy mood. The mess at the state park seems like it happened a thousand miles from here, a hundred years ago."

As we continued down the street, I hesitated to break the mood. "I talked to a couple of women at the laundromat. One of them knew of Tedeschi. Her landlady told her Al was spreading STDs all over town."

"Let's leave our jobs behind for at least tonight. Okay?"

I nodded. "They're gone."

We'd just ordered supper when my cell phone buzzed. I got up from the table and connected the call as I walked outside. "Fletcher."

"Were you waiting for me to hear about the gunfight at the OK Corral on the news before you called?" Matt Mattson asked.

"I got distracted."

"I hope it was because you were too busy filling out the incident report after your interviews with the local police and county attorney."

"Something like that," I said, evading the issue.

"Ginny Goins called from Montezuma's Castle to assure me you and Jill were both safe and unharmed."

"There you go! We're safe, unharmed, and about to eat supper. I'll call you tomorrow."

"Listen, Doug, I'll be getting calls from my bosses and the head of the Park

Service Investigative Bureau. I want to be able to speak with them from a position of knowledge and confidence. Assure me that you did the right thing and represented the Park Service well."

"We were fine, upstanding representatives of the Park Service and Padre Island National Seashore. You should be proud of us."

"Cut the B.S. Tell me what happened."

"Can I call you back? Jill and I were about to eat supper when my phone rang."

Matt sighed and said, "Please give me a quick recap so I don't sound like an idiot if one of our bosses asks me for an update on your investigation."

I exhaled and leaned against the restaurant façade. "It started when we rented a couple horses."

"Okay, now I know you're pulling my leg. You hate horses."

"Jill talked me into riding rather than walking the trails leading in and out of Tuzigoot…"

I spent ten minutes updating Matt and answering his questions. He wanted more details, but his call-waiting notified him that the NPS regional superintendent was calling. "We'll talk more, but I think I've got enough information to throw oil on troubled water if I need to." He paused. "You guys did great. Keep me informed."

When I returned, Jill looked concerned. I took her hand and smiled. "It was Matt. He wanted to know today's whole story before the chain of command telephone cascade got it all twisted."

"Are we…is everything okay?"

"His parting words were, 'You guys did great.'"

Letting out a breath, Jill closed her eyes. "I know we did the right thing but sometimes, depending on the viewpoint, the optics look very wrong."

"We're good." I looked around for our waiter. "Did you order a bottle of wine?"

"Manuel is checking the wine cellar for a bottle of '*muy bueno*' Chianti to go with the Veal parmesan I've ordered for us."

I chuckled.

"What?"

"I find it ironic that Manuel is looking for a *muy bueno* Italian red wine."

Jill rolled her eyes as a young woman in a white blouse and black apron brought two salads and set them in front of us. "Caesar salads, no anchovies. Would you like parmesan grated onto them?"

"That'd be great," I said. She grated until we signaled for her to stop, then she stepped away.

I took a bite of salad and smiled. "You know I like anchovies on my Caesar salads."

"But I don't like your anchovy breath. If you have any inkling there may be romance later tonight, you'll be happy there aren't anchovies on your salad." I was mulling a smart remark when Jill cut me off. "And don't tell me some lie about preferring anchovies to a romantic interlude. I know better."

Verbally cut off at the knees, I ate my salad in silence.

"I'd like to finish our ride tomorrow."

"You'd be happy if we spent every day on a horse. I might prefer resting my saddle sores for a day."

"You were only in the saddle for like two hours. Cowboys spend eight or ten hours a day on their horses."

"I bet they develop butt calluses."

Manuel arrived with a dusty wine bottle wrapped in basket-weave net. He made a ceremony of wiping it and presenting it for my inspection. "This was in a back corner. I suspect the owner was hiding it for his friends."

"I'm not sure my palate or wallet will appreciate that fine bottle of wine."

Manuel's sly smile made me uncomfortable. He cut the foil and produced a corkscrew despite my effort to stop him. "It's an odd bottle, not on the wine list. I have no idea what to charge, so I'll charge you the same as I would for the house wine." He poured a little in my glass and said, "Swirl it in the glass to let it open, then take a bite of bread to cleanse your palate before you taste it."

I sniffed the bouquet. "We've been tasting wine all over town and I haven't had anything like this."

Manuel nodded. "The local wines are young, and the Arizona soil doesn't give the grapes the rich flavor of this wine. Now, taste it."

I sipped, using the techniques taught by the wine tasting rooms. The rich flavor filled my mouth. Manuel read my expression and poured for Jill, who was beyond intrigued.

Repeating the procedure, she sniffed, then tasted the wine. "This is lovely."

Smiling, Manuel poured for me. "This wine is like a fine woman. She may be pretty in her youth, but like your wife, a bit of age adds intrigue and depth that no youngster has. Enjoy."

Jill sipped her wine and raised her eyebrows. "Do I have intrigue and depth?"

I pushed my salad plate aside and reached out, taking her hand. "My limited cop vocabulary lacks the adjectives to describe you."

"Try."

I squeezed her hand. "You're…incredible."

"I like incredible."

The moment was nearly broken when Manuel arrived with our Veal parmesan. He paused, looking back and forth between us. "Too soon?"

I let go of Jill's hand and leaned back. "Your timing is perfect."

Manuel set the plates down and took the salads. "*Bon appétit!*"

Jill started to laugh as Manuel walked away. "Somehow, *bon appétit* sounds very wrong with a Spanish accent."

Manuel doted on us, filling our wine glasses and delivering warm bread. Jill pushed back her plate after finishing half her entree. "I'm stuffed."

"I needed a break like this."

"To rest your sore butt?"

"To rest my cynical mind. I sometimes need to be reminded of what's important. I get too deep into the cases and…"

"And what?"

"They'll either be solved, or not. Five years from now they won't matter, but you will."

"I know you're not a horse person, but I really miss riding. This case has been interesting, *and* it's got me on a horse."

"Instead of looking for a house in Port Aransas, maybe we should talk to a realtor about acreage outside Corpus Christi."

Jill's eyes sparkled. "You've had too much sun and wine. You've become irrational."

"Maybe I've become a convert."

"Pay the bill while I look for my husband. Someone's taken over his body and is talking crazy."

"It's an option."

Jill shook her head. "I like Port Aransas, walking the beach, and I like being by Matt and Mandy. I'd miss that if we lived on a ranch outside town."

"But…"

"That was the younger, less intriguing and refined me talking. The mature me knows there'll be time for riding after we retire to South Dakota."

I grimaced. "I hate winter more than I dislike horses."

Jill set her napkin on the table and stood. "Leave Manuel a nice tip while I use the ladies' room."

Manuel appeared with a plastic folio. I handed him my VISA card without looking at the bill. He glanced at Jill as she threaded her way through the dining room. "Your wife is a classy lady. She seems very wise."

"She's more than I deserve."

Manuel shook his head. "No *señor*, you seem well matched. I think you've both been around long enough to know what's important."

"How can you tell?"

"The way you look at each other. I see lots of people. Some put on airs to impress their dates. Some couples are indifferent and impolite. You two are *simpáticas*: You respect and care for each other."

Manuel was back with my card before Jill returned. I looked at the total, then up at Manuel. "You didn't charge us for the wine."

Manuel smiled and cocked his head. "It's too late to correct that minor error. I've already run your card."

I added a $40 tip and signed the slip. "*Gracias*."

Jill returned as Manuel walked away. "All set?" she asked.

I put my napkin on the table and stood. "All set."

Holding my hand as we walked down the street, Jill stared at the clear sky. "I liked living in Arizona. Flagstaff is a medium-sized city and I like that it has a winter, spring, and fall. There was snow, but not the brutal Black Hills cold and blizzards."

"Are you telling me you'd like to retire here?"

"No, I'm just telling you what's on my mind. We'll own a ranch and horses in Spearfish."

Three cowboys spilled out of a bar ahead of us. They staggered, laughing about whatever had happened inside. Jill squeezed my hand and pulled me into a recessed door, to get off the sidewalk. The three guys lurched toward us spewing loud obscenities. I turned so the gun on my right hip was away from the sidewalk and pulled Jill into an embrace with my left arm.

The guy who stopped in front of us looked barely old enough to drink. But he was drunk and his shirt disheveled. "You two should get a room." His buddies stopped to see what had caught his attention.

Jill leaned her head against my chest, trying to look at ease, but I felt her tension. "Move along, guys."

I had my hand on the pistol. They didn't act threatening, but I'd dealt with enough drunks to know the situation could turn ugly in a fraction of a second.

The tallest cowboy sniffled, then spit at my feet. "You gonna let the woman talk for you?"

"She said all that needed to be said. Just move along."

Eyeing Jill, the first guy cocked his head. "Not much upstairs or in the caboose. I prefer my women with a little more meat on their bones."

The tall cowboy shook his head. "I prefer experience over looks. She looks like someone who knows how to please a man."

"Are any of you sober enough to drive home?" I asked.

The change in direction caught them off guard. "Why? Are you planning to have us arrested for a DUI?"

"The thought had crossed my mind," I said.

Jill put up her left hand. "Guys, we've all had a nice night. Let's leave it at that and we'll all go our separate ways."

The guy closest to Jill took a step forward and reached out, like he was going to hug her. "I like a take-charge kind of woman."

Jill's hand shot out and her knuckle struck his solar plexus. Then his body spasmed as he gasped. Bent at the waist, he tried to catch his breath. Jill's left hand was still up, but her right was in a fist. "Take him home and put him in bed," she warned.

Gasping, the aggressor rubbed his chest as I eased my gun from the holster on my hip. I lifted my golf shirt, exposing my badge. "The fun's over, guys. Leave."

"Geez, Lance," the tallest guy said, putting his arm over his injured buddy's shoulder. "You sure can pick 'em. Let's leave the cop and go."

"Good plan," I said.

Watching them walk away, Jill put her arm around my waist. "I hate drunk idiots."

"I wonder what story that cowboy is going to tell his buddies about the bruise you caused?"

Jill pulled me onto the sidewalk. "Frankly my dear, I don't give a damn."

* * *

Back in our room I put my gun and badge on the nightstand. Jill went into the bathroom and later emerged wearing a short nightgown. She plumped two pillows, then leaned against them.

"You don't look like you're ready to sleep," I said, stripping off my shirt.

"No. I'm too keyed up after the confrontation with the idiots." She paused. "We probably should've called the local cops and alerted them to the potential drunk drivers."

"We never saw them get into a vehicle."

Watching me slip my shoes and socks off, Jill leaned over and put her hand on my side. "I'm glad I wasn't facing those three alone. Imagine some poor waitress getting off work and running into them on the way to her car or walking home."

"Yeah, wolf packs are dangerous. Drunken idiots feed off each other. On the other hand, they're not our problem. We've got a case of our own to deal with."

"I want to finish riding the Tuzigoot trails tomorrow."

"I'll have a blistered butt."

Jill's hand slid from my side to the inside of my thigh. "Poor baby. Let me massage those sores for you."

Leaning back, I kissed her. "Your hand isn't on my sores."

"I thought you like my hand right where it is."

"Yeah, we can work on the blisters later."

Chapter 12

Jill called Hoofbeats Ranch while I refilled our breakfast coffees. "That'll be great, Megan." She ended the call and slipped her cell phone into her back pocket. "She'll have Lash and Weed saddled and ready for us in half an hour. Megan said she'd put extra padding on Weed's saddle to help ease your blisters."

I set the Styrofoam cups on the table and sat down. "Really?"

"Hell no." Jill laughed and said, "You'll have to put your big boy pants on and deal with it."

"I'm starting to feel like the punchline in a joke."

With her coffee cup to her lips, Jill nodded. "The word will get around."

Rob Henderson walked into the breakfast area, spied us, nodded, then drew a cup of coffee from the urn.

"I wonder what brings Rob here so early?" I asked.

He sat in the third chair at our table and put his Stetson on the fourth chair. "Sounds like you two had an interesting evening."

“We had a nice dinner at the Italian restaurant.”

“And an eventful walk back to the hotel.”

Jill glanced at him. “I don’t understand.”

“The Cottonwood cops pulled over a truckload of drunks last night. They told the jailer a crazy story about some skinny woman punching one of them and a cop who flashed a badge at them and told them to go before he beat the shit out of them.”

“Interesting story,” I said. “Pure fiction, I assume.”

Wrinkling his nose to hide his smile, Rob sipped his coffee. “The couple they described sounds a lot like you two.”

“Coincidence.”

“They want the woman arrested for assault.”

Jill raised her eyebrows. “Too bad they don’t know who the man and woman were.”

Henderson laughed. “Yeah, too bad.”

“Do you think they’ll remember any of that fantasy after they sober up?” I asked.

“Who knows. I can tell you that the Cottonwood cops and jailers got quite a chuckle out of the story about three cowboys getting beaten up by a skinny woman, then scared off by a guy with a fake cop’s badge.”

“Are the Cottonwood cops going to follow up?” Jill asked.

"Oh, hell no. They're still laughing about the fantasy created by three drunks."

"I assume Cottonwood has bigger crimes to pursue than a woman who punched a guy who was trying to kiss her."

Obviously willing to let the topic die, Henderson asked, "What are you two planning to do today?"

"We're going to finish our ride on the Tuzigoot trails," Jill replied.

Drinking the last of his coffee Henderson stood. "Try not to shoot anyone today."

Digging her new phone out, Jill shook her head. "I've got to warn Matt that I punched a guy last night."

With my hand on hers, I stopped her. "Don't stir the hornet's nest. It sounds like the local cops are going to mark it up as the ravings of a bunch of drunk cowboys."

"But…"

"If you tell Matt, we'll have to file an incident report. It'll get way too much visibility. Trust me on this one." Flashing back to our previous days' ride I asked, "Al Tedeschi's phone wasn't recovered with his body. Have you checked with his carrier to see when it was last active?"

"I'm way ahead of you on that question," Rob replied. "His phone hasn't been on since the night he was murdered. The last time it pinged a cell tower was early the evening he was killed. He'd been near Cottonwood, but the cell phone company couldn't give me an exact location."

"I don't suppose his last text was to his killer saying, 'meet me at Tuzigoot.'"

Chuckling, Henderson shook his head. "Al wasn't a tech guy. According to Al's cell phone carrier, he had a basic phone and he'd never texted anyone. His last call was to the 45-70 Saloon at seven o'clock, and no one there remembers his call."

"I wonder if his phone is somewhere along the trail where it fell out of his pocket?" Jill asked, rhetorically.

"Who knows," Henderson replied as he stood. "It could be almost anywhere. Hell, the killer might've thrown it in the swamp when he unloaded the body. I asked the phone carrier to notify me if it pings a tower, but I think the phone is long gone." Putting on his Stetson, Rob smiled, "Have fun on your horse ride. And, like I said, try not to shoot anyone today."

Jill stood and put her phone in her pocket while I gathered remnants of our breakfast and coffee. Carrying our cups to the coffee urn, I'd planned to fill and cover them. "Honey, horses don't have cup holders."

I tilted back my head, then poured an inch of coffee into the cup. "Fine, I'll drink this on the way to the riding school."

As promised, Lash and Weed were saddled and tied to a hitching post outside the Hoofbeats Ranch office. Megan looked up from her computer when she heard the office door open. She smiled and looked me up and down. "My oh my. Don't you look like a real cowboy."

"Smartass," I replied.

"How are your butt blisters today?"

I looked at Jill, who was beaming. "My butt is just fine, thanks."

"I've got some liniment we use on the horses in the barn. You could rub some on your butt to see if that makes it better." A grin spread across her face. "I think it's turpentine based, so you probably want to make sure you don't get any on your…personals."

"The liniment won't be necessary. And I appreciate your concern about my personals."

"The boys are ready to go," Megan said. "Grab yourselves a couple bottles of water and I'll see you whenever you get back."

Being stiff from the previous day's ride, I struggled to mount the saddle. Jill watched in amusement and took great delight in watching me ease my butt into the saddle. "Whenever you're ready, dear," she said.

I waved her on and let the horse follow without offering encouragement. "I think Weed likes me."

"Don't let it go to your head. If he senses you're not in control, he'll give you trouble."

Half an hour later we were passing Dead Horse Ranch State Park. I noticed a flash of orange through the cottonwoods. Spurring Lash resulted in a look of disdain. At least, that's how I interpreted his glance at me. I spurred him a bit harder, and he picked up the pace until we were alongside Jill and Lash.

"Our stalker is following us from across the river."

Without looking back, Jill nodded. "You keep riding ahead, and I'll circle back to the ford in the river."

"What's your plan?"

"I'll see if I can approach Gunner without scaring him off."

"Do you think Weed will let me go on without you and Lash?"

Jill's eye roll was her answer. "Which one of you is the rider and which is the horse?"

She slowed Lash and turned toward the river. Weed wanted to follow, but after a test of wills, I won, and we continued down the trail, watching Jill and Lash ride toward the river.

The orange helmet stopped as Jill approached. I saw her get down from the saddle and lead Lash through the cottonwoods across the river. I couldn't see much of Gunner except for the helmet, but he didn't ride away. After a few moments, the orange helmet started moving toward me. Gunner was alongside Jill as they crossed the Verde River.

"Gunner, this is my partner, Doug."

I nodded to Gunner who seemed ready to bolt. "Nice to meet you."

Gunner's head dipped slightly, but he looked extremely uneasy.

"I invited Gunner and Mojo to ride with us because they know these trails better than anyone. He rides them every day."

"Who's Mojo?" I asked.

Jill nodded to Gunner's horse. "Mojo is Gunner's gelding."

Gunner watched Jill as if he was in awe of her. Then he looked at me and nodded. "Every day."

Jill led the way and Gunner quickly spurred Mojo to ride alongside her. Weed and I followed, unable to understand Jill's monologue. She chatted and Gunner rode along, staring at her like a lost puppy. They stopped when we got to the Tuzigoot trail that led to the Swamp.

"What's down here, Gunner?" I asked.

Blinking and looking uneasy, Gunner considered the question. "Well, there was a dead guy down there last week." Gunner paused in thought. "But he's gone now. A whole bunch of people came and took him away."

Jill was ready to ride on, but I stopped her. "How long was the dead guy there, Gunner?"

The expression on Gunner's face made me think time was a relative thing for him. I suspected that other than today and yesterday, his concept of the passing of time might not be exactly measured in hours, days, and weeks.

"Days."

"Did you know he was there before the cops came to haul his body away?"

"Yeah. He was eaten up by the vultures before the rangers came."

"Do you ride this trail every day?"

Gunner looked suddenly uneasy, and I feared he was about ready to bolt.

"It's okay. You're not in trouble for riding here. I'm just trying to understand how long the man was lying here before the rangers came to pick him up."

Gunner's helmet bobbed. "I came after the rangers left at night. I don't think they want me on the trails inside the park."

"Do you remember how many days the guy's body was by the swamp?"

After blinking, Gunner said, "The first day the vultures ate his eyes and face. I've seen them do that to injured deer. Austin said they do that so the deer can't see to escape. It didn't matter this time because the guy was already dead. So, I don't know why the vultures pecked his eyes. I suppose it's just a thing they do."

"Did the rangers come the next day?"

"No. The vultures ripped the guy's shirt and ate his innards." Gunner paused and looked at his hands. "They didn't eat his hands. There must be no meat on people's hands because the vultures never eat them."

"Did the rangers come the next day?"

"They came after the vultures tried to rip the guy's jeans. Levis must be really tough because the vultures couldn't tear his jeans. They tried, but it just didn't work. The rangers came the next day."

I'd been so focused on establishing the timeline, I missed the basic question. Jill leaned forward. "Gunner, did you see who brought him here?"

That question rattled Gunner and he shook his head. "No!" He sat shaking his head for a minute. "I wasn't here when they brought him. It must've been at night. I have to be home before dark."

Jill's voice was gentle and reassuring. "Do you know who brought the guy here?"

"I didn't see."

"I understand, but do you know who killed him and brought him here?"

"Bad people did it. They brought him here so the vultures would eat him up,"

I glanced at Jill and mouthed "Good question." Then I turned back to Gunner. "Which way did they come from?"

He immediately pointed north. "That way."

"You're sure?" I asked.

Gunner nodded. "That's the direction their hoofprints went."

"What's up there?"

"Clarkdale, Winston's ranch, the Lazy L Ranch, Parker's ranch. Then it goes all the way to Sedona if you keep riding."

"Did you follow the hoofprints?" Jill asked.

"Some, but I have to be home before dark."

"How far did you follow them?" I asked.

Gunner turned toward me and frowned. "I already told you. I followed until I had to go home."

Jill and Lash started down the dead-end trail to the swamp. I spurred Weed and caught up with Jill and Gunner. "Why are we going here? We've already walked this trail in and back out."

Jill nodded toward the brushy ground around the trail. "Things look different on horseback. You're higher, so you're looking down into the brush, and you don't have to concentrate on your footing."

I let Weed trail Jill and Gunner, now aware of the ground around us. A lizard scampered away from the trail, disappearing into a bush. I saw the top of the ground-hugging cacti and there were dozens of saguaro cacti on the hillside above us, something I hadn't noticed on foot. We also traveled faster on horseback and what had been a long hot walk, was over in ten minutes. Gathering at the end of the trail overlooking the pond, I could see cattails surrounding the swampy area.

Without a word, Gunner dismounted and led Mojo to the spot where Tedeschi's body was found. "The dead guy was here."

I looked around the area and there wasn't a nearby tree or even a high bush. "Did you see the vultures circling?"

"They don't circle when they've got something to eat," Gunner replied. "They just land and peck off chunks and eat them. It's messy."

"Did you see anything unusual here before the rangers came?"

"There was a dead guy and vultures. That's unusual."

Sensing my frustration with Gunner's answers, Jill smirked. "Other than the dead guy and vultures, was there anything else unusual?"

Apparently ignoring Jill's question, Gunner mounted Mojo, and then he looked at her. "There were hoof prints. Nobody else rides down here."

"What did you notice about the hoof prints, Gunner?"

"There were two sets of hoof prints. One was wider, and the other was made by a bar horseshoe. There aren't many horses with bar shoes."

"You're sure there were only two sets of hoof prints?" I asked.

"There were three after I rode out here."

I saw Jill's smile. She was enjoying Gunner's matter of fact answers. He didn't try to interpret or embellish the information, he just stated what he knew.

"Did you know who the dead guy was?" I asked.

Gunner shook his head. "The vultures ate his face." Gunner spurred Mojo and started back down the trail. I shrugged at Jill, and we followed him.

At the river trail, Gunner turned left. "Wait," I said. He stopped and stared at me. "Would you ride the rest of the trail with us?"

Gunner looked at the sky, then shook his head. "Lunchtime soon."

"Is there a place to eat in Clarkdale?" Jill asked.

With a frown, Gunner considered the question. "Mom and I go to the Rooster sometimes."

"Would you like to eat lunch with us at the Rooster?" Jill asked.

"Can't. No money."

Jill smiled, radiating reassurance. "You're helping us. I'd like to buy your lunch."

After a bit of thought, Gunner nodded. "Okay."

We turned north and followed the Verde River over the Tuzigoot National Monument access road and on toward Clarkdale. I noticed Gunner studying the ground around the trail like he was searching for something.

"What are you looking for?" I asked.

"Stuff I can sell."

"What kind of stuff do you find?" I asked.

"I found a backpack once. A guy paid me five bucks for it."

"Was it empty?"

"Naw, it had some clothes in it, but they didn't fit me."

My interest was piqued. "Did you find the backpack about the time the dead guy was found?"

"No, that was when the river went down, after the monsoon. I found lots of stuff then."

Pulling teeth would've been easier than trying to engage Gunner in a conversation. "What other valuable things have you found?"

"A guy paid me ten bucks to show him where I found a kayak."

"Kayaks are very valuable," I said. "You could've hauled it into town and got more than ten dollars for it."

"I had no way to get it into town. So, the guy paid me, and I showed him. No work for me."

We rode in silence until we were across the river from a housing development. Gunner sped up and rode alongside Jill. "There's a ford before we get to the Rooster. I'll show you."

Gunner led us toward the cottonwoods and down a path that crossed the river. Knowing his destination, he sped up and we followed. Within a few minutes we were behind a building. The aroma of frying onions and burgers wafted on the breeze. Gunner tied Mojo to a tree behind the building, as if he'd done it a thousand times before, then waited for us.

"Here's The Rooster. I like hamburgers with pickles."

Gunner was inside before I was off the horse. "I think you've sweet-talked Gunner into eating at his favorite place."

Gunner was sitting on a stool at the lunch counter, chatting with a heavyset woman. She seemed surprised when we sat on the stools on either side of him.

"My, my Gunner. You've got friends with guns and badges."

Nodding, Gunner looked over the woman's shoulder. "I'd like a Coke with ice, and a hamburger with pickles."

With a smile, the woman nodded. "The usual." She turned to Jill and me. "And what will Gunner's friends have?"

Jill looked at the menu board behind the counter. "I think I'll try a bowl of vegetable soup and Diet Coke."

"I think I'll have Gunner's usual, with fried onions and fries."

"Got it. I'm Nettie. If you need anything, just holler." We watched the waitress post our orders on a clip. "Do you ever take your helmet off, Gunner?"

"Mom says I have to wear it whenever I'm riding. It protects my head."

Jill nodded. "Your mom is very wise."

"People say she's smart. I've never heard anyone say she was wise. Is wise smarter than plain smart?"

"Smart is book learning," Jill replied. "Wise means using your head."

Gunner looked perplexed by the answer. "Mom doesn't have a lot of book learning, but she's smart anyway."

Nettie delivered our beverages and straws, then leaned on the counter. "Is that enough ice, Gunner?"

He stripped off the paper wrapper and pushed the straw into the glass. Swirling it in the drink, he nodded. Nettie looked at me. How's your ice?" she asked with a wink.

"It's just about perfect," I replied.

"What brings you two to The Red Rooster with my friend Gunner?"

"We're out riding."

Nettie cocked her head, then looked at Jill. "I've never heard of a cop just out riding."

"We're investigating the Tedeschi murder."

Drawing a breath, Nettie shook her head. "Leave well enough alone. He was a boil on the butt of humanity."

"You didn't have much time for Al?" Jill asked.

"My daughter dated him until he got bored. He was old enough to be her father, but off they went, strutting around town like he was king and she was the queen in waiting."

"We've heard he dates a lot of women."

Gunner was suddenly interested in the conversation. He turned to Jill. "Mom says he..." Gunner paused. "Mom told me not to use the word she calls Mr. Tedeschi. She said it's swearing."

Nettie chuckled. "I bet that swear word rhymes with trucker."

Gunner nodded. "It starts with F, but that's all Mom will let me say."

A bell sounded on the pass through, and Nettie stood. "That'll be your lunch."

She set the plates on the counter and Gunner ate like he was afraid someone would steal his burger. "Would you like some of my fries, Gunner?" I asked, pushing the huge basket of fries toward him.

He looked at them hungrily. "I like to dip them in mayo."

"Nettie, can we get some mayo for Gunner to dip?"

Nettie returned with a paper cup filled with mayonnaise, setting it between us. "Gunner, you've hit the big time. You're eating fries with your burger and Coke."

Gunner grabbed handfuls of fries, dipped them, and crammed them into his mouth. He dipped the next handful before he'd finished chewing the first. Nettie put her hand on Gunner's arm. "Slow down. Nobody's going to steal them."

Gunner nodded and slowed his chewing. "Yes, ma'am."

"How's your soup?" Nettie asked.

"It's excellent! If we weren't on horseback, I'd take a quart home with me."

"I've never heard that one before," Nettie said with a laugh. She tore three bills off her pad and slid one in front of me. "Are you treating Gunner, or is he paying for himself?"

Jill put out her hand. "I've got all three."

Gunner looked at her and smiled. "I can pay for part." He got up and walked out of the café.

Looking at the bills, Jill handed Nettie a twenty. "I've got it. And I don't need any change."

Nettie smiled and accepted the money as Gunner rushed back in with a spur hanging from his hand. He held it out to Nettie, "How much is this worth?"

I looked around at the café's walls. They were adorned with rusty signs and antiques.

"This nice lady already paid for your lunch. Save your spur for next time."

Jill put out her hand. "Where did you find this, Gunner?"

"It was on the trail the day after the dead guy showed up. Would you like to buy it?"

Jill took the spur and examined the broken leather strap. It was a basic spur, without the fancy markings I'd seen at the tack shop. She looked at me, then back to Gunner. "Will you take twenty for it?"

Gunner shook his head. "Twenty cents isn't enough. I think it's worth two dollars."

Jill reached in her pocket and peeled a twenty dollar bill off, then handed it to Gunner. "Twenty dollars."

Gunner looked at the spur, then at the cash. "Look here. It's broken here where the leather ripped next to the hole. It won't even work."

Jill waved the bill. "It's okay, Gunner. I'll pay twenty, but you have to show me where you found it."

Gunner set the spur on the counter and pushed it toward Jill, as if he was afraid their hands might touch. Then, he snatched the bill out of her hand and spun around on his stool. Wondering what was going on, I watched him pull off his right boot and drop it on the floor, exposing a dirty white sock with holes in both the toe and heel. He slid up his pants leg, then carefully folded the bill twice before sliding into the top of his sock.

Completely mesmerized by the process, Jill had to poke my arm to get my attention. "Look at the initials on the spur."

I took the spur from her and studied the leather. Embossed in the leather many years ago were the letters A and T, now barely visible through the wear and scratches. Further down the strap was a hole with the leather torn away on one side.

Gunner pulled his boot on and spun around on the stool. "Are we going now?"

While watching us, Nettie continued to smile. She put her hand on Jill's arm as we stood. I followed Gunner out the door while Jill and Nettie talked.

Gunner was ready to ride when I stopped him. "Hold on a second until Jill comes out."

Gunner stopped and stared at the door, as if willing Jill to hurry. Studying his face, I realized he was older than I'd thought. He'd spent a lot of his time in the sun, tanning his face deeply, but in addition to his tan, there was a leathery appearance to his skin that only came with age. "How old are you, Gunner?"

Looking away from the door, he squinted. "Why?"

"I'm just curious. What year were you born?"

"My birthday is May twenty seventh."

"What year?"

The question seemed to stump him. "Mom says I'm old enough to know I shouldn't get into trouble."

I looked at the fringe of dark, greasy hair exposed around the edges of the orange football helmet. A bead of sweat ran down his neck and I guessed Gunner was at least thirty.

"Hold my reins," he said, jamming the leather into my hand. He turned, pulled down his zipper, and peed on a tree. The car driving past didn't seem to care about Gunner's exposure; perhaps someone who knew about him. He zipped up just as Jill opened the café door. "Coke makes me hafta pee," he said, taking the reins.

Jill stepped around the puddle and untied her horse. "Okay, Gunner, let's see where you found this spur."

In one fluid motion, Gunner mounted Mojo and they wheeled around, as if the horse knew where we were going. My attempt to get on the saddle was less graceful. Wanting to stay with the herd, Weed was moving away while I had one foot in the stirrup but still trying to get momentum to pull myself into the saddle. I had to pull my foot out of the stirrup. Then, Weed and I had a discussion about our partnership, or lack thereof. I mentioned that I was armed, with little response from him. I guess he sensed I wouldn't shoot him over mounting etiquette, but still… With Jill and Gunner nearly to the river I settled in the saddle, which was more than Weed could bear. Despite my protest, we galloped to catch up, irritating my already sore butt.

Grinning, Jill stopped Lash and let me catch up to them. "Are you having problems, dear?"

"Weed and I had a minor difference of opinion about whether I needed to be in the saddle before he took off. We've got it settled now."

"You are such a city kid."

"Hey," I said as we followed Gunner, "at least I'm riding a horse. I haven't fallen off, nor have I embarrassed myself."

Jill snorted. "You don't even know when to be embarrassed. Have you forgotten peeing in your pants?"

After fording the river, Gunner turned north onto the path. His pace was leisurely, and although he wanted to ride next to Jill, he didn't say a word. I saw him glance at her a few times and I had the impression he had a crush on my wife.

Gunner reined Mojo in and said, "Whoa." It was literally the only word he'd spoken since we left the Red Rooster Café. He pointed to a spot next to the trail. "It was here." He pointed to a spot under a cottonwood branch.

We dismounted and Jill squatted down to study the spot Gunner had pointed out. "Was it exactly here, Gunner?"

"Yes ma'am. It was under that branch."

I leaned over Jill and looked at the head-high branch that leaned toward the trail. "The bark has been scuffed.

With her phone in one hand and reins in the other, Jill took a picture of the scuff marks on the tree and the spot Gunner had identified as the place he'd found the spur. Jamming her phone into her back pocket, Jill turned to Gunner and me.

"The spur's leather was old and scraped up, but it didn't break while Al was riding. If I had to guess, I'd say Al's boot was sticking out and the spur caught on the branch with enough resistance to tear the leather."

Gunner shook his head. "No one's boots are that high when they're riding."

"Maybe Al Tedeschi was tied across the saddle with his spurs sticking up," Jill replied.

"Take a picture of the spur and send it to Rob Henderson. Ask him if Tedeschi had one spur on when they recovered his body and if the other spur matches this."

Gunner was deep in thought. "Nobody loses a spur while they're riding."

"Who owns the nearest ranch, Gunner?"

"That'd be the Lazy L. It's not really a ranch anymore. They bring in city people so they can pretend to be cowboys."

"Tedeschi owns it," I said.

Gunner nodded. "So far."

Jill finished emailing the spur picture and turned to Gunner. "What do you mean, so far?"

"They're selling. Everyone says so in town. I heard people saying that old lady Tedeschi is selling now that she's rid of that old..." Gunner paused and looked at Jill, "That's the word Mom told me not to say anymore."

Gunner rode with us until we got to Dead Horse Ranch State Park. He stopped and looked at Jill, obviously searching for words. "Thanks for lunch, ma'am."

"You're welcome."

Gunner turned Mojo toward the river, then stopped. Looking over his shoulder he said, "You're smart, like my mom."

Jill looked at me as the horses started back down the trail to Hoofbeats Ranch. "I'm smart, like Gunner's mom."

"You're way smarter than Gunner's mom, and cuter."

"You've never met Gunner's mom."

"She can't hold a candle to you."

Jill was deep in thought as we approached the riding stable. I suspected she was melancholy about our horses at her parents' South Dakota ranch, but was surprised when she said, "There aren't many places with horses north of where Gunner found the broken spur."

"As a rational person, I agree. As a cop or prosecutor, I'd say the chain of evidence for the spur was deeply compromised when Gunner removed it from the spot where he'd found it."

"Gunner could testify…" Jill blew out a breath. "I can't picture Gunner testifying in court."

"Any half-wit defense attorney would pick him apart like a vulture on a carcass."

Chuckling, Jill shook her head. "You've gone cowboy. No Minnesota cop would use a vulture analogy."

"It's the hat and boots. I'm sure I'll be transformed back when I buy a new Minnesota Twins cap."

"I haven't seen any of them around town."

"There's a computer in the hotel lobby. I'm sure I can order one from Amazon."

We dismounted at the riding school. Weed stood still while I slid down from the saddle. I'd like to think we'd bonded, but I suspected he was just tired. Megan met us at the office door, smiling. "How was lunch at The Red Rooster?"

"They have great vegetable soup," Jill said.

With a grin, Megan looked at me. "I heard Gunner wiped out your fries."

"He was a hungry man." I paused. "How old is Gunner?"

"I'm not sure. His rodeo accident was more than ten years ago. I'm sure he was in his twenties when he was on the rodeo circuit. I suppose that makes him almost forty."

"He acts and talks like a ten-year-old," I said.

Nodding toward the office, Megan said, "I think of him as a grade school kid in a man's body. He's very shy, even around people he knows. I'm surprised you got him to ride with you."

"Jill talked to him, and I think he has a crush on her."

Megan sat at the desk and gestured for us to sit in her dusty guest chairs. "Gunner's mom looks like a tired, weathered version of Jill."

"I think we're done riding," Jill said, digging out a charge card from her back pocket. "How much do we owe you?"

"Our published $60/hour rates are based on guided rides. Since you didn't need a guide, and you rode for two entire days, I suppose $100 per horse for each day would cover it."

I stopped Jill before she handed Megan her card. "Megan, let's look at your trail map before we settle up."

We walked to the laminated map near the door. "What are you looking for?"

I traced the trail alongside the river with my finger. "We went past Dead Horse Ranch State Park, then cut across Tuzigoot. We had lunch in Clarkdale, then Gunner led us to a spot here, where he found what might be a piece of evidence."

Nodding, Megan watched. "I heard he sold Jill a broken spur. Do you think that has something to do with Al's murder?"

"Let's assume it does. Gunner showed us this spot, where he found the spur. What's farther up this trail?"

Tracing a dotted trail following the Verde River, Megan said, "We've ridden all the way to Sedona. We don't advertise trail rides past Clarkdale but if we have experienced riders looking for a day trip, we'll take them to SOB Canyon."

"SOB Canyon?" I asked.

"That's what the locals call it. I think the official name is Sycamore Canyon."

"Are there ranches up there?"

Megan moved her finger over the area beyond Clarkdale. "There are old homesteads up there, but the last occupied ranch is Paysons', here." She pointed to a spot halfway between Clarkdale and SOB Canyon.

"Would Paysons have a reason to kill Al Tedeschi?"

Megan's look was priceless. "Everyone had a reason to hate Al. I'm not sure whose grudge would lead to killing him."

"We found horseshoe prints made by a bar shoe," Jill said, turning away from the map.

"I suppose anyone who has a horse with a soft heel would use a bar shoe. They're not common, but they're around."

Jill pondered that. "Should we ride further up the trail tomorrow? We could look for bar horseshoe prints and talk to Paysons."

"Let's spend another day in Cottonwood and see where that leads us. Settle up with Megan."

Megan accepted Jill's charge card and went to her desk. "I have a couple groups riding in the next few days. Let me know a day ahead and I can have Lash and Weed ready for you."

* * *

Fingering the spur as we left Hoofbeats Ranch, Jill was deep in thought.

"Call Rob Henderson. We need to give him the spur and strategize."

"Let's shower and change first. We both smell like horses."

"If you call him now, he might meet us for supper."

Jill took out her phone and punched in Rob's number. She put it on speakerphone as it rang. "Hi, Rob. This is Jill Fletcher. Can we meet for supper?"

Laughing, Rob said, "I've got a wife who expects me to sit across from her at dinner once in a while. I'll have to pass." A woman's voice said something indistinct in the background.

"I get that. Let's make it lunch," Jill replied.

"Hang on, Jill. The home boss just informed me she's made enough meatloaf to feed an army. She's wondering if you'd like to come over to our house for dinner. She's heard me talking about you two, and I think she'd like to meet you."

The woman's voice became more distinct, then she spoke into the phone. "Hi, this is Skip, Rob's wife. Yes, I'd like to meet you, and I hope a quiet home cooked meal might be a nice change from eating at restaurants.”

“What time do you want us?” Jill asked.

“The meatloaf and potatoes will come out of the oven at six. If that’s too early, I can turn the oven down.”

Jill glanced at her watch. “Six will be fine. Where do you live?”

Rob came back on the phone. “Take a right at the second Cottonwood stop light and go up the hill five blocks. Turn left and we’re the third house on the right. It’s the white house with the sheriff’s car parked in the driveway.”

“Got it! We’ll see you at six.” Jill ended the call. “You’re going to have to shower quickly if we’re going to make it by six.”

“Me? I’m not the one who dawdles for half an hour using up all the hot water.”

“I have longer hair and it takes a while for me to wash and rinse it.” Without a witty response from me, she went on. “You’re clueless, aren’t you?”

“I am not clueless.”

“No, you’re a brilliant detective who’s clueless about women.”

“I’ve got news for you. Women don’t come with an instruction manual, and the rules change as you play the game.”

"At least you've got that much figured out; you know that I determine the bathroom rules, and you have to follow along."

I turned into the hotel parking lot and got out of the pickup. "You get the shower first," I said.

Jill smiled. "At least you've got that rule right."

Chapter 13

Rob Henderson met us at the front door as the rich aroma of meatloaf filled the air. I handed him a bottle of wine from the case we'd purchased. He ushered us in, then looked at the wine. "I'm not sure meatloaf deserves wine."

While Rob was slender, Skip Henderson had a matronly build. She engulfed Jill in a hug. "Rob has talked endlessly about you two. I'm so pleased to finally meet you." She hugged me and pecked me on the cheek. "You're the one who doesn't like horses."

"I'm not a big fan," I said as Rob urged me into the dining room in their modest rambler.

Skip put her arm around Jill's waist and in a stage whisper said, "I heard he peed his pants when his horse broke into a gallop."

I glared at Rob who gave me a, *I didn't tell her,* gesture. He dug a corkscrew out of an antique sideboard while Jill followed Skip into the kitchen. "It's been so long since we've had wine, we should probably check the wine glasses for spiders."

I pulled the evidence bag containing the spur from my back pocket and set it on the sideboard. "You need to put this into evidence."

Rob opened the wine, took down four glasses, and poured. "You're not going to hang onto that?"

"It's your case, Rob."

After setting the ladies' wine glasses on the table, Rob picked up the evidence bag and examined the spur. "Fletcher, you're the strangest Fed I've ever worked with."

"I told you when we arrived that our job was helping with *your* case. It's not, nor will it ever be, *my* case."

Rob took out a pen and signed the chain of evidence tag on the bag. "I know you said that, but I've had so many Feds blow smoke up my butt about how they were here to help me, I've grown skeptical."

I lifted my wine glass to Rob. "To cynical cops."

Rob shook his head. "Absent friends." The traditional toast to friends and associates who preceded us in death. We touched our glasses and sipped the wine. "This isn't bad."

"We liked it and I've got most of a case to drink up so I don't have to ship it back to Texas." Jill and Skip laughed in the other room. "Do you think they're laughing at you or me?"

"Whew, that's a tough call, Doug. I've stumbled on so many marital landmines that I'm afraid to take a step."

"Jill says I like the taste of boot leather so much that I keep sticking my foot in my mouth." I nodded toward the spur on the sideboard. "Does that spur fit anything in your case?"

Rob took out his phone and pulled up a photo file. He scrolled down, then enlarged a photo before handing the phone to me. "This is the spur on Al Tedeschi's left boot."

After leafing through a series of photos, I handed the phone back to him. "I think Gunner found gold."

Jill walked in carrying a bowl of foil wrapped baked potatoes, followed by Skip carrying a platter of sliced meatloaf and a steaming bowl of green beans. Skip set the platter down and said, "Grab a chair and sit yourselves down while I get some ketchup."

Rob held a chair for Jill, and we sat as Skip rushed back with a bottle of ketchup. "I poured tomatoes on top, but Rob likes a dash of ketchup, too."

Rob handed the platter of meat to Jill. "Please, help yourself."

"This is a treat. Your meal reminds me of my mom's meatloaf dinners."

"It's nothing fancy. If Rob had given me a little notice, I could've whipped up a Yankee pot roast or something."

Jill took a potato and passed the bowl. "There's nothing you could've served us that would've tasted any better than this."

Rob cut off a corner of meatloaf and popped it into his mouth. "That's high praise for a meal you haven't tasted yet."

Skip noticed the evidence bag. "Is that what Gunner sold you, Jill?"

Rob held up his fork while he swallowed. "It is, and it matches the spur on the victim's boot."

Jill looked at Skip and asked, "Are criminal cases a regular part of your dinner conversations?"

"For thirty-three years now. Our kids grew up knowing more about the collection and handling of evidence than most first-year public defenders. How about you two?"

Jill laughed. "We met when Doug was working for me and explained the intricacies of criminal investigations."

"That didn't scare you off?" Rob asked.

"I found it fascinating. I waited for his nightly call."

With a sly smile, Skip said, "Was that because of the caller or the subject matter?"

"It was a little of each. I was the Flagstaff superintendent and...it was lonely at the top. Doug treated me as an equal and we became friends. Then, there was a wilderness trek searching for the source of a body recovered after a flash flood. I discovered how much I'd been missing by making my career my life." Jill paused, uncomfortable taking that conversation any further. "How did you two meet?"

"We were high school sweethearts," Skip said. "We got married shortly after graduation."

Rob laughed, "And four months before the birth of Rob Junior."

Conversation drifted to life in Cottonwood, our Texas assignment, then our cross-country investigations.

Rob ate his last bite of meatloaf and leaned back with his wine glass in hand. "As much as your investigations around the country sound interesting, I think it'd be hard to investigate a crime without local knowledge. It sounds trite, but when something happens, we round up the usual suspects and ninety-nine percent of the time, we've solved the crime in a few hours."

"I like to believe we bring in an unbiased view," I said.

Skip started gathering our plates. "You only get called to investigate crimes where the local cops haven't been able to solve a crime by looking at the usual suspects.

That's got to be both interesting and challenging."

Helping with the cleanup, Jill said, "We rely on local experts, like Rob, to fill in the local scene."

I poured the last of the wine into our glasses. "That's also why we say we're helping the local law enforcement people, not taking over their investigations. We rarely solve a case alone. Our role is to supply the time and unbiased perspective that adds to what's already being done."

Rob waited until Jill and Skip were in the kitchen, then he leaned toward me. "I did a little research. You and Jill have been in the news a half dozen times, and each time you're standing in the background when the local police chief or sheriff has a news conference. You're mentioned as resources, not the key investigators. How do your bosses feel about that?"

"They know what we've done, and what we've contributed."

"But you're never thumping your chest, bragging about solving the crime."

Skip and Jill walked in carrying plates, each with a slice of pie. "I'm sorry," Skip said, as she placed a plate in front of me. "I didn't have time to make something so this is store-bought apple pie."

"I'm sure it's not as good as you'd make yourself, but it's much appreciated."

Jill placed a napkin on her lap, then paused deep in thought. "You know why we're different, Rob? We're Park Service investigators who don't work for a police agency. The National Park Service is concerned about safety in the parks, not in being police. We're happy to help our local law enforcement agencies, knowing how important your support is and realizing the Park Service has to depend on you long after Doug and I are back in Texas."

After breaking the back crust off her pie, Skip looked at Jill. "I heard that Gunner has been helping you."

"He found the missing spur that matches the one on Al Tedeschi's boot."

"Gunner is simple, but he's not dumb," Skip said, cutting a piece of pie with the edge of her fork. "He sees a lot and knows more than he says."

I looked at Rob, who'd become quiet. "Should we question Gunner?"

"I assume you tried to have a conversation with him while you were riding."

I nodded. "Gunner is a man of few words."

"Exactly. You could question him all day long and never get more than a one-word answer. Afterwards, you'd question the veracity of what he'd told you."

Jill was shaking her head. "I disagree. I think everything Gunner told us was the truth."

"It was the truth as Gunner saw it. I think he sees life through a different lens than the rest of us," Rob said.

Skip stopped eating and considered what she'd heard. "I think Gunner is a special person with special gifts. For him, the world is a simpler place, uncluttered with human emotions, hatred, or prejudice. He lives in the moment."

"He told us about seeing Al's body days before it was discovered by a hiker," I said. "Although he didn't know the significance of the spur, he showed us the exact spot he'd found it. I wonder what else he knows? Unless we ask the right questions, we'll never know."

Rob ate the last bite of his pie and set his napkin on the table. "Gunner is intimidated by me. He turns away when I say hi."

"He was following Jill like a lost puppy," I said, pushing my empty pie plate away. "I'm sure Gunner would answer her questions."

Jill shook her head. "We asked him every question that came to mind. I don't know what else I'd ask him. And the only place we've seen him is riding by Dead Horse Ranch State Park. I don't know where else he rides or where we'd find him."

Skip gathered the pie plates and said, "He and his mom live on a couple acres on the edge of old Cottonwood. You could probably catch him there at mealtime."

"That's right," Jill said. "He checked the sun several times during the day to determine when he had to be home for meals."

Skip was getting into it and set the pie plates aside. "What do you hope to learn from Gunner?"

Cocking her head, Jill stared at me. "He told us he noticed two sets of hoofprints but didn't see anyone riding on the trail where Al was recovered."

"And we're reasonably certain Al's body was carried there on horseback. It was transported after the park closed and probably after dark," I added.

Skip stared out the window. "Maybe you're trying to determine what Gunner didn't see."

Rob frowned. "Huh?"

"Maybe you need to ask Gunner what's changed. Maybe he's seen something in the past that's no longer there."

Rob shook his head. "The swamp trail has been traveled by dozens of people since Al's body was found. It's changed a lot."

Skip sighed. "Think outside the box, Rob. Gunner rides all over the area. He found the spur like a mile from the swamp. Maybe the important piece is miles from the park."

Jill raised her eyebrows. "Megan pointed out trails going all the way from Cottonwood to Sedona, and beyond. We're reasonably certain his body was moved from somewhere north of the park."

"What's common to all the places you're considering?" Skip asked.

"His body was found by the marsh and all the trails we're riding follow the river," Jill explained.

Skip held her knuckle to her upper lip as she thought. "Water is scarce here. Maybe his death has more to do with water than Al's bimbos."

Jill sat up. "Gunner said Al's wife is going to sell the ranch. Someone told us that the water rights were worth more than the ranch land."

I shook my head. "Murder is usually about love, drugs, or money. I have a hard time believing Al was murdered because of water."

Skip smiled. "You're from Minnesota, the land of ten thousand lakes. In Arizona, water is more than money, it's life and death."

"Let's take a ride," I said.

"Now?" Rob asked.

"Yes, I think I'd like to sample some Tedeschi wine at their tasting room."

Skip laughed. "This is like free association. I say water and Doug says wine. It's almost Biblical."

Jill picked up the pie plates. "Let's load the dishwasher." As she and Skip walked into the kitchen she added, "If something is Doug's idea, I can assure you the thought isn't Biblical."

* * *

The four of us took the Park Service pickup to old Cottonwood rather than having two people ride in the back seat of Rob's county cruiser looking like arrestees. Parking was tough, so we found a spot in front of the hotel and walked the three blocks to the Tedeschi Winery tasting room. Unlike most of the other light and airy tasting rooms, Tedeschi's was painted black. Track lighting provided bright areas over the tasting bar and cash register, leaving the rest of the room in subdued darkness.

A young man was pouring wine samples for four people seated at the bar. He glanced up when the door opened, then did a double take when he spotted Rob. Taking four seats in the most remote corner of the tasting bar, our group had a good view of the room. As my eyes adjusted to the dim lighting, I noticed two couples sitting at small tables along the wall. The rest of the tables were empty, probably typical for the weekday evening tourist business.

The young man excused himself from his foursome of customers, took four wine glasses from under the counter, and set them down in front of us. "Hey, Rob. I don't remember seeing you in here before."

"Hi, Carlton. We had some friends over for dinner and they suggested having a glass of wine. This is my wife, Skip, and these are our friends, Jill and Doug Fletcher."

After handing us wine menus, Carlton said, "If you're here to taste, I suggest starting with the dry reds at the top of the list. If you're here for dessert, I've got a fruity cherry wine and a port-style red fortified with brandy." His eyes locked on Jill's Glock pistol. "I don't see many women open carrying."

Smiling, Jill nodded. "I feel naked without my Glock."

The comment left Carlton Tedeschi speechless. "Um, I see."

Rob broke into laughter. "The Fletchers are Park Service investigators assigned to your father's murder case."

"I apologize for my wife's flippant comment," I said. "We offer our condolences in this difficult time."

Carlton straightened the row of wine glasses in front of us, then drew a breath and blew it out. "It's been a tough week." After a moment's hesitation, he brought out another glass and a bottle of red wine. He poured five glasses half full, then raised one of the glasses. "I'd be honored if you'd join me in a toast to Dad."

We each touched the rim of our wine glass to Carlton's, then took a sip.

After swallowing, Jill held the glass under her nose and inhaled. She looked at the tasting menu. "This is delicious. What is it?"

Carlton swirled the wine in his glass, then breathed in the aroma. "It's not on the list. I made a test batch, blending cabernet franc grapes from our ranch with some zinfandel and petite syrah from the Sierra Nevada foothills. We only bottled a dozen cases and most of them went to the Lazy L for a wine tasting group. I keep a few bottles under the bar for my friends."

Smiling, Rob tipped his glass to Carlton. "I'm honored. Thanks."

The other group gestured to Carlton, and he excused himself. Watching him leave, Jill whispered, "I'd have sworn he was ready to pee in his pants when he saw you walk in, Rob."

Rob swirled his wine and nodded. Skip leaned close and said, "Carlton sowed some wild oats as a teen. He really cleaned up his behavior when he got into viniculture. The vines were planted by his grandparents and had languished under Al. Carlton got interested and nursed them back to health, then started bottling his own wines."

"Are the rest of his wines any good?" Jill asked.

Rob shrugged. "I've never had any of his wines before tonight."

Carlton walked back to us, carrying another bottle of wine. "When you're through with the red blend, I'd like you to try my port."

I held up my still half-full wine glass. "You'd better give us a minute to savor this."

The foursome stood and Carlton went back to them, selling them a few bottles that he wrapped in paper bags. He walked them out the door and waved goodbye, then returned to us. He took out five new glasses and poured the glasses half full. I'd watched the one-ounce tasting pours the other group got, and we were getting glasses with about five or six ounces.

Carlton slid the glasses to us, then stood across from Jill. "You seem to be the wine aficionado in this group. Tell me what you think of this."

Wetting her lips, Jill paused. "I'm just a South Dakota ranch girl, hardly a wine aficionado."

"I could tell by the way you breathed in the bouquet and rolled the wine in your mouth that you were really appreciating its character."

With a swirl of the glass, Jill held the wine up to the light. Then, she breathed in the bouquet and took a sip. She closed her eyes for a second, then swallowed. "Oh, my."

Carlton smiled. "I tried a lot of blends to come up with this. It's fortified with French cognac."

I tasted a sample and felt the warmth from the cognac. "I'll be ready for a nap after a glass of this," I said.

Carlton turned the bottle and cradled it in his hand so we could see the label. "I chose the Kokopelli symbol on the label. It's the Navajo/Hopi symbol of mischief and fertility. A female customer told me I should rename it 'Love Potion #9'."

Skip pushed aside her nearly empty glass of the first red and sampled the port. Her eyes twinkled and she grinned. "Yes, I could see a few cowboys getting lucky after pouring their gals a couple glasses of this."

Jill pulled her charge card from a back pocket and slid it across the bar. "Wrap up two bottles of the love potion wine: one for me, and one for Skip. I'm paying the tasting fee, too."

"There's no charge. You guys are trying to help find Dad's killer. This is one way I can thank you."

Jill shook her head. "We're paying. Federal officers can't accept gifts, and this might cloud my judgment."

Carlton smiled and took Jill's card. "People have said a lot of things after drinking wine samples, but you're the first who's said it might cloud your judgment."

Sipping the port, Skip made a yummy sound. "This brings back memories of holiday dinners when my father would pull out a bottle of Mogen David wine and serve it in water glasses. Do you remember that, Rob?"

Holding up his glass, Rob shook his head. "This does *not* remind me of your dad's wine."

We were laughing when Carlton returned with two bottles and a charge slip for Jill to sign. "I'm pleased you're enjoying the wine." After Jill signed the slip, he paused and looked at Rob. "I've never thanked you for not hauling my butt off to jail."

"You were doing the same stuff a lot of stupid kids have done for decades. I didn't see any point in dragging you in front of a judge when I knew your dad would dole out all the punishment required."

"You've got that right. After you hauled me home drunk, Dad had me up at dawn loading bales of hay into the barn. I've never sweated so much in my entire life."

After tucking away her charge card, Jill changed the topic. "How did you rescue the vineyard?"

"I cut back the stalks to stimulate new growth, tilled up the weeds between the rows, and irrigated the vines. Within four years, the yield went from a few bottles of barely drinkable swill to a few hundred cases of quality wine."

"Irrigation is tough back in South Dakota. My family had to drill wells that are hundreds of feet deep to get enough water to grow enough hay for a winter."

"The family ranch has water rights to some Verde River water. I have to use drip irrigation to minimize the water use and get the water where the vines need it."

"Are you planning to expand?"

Carlton shook his head. "We've got as many vines as the ranch will support and even if I planted more, I'd have to buy water rights from someone to irrigate the expanded vineyard. I make enough to support my few employees, but I can't see how I could cover my additional costs if I had to buy water."

"Doug's from Minnesota and he doesn't get the water rights problems," Jill explained.

"Yeah, what's your state nickname? 'The land of ten million lakes?'"

"Ten thousand lakes," I replied. "And some of them are hardly more than ponds."

"Dad split the ranch water allocation between the vineyard and the Lazy L when he started the dude ranch and gave up raising beef. We each have just enough water to meet our needs with none to spare."

"I hope he put that in his will," Jill said. "I'd hate to see you lose the water you need for the vineyard."

Jill's comment made Carlton uneasy. "Yeah, I think I'm okay."

"We heard a rumor that your mother wants to sell the ranch to a developer."

Carlton leaned on the counter. "The ranch isn't hers to sell. Dad's will leaves her the house, but the rest of the ranch belongs to Theresa and me."

"And the water rights?" Jill asked.

"The water rights are attached to the acreage, not the house."

Rob stood and put his hand out to Carlton. "Some of us have to work in the morning. Thanks for sharing your special wines with us."

Carlton's eyes got misty as he shook our hands. "Find the bastards who killed Dad."

Nodding, I shook his hand. "We'll do everything we can."

Rob hung back as we walked out the door. The sidewalks were empty as we waited outside the tasting room. Skip held up the paper-wrapped bottle Jill had given her. "Thanks. This is heavenly."

Rob joined us and held my elbow as the women walked toward the pickup. "I told Carlton that you and Jill were the Park Service A Team. That pleased him."

"I hope you didn't oversell our capabilities."

"I doubt that." Rob paused. "He seemed sincerely sad about his father's death. I'm inclined to remove him from the list of possible killers."

"Yeah, he's either very sad or one hell of an actor."

Skip slowed and let us catch up. "Carlton isn't an actor. He's always worn his heart on his sleeve. He's not Al's killer."

"He was emphatic about the ranch and water rights ownership," I said. "I think the rumor about Robyn selling off the ranch is just that; a rumor."

We chatted about Tedeschi family dynamics on the drive back to Skip and Rob's home. I parked at the curb to let them out, but Skip, who'd been riding in the backseat with Jill, leaned her arms on the seatback. "You need to talk to Gunner and his mother."

I looked at Rob. "You know her. Why don't *you* talk to her?"

"Caroline and I have a history. It'd be less confrontational if you and Jill spoke to her."

Nodding, Skip added, "It might be even better if just Jill spoke to Caroline. Her history with men is…complicated. I think she might tell Jill things she wouldn't say around Doug or Rob."

With emphatic hugs, Skip wished us goodnight. Rob shook my hand and gave Jill an obligatory hug that involved barely touching shoulders.

"What do you think about interviewing Gunner's mom?" I asked.

Jill considered that question for several blocks. "I'm not sure we'll get anything out of her. Skip's theory about Gunner noticing changes has me confused. It sounds stupid but, Gunner doesn't know what he doesn't know."

"You should write that down," I said playfully.

"It's like this whole investigation. We aren't smart enough to ask the quintessential question because we're not smart enough to know what's missing from the picture."

"On the other hand, there's no harm in speaking with Gunner's mother."

"I might not be ready to talk to a woman who's so distrustful of men that she won't open up to you or Rob."

With only one very narrow parking spot open in the hotel parking lot, I elected to park a block away on a side street. Jill carried her wine bottle, silently mulling the issue of interviewing Gunner's mother.

"Don't worry about it. You're a great interviewer."

The glare I got in response was telling.

"Don't glare at me. You *are* a great interviewer. You get people to spill things I'd never get out of them."

"Right."

After brushing her teeth and hair, Jill climbed in bed beside me. "We need to interview Robyn Tedeschi."

"I've been holding off, assuming we'd get something to rattle her. Maybe something to use as leverage so she'd open up."

"What if that item never shows up?"

"Then we knock on her door and express our profound sadness about the loss of her husband."

"Her husband was a womanizing jerk. She'll probably be dancing on his grave before the dirt settles." Jill snuggled into me, then rolled onto her back. "Do you have any Tylenol in your travel bag? I think the wine is wearing off and I'm starting to get a headache."

"There's a bottle in the side pocket. I'm not sure how many are left."

The trilling of Jill's cell phone jarred me. I reached across the bed for it, succeeding only in knocking it off the nightstand and onto the floor. Jill stepped out of the bathroom and snatched it off the floor.

Catching the call before it rolled over to voicemail, she answered, then quickly stepped into the bathroom. That usually meant the call was from Mandy Mattson who wanted to talk "about girl stuff" or complain about something our boss, Matt, had done. The clock said it was just past nine, yet the combination of heavy dinner and wine made me feel like it was much later. I rolled away from the bathroom door and closed my eyes.

When the bathroom door opened, I was half asleep. "Yes, he's right here. I'll hand him the phone."

"Who is it?" I asked, trying to get my eyes to adjust after being nearly asleep. Jill didn't answer, just extended the phone to me.

"Fletcher," I said, anticipating that the caller was someone from the Park Service.

"I know you're Fletcher," my mother said. "Why don't you just say, 'hello' like a normal person?"

"What's up, Mom?"

"I thought I'd better let you know we're at the hospital with Rickowskis. Molly fell off the back step and hurt her wrist. They're taking x-rays, but I'm sure it's broken."

"Did she miss a step or…?"

"She doesn't remember the fall. Al heard a crash and rushed out. Molly was dazed and Al assumed she banged her head. I'm not as sure about the sequence of events."

Jill leaned against pillows with her arms wrapped around her knees. "Do you think she had a stroke?"

"She was talking without slurring her words. Her arms and legs seemed to be functioning, so I don't think it was a stroke."

"What are you planning to do?"

"Chet and I are staying at the hospital with Al until they're through testing Molly and ready to discharge her."

"And if they don't discharge her tonight?"

"I suppose we'll be sitting here until some decision is made."

"Keep us posted."

"Doug…"

"What Mom?"

"Can you guys fly back? Al's pretty much a wreck and he's hopeless around the kitchen."

"Jill and I will talk about our options for getting out of here after I get off the phone. Call us when you know more."

"Doug…"

I closed my eyes. "What Mom?"

"Al wants you to move home. He's afraid Molly will be somehow unable to take care of the house and he'd like you two around to help out."

Pinching the bridge of my nose, I looked at Jill. "Did you discuss that option with Jill?"

"She said you'd have to talk about it."

"I don't see a move to Spearfish in our immediate future."

"Doug, you know that Jill owns more than a section of land here."

"We're not making that decision tonight based on one phone conversation. Call us in the morning unless something unexpected happens tonight." After ending the call, I handed the phone back to Jill. "They want us to move to South Dakota to take care of your father."

"I didn't slam that door."

"I'm not having that discussion after a bottle of wine and a five-minute phone conversation with my mother."

Jill nodded and set the phone on her nightstand. She plugged it into the charger, then turned off the light. "You know I love you."

"And I love you," I said, squeezing her hand.

"Where we live isn't important. Us being together is what's important."

Sighing, I rolled over. "I don't want to live anywhere that has blizzards."

"Maybe global warming will change the Black Hills and the area will become a resort mecca."

"And maybe pigs will fly." I rolled over. "Goodnight, dear."

I felt a sharp pain in my back. "What?"

"I want a proper goodnight kiss, not a goodnight, dear."

I rolled over and pressed my lips against Jill's. She pulled me close and buried her face in my shoulder. "I'm so afraid."

"I know. So am I."

Chapter 14

My mother didn't call back that night and it was too early to call them when we left the hotel in the morning. I navigated the vague directions to Gunner's and found an aging single-story ranch house with a weedy yard and a pickup sitting atop blocks. There was a lean-to behind the house, and an ancient Buick with oxidized blue paint was parked outside the garage.

I drove past the house and turned around so I could park directly in front of it. "You're sure you don't want to come along?" Jill asked as she unbuckled her seatbelt.

"Skip felt that Caroline would respond better to you alone."

"What if she meets me at the front door with a shotgun?"

"Back away slowly with your hands in the air. Speak softly, like you would if you came across a bear on a backcountry hike."

"I don't believe that really works with either bears or angry homeowners."

A few moments after Jill's knock on the storm door, a shadow appeared behind the screen. I couldn't hear the conversation from the pickup. After a minute or so, the storm door opened and a stick-thin woman, with a cigarette dangling from her fingers, held the door open for Jill to enter.

Expecting a prolonged wait, I considered driving into town for a cup of coffee. Then, being a recently trained and considerate husband, I decided not to leave on an errand that might last longer than Jill's conversation with Gunner's mom. Instead, I reluctantly dialed my mother's cell phone.

"Douglas?"

"How's Molly doing?"

"You never call me anymore. Is Jill okay?"

"She's fine, Mom. I called to check on Molly."

"But you never call me unless the world is ending."

Sighing, I tried again. "You called last night to tell us Molly was being treated for an injury. I'm following up to see what the doctor told you."

"He didn't talk to me at all."

"Mom," I said, trying to hide my exasperation, "I assume the doctor spoke with Al, who relayed the information about Molly's condition to you."

"Well, yes. That's what happened."

"And?"

"What time is it there? Are you still on that stupid Arizona time that's an hour different from us even though you're in the same time zone?"

"We are in the Mountain Time Zone. But Arizona doesn't change to Daylight Savings time. It's just after eight here. It's just after nine in Spearfish."

"We're in Rapid City."

"Mom, Rapid City and Spearfish are both in the same time zone."

"Oh, right. I'm accustomed to being in the Central Time Zone and I'm not sure where it changes from Central to Mountain Time."

I pinched the bridge of my nose. "How is Molly?"

"We haven't gone to the hospital yet. It's too early."

"What was the diagnosis last night?"

"I'm fine."

"Not your diagnosis, Mom. What's wrong with Molly?"

"I thought I told you last night. She fell off the step."

I leaned my head back and closed my eyes. "I'll have Jill call you."

"Why would Jill call me? We're already talking on the phone."

"Why did Molly fall off the step, and how badly was she injured?"

"We won't know until after her surgery."

"What surgery?"

"The surgery to repair her broken wrist."

After a hopeful look toward Gunner's front door, I decided Jill wouldn't be coming to my immediate rescue. "Jill wants to know why her mother fell off the step."

"Tell her the doctor is running some tests to check her brain. He thinks she had some sort of brain thing, like a minor stroke. They're waiting until after her wrist surgery to run those tests."

"Finally."

"Finally, what?"

"I didn't mean to say that out loud."

"You said, 'finally.' Are you relieved that they're testing her brain function?"

I bit my tongue and didn't suggest that Molly's brain function wasn't the only one that needed testing. "Yes, I'm pleased that they're trying to get to the root of the problem."

"When are you and Jill flying back?"

"We were waiting until we talked to you this morning and knew more about Molly's prognosis."

The pause was so long I thought the connection had been lost. "Well, I suppose if you're not coming home, Chet and I will have to move to Rickowski's. Al doesn't even know how to fry an egg."

"Mom, it'll get sorted out, and the solution probably won't involve Jill and me moving to South Dakota."

"But we all want you to move here."

"Jill and I have careers. We can't just move there."

"But Chet's giving Jill his ranch and you have horses here."

"Horses aren't a selling point."

"But…"

"Mom, we're in the middle of a murder investigation. We can't just leave."

"Why not? Will the dead person be any more dead if someone else takes over?"

"We're very close to solving the murder and it would be unethical for us to leave at this point."

"It's unethical to sit in Arizona when your mother-in-law is dying in the hospital."

"You just said she has a broken wrist. That won't be the cause of her death."

"Fine. You always were an obstinate child."

"Mom, I'm nearly fifty years old. I'm hardly a child, and I'm not obstinate. I'm practical."

"Put Jill on the phone."

"She's interviewing someone."

"Put her on the phone, Douglas."

"I'm not with her. She's doing the interview alone."

"What? We spoke about this. You need to watch over her. How can you let her wander off to interview some…stranger without you? She could be shot, or raped, or who knows what."

"She won't be raped. She's interviewing a woman."

"That's not the point. You need to look out for her."

"Call Jill after Molly is out of surgery." I paused and added, "I love you, Mom."

"I love you too, but I'm very pleased you're married to Jill. She knows how to have a conversation."

I ended the call and tossed the phone onto the dashboard. It slid across the windshield and fell to the floor on the opposite side of the pickup. "Shit." Shaking my head over the infuriating conversation, I stared at the floorboard, trying to see the phone on the shaded floor. After checking the door again and not seeing Jill, I decided to retrieve the phone.

My shoulders were twisted so I could reach under the seat when someone asked, "Whatcha doing?"

Banging my head on the underside of the dash, I backed out of the pickup and turned to Gunner. "I lost my phone under the seat."

Bobbing his orange helmet, Gunner nodded his understanding. "Mom asked if you wanted a cup of coffee."

"Sure, that would be nice."

Without further comment, Gunner turned and walked toward the house. I slammed the pickup door and followed. The inside of the house was dark and spartan.

Faded living room drapes filtered the stark Arizona sunlight. We walked through the living room, furnished with only two overstuffed chairs far past their expected life, and an old television sitting on top of a wooden table. The hallway was lined with rodeo pictures, apparently taken before Gunner's injury. In most of the photos, the dark-haired young man was waving his left hand over his head while riding a bucking bronco.

In the kitchen, Jill and Caroline were sitting at a yellow Formica table with mismatched wooden chairs. A coffee carafe was between them, next to an ashtray holding a half dozen butts. Cigarette-smoke haze hung in the air. Gunner sat in a chair in the corner.

Caroline pulled a chair away from the table, then walked to the sink where she rinsed a coffee cup and wiped it dry. "How do you take your coffee?"

"Black is fine," I said, taking the chair she'd pulled back.

Caroline poured coffee for me, then topped off Jill's cup before refilling her own. "Jill says Gunner's been helping you."

"He found the only clue we've got."

Caroline sat in the chair and looked at me. Her face was heavily lined, the combination of cigarette smoke and Arizona sun adding years to her appearance. "I told your partner she overpaid Gunner for the spur he sold her."

"It was valuable to us and Gunner deserved the reward."

Caroline laughed and looked at Gunner. "You hear that? You've been paid a reward."

Gunner's focus was on Jill. He watched her every move and didn't respond to his mother's comments.

"Jill says she'd like to hire Gunner to guide the two of you on the trails beyond the river."

Hiding my surprise, I said, "We think he might be able to help us."

Caroline shook her head. "If Gunner's the best resource you've got, you're scraping the bottom of the barrel."

Jill looked toward the corner. "Gunner sees things other people miss. Most people's minds are elsewhere when they're riding and talking. Gunner knows the trails and sees more than other people do."

Shrugging, Caroline looked at Gunner. "You're welcome to ask him to ride with you, but you don't need to pay him. He's going to ride whether he's with you or alone."

I looked at the lean-to shed in the backyard where Gunner's horse was in a stall. Mojo's bridle hung from a peg and the saddle sat on a sawhorse near two bales of hay. "We'll buy a dozen bales of hay for each day Gunner guides us."

Frowning, Caroline stared at me. "A dozen bales a day?"

"Two dozen," Jill said, "but that's as high as we'll go. And we'll have them delivered."

With her eyes narrowing, Caroline said, "We don't take charity."

Jill looked out the kitchen window. "It looks like Mojo is about four days away from eating dirt."

"You paid Gunner twenty bucks yesterday. That'll pay for a few bales of hay."

"You can use that after our hay delivery runs out."

Caroline leaned away from Jill and spoke to Gunner. "Are you willing to ride with Jill and…I don't know your name, sir."

"Sorry, I'm Doug Fletcher."

"Will you ride with Jill and Doug, Gunner?"

He looked at Jill and smiled. "I think so."

Gunner's mom shrugged. "Fine. He can go with you, but I want him home for supper."

"Where do you work, Caroline?" I asked.

"I do accounts for the feed store. They're flexible with my hours so I can deal with Gunner."

"How about Gunner's dad?"

When her coughing stopped, Caroline shook her head. "Harlan couldn't cope with a handicapped son. He went out to buy a bottle one night and never came back."

"That stinks."

"It's better than being saddled with someone like Al Tedeschi who's buying drinks for every woman in town and sleeping with half of them."

Jill nodded. "It sounds like he was a real piece of work."

"Believe me, you don't know the half of it." Caroline paused and blew out a breath. "Robyn deserved him."

"What do you mean?" I asked.

"She's an A-number-one bitch. She drove Al from the house and into the arms of those other women."

"What do you mean?"

"Al was a wheeler and dealer, but she squeezed money out of people like they were sponges. If someone billed her ten bucks, she'd pay five and tell them they should be happy with it. Truth be told, she seemed to know what everyone made on their goods and services, and she paid their cost and not a penny more. Nobody lost money on her business, but they sure didn't make any profit to cover expenses and overhead."

Jill nodded. "We knew some ranchers like that in South Dakota. Most of them antagonized their neighbors. They'd last until a drought or blizzard put them in a bind, then they'd reach out expecting people they'd shunned to help them out."

"I bet that didn't work out well for them," Caroline said.

"Most sold off or went bankrupt after a couple years. The rest of us are more than happy to help each other out with roundups and branding. My dad considered our neighbors his family. I was taught that you always do anything you can for your family."

Changing the topic, I said, "We heard Robyn Tedeschi is going to sell the ranch and water rights to a developer."

Caroline shook a cigarette out of a pack and lit it. "That's not going to happen."

"Why not?" I asked.

"They've got water rights, but not enough for a residential community. They barely have enough to grow hay and grapes. People who buy houses want to shower, wash clothes, grow flowers, and have green golf courses. Tedeschis don't have enough water for all that...even if Robyn could sell."

"Why couldn't she sell?"

"Well, I heard there are two reasons: Al gave the ranch to Carlton and Theresa. And the county won't let them develop."

"I'd think the county would like the real estate taxes."

"Tedeschis outsmarted themselves by having the ranch rezoned as a business when they opened the dude ranch. Word is that the county won't rezone their land as residential. They're looking at all the business development in Phoenix, Sedona, and along the I-17 corridor. The county board figures some day that land will be prime business development."

"Robyn could sell it as a business site."

"Nobody wants to put a business that far out, at least not yet. They're stuck growing grapes and catering to city folks who want to play cowboy for the time being."

"I'm sure Robyn is smart enough to know she can hang on until business development spreads this far."

Caroline snorted. "Robyn isn't a patient woman. Now that Al's gone, she wants to take her money and run."

"Run where?"

"Robyn wants to be a socialite instead of a rancher. What have you heard, Gunner?"

Startled by being included in the conversation, Gunner stuttered, "D-d-d-denver. Robyn and Butch are moving to Denver."

Jill looked at me, then back at Caroline. "Who's Butch?"

"Al had his ladies. Robyn's got her boy toy, Butch Compton."

"Is Butch someone local?"

"Butch is from Prescott," Gunner said.

Caroline nodded. "Butch was a cook at the brew pub until Robyn 'realized his talents' and hired him as the Lazy L trail boss. He's the eye candy she keeps around to entertain the female clientele. He's cute, well built, and flirtatious—everything you could ask for in a trail boss. He leads trail rides into the high country, tells stories, and flirts with the women."

"Who else works at the ranch besides Butch?"

"Anna Weise cooks, Harrison Brigham takes care of the stable, and Rose Bunch manages the children's programs."

"Are there any other interesting dynamics at the Lazy L?"

"Now, you'd be moving into rumor and speculation. Harrison is a mean drunk who abuses his girlfriends and picks fights with the cowboys in town. Rose has a crush on Butch and is trying hard to catch his eye without getting fired."

"We met Anna in town."

Caroline smiled. "Anna is my type of woman. She doesn't drink, swears like a mule skinner, and doesn't take shit from anyone. She's the one person who can tell Robyn off and get away with it. The rest of the employees are misfits who don't have other options. Robyn pays them next to nothing, then deducts room and board from their wages. There's a lot of turnover."

"They don't sound like the kind of employees you'd want around your customers," Jill said.

"That's where Harrison comes in. He keeps the 'hired help' in line, with his fists if necessary."

When Caroline was through, Jill digested her comments. "We heard that Theresa entertains her friends when they don't have paying guests."

Taking a drag on her cigarette, Caroline weighed her answer. "I've never been invited to a party at the Lazy L."

"That's not exactly what I asked."

With the question dangling, Caroline stubbed out her cigarette and topped off our coffee. "Gunner, check the mail." Without response, Gunner got up and walked out the back door. "Here's the thing, Theresa is a female version of Al. She has parties and there are people staggering out of the ranch all the next day. As far as I know, she's never tied herself to one man, but she seems to…find comfort where she can. She doesn't seem concerned about the marital status of her friends, so there are some town people who don't appreciate her business."

Gunner walked in empty handed. "No mail, Ma."

Jill smiled at Gunner. "Do you ever see the people who are driving away from the Lazy L?"

"People come and people go."

"Do you recognize any of them?"

"Sometimes."

Jill looked at Caroline. "I wonder if Gunner saw Al's killer?"

"Gunner, have you seen anyone bring a body out of the Lazy L draped across a saddle?" I asked.

"No."

I was hit with the obvious question. Gunner wasn't out after dark, but he was in the morning. "Did you see someone lead an empty horse back to the Lazy L the day you saw Al's body by the swamp?"

"Yep."

Jill's eyes lit up. "Who was leading the horse?"

"Couldn't see his face. He was riding away."

"Did it look like someone you knew?"

"Couldn't see his face."

"Did you recognize the horse or..." Jill stopped. "Was it a man or a woman leading the horse?"

Gunner cocked his head and wrinkled his nose. "No ponytail. But I didn't see his face."

Caroline raised her eyebrows. "Theresa has long hair. Robyn and Anna wear their hair shorter."

Gunner shook his head. "Not Theresa. She wears a different hat and she's mean."

Jill turned. "Tell me about the rider's hat and shirt."

"It was just a hat. Couldn't see the shirt because he was wearing a vest."

Caroline got into it. "Harrison wears a baseball cap backwards, like a biker. Was it that kind of hat, Gunner?"

"It was a regular hat, like everyone wears. Not Harrison's stupid cap. People laugh at Harrison because he wears his stupid cap backwards. He doesn't wear a real hat."

Jill's eyes lit up. "Could you see the hatband, Gunner?"

"He was too far away."

"Tell me about the horses. What did they look like?"

"The man was on a sorrel with a white front sock. The other horse was gray…with spots."

That meant something to Jill. I could tell she was struggling to contain her excitement. "Was the gray horse bigger than the sorrel?"

"Bigger."

"Did the gray horse have a saddle?"

Gunner thought. "It had a sawbuck saddle."

"Sawbuck saddle?" I asked.

"It's the saddle an outfitter uses to haul gear," Jill explained. She looked at Gunner. "Was there anything on the sawbuck saddle?"

"It was empty." Gunner squirmed. "Can I ride now?"

"One more question, Gunner. Did you see the person with the two horses ride into the Lazy L?"

"They were on that trail."

"But did you see them go into the Lazy L Ranch?"

Gunner shook his head and stood. "It's time to ride." He turned and walked out the door.

Lighting another cigarette, Caroline smiled. "That was good, right?"

Jill blew out a breath. "That was very good. If we find horses that match Gunner's description, we've narrowed down the ranch where Al was killed and the list of potential murderers."

Caroline waved at the cloud of smoke she blew toward the ceiling. "Eliminating Harrison takes one feisty guy off the list."

I stood. "It leaves just about everyone else in the county on the list."

With Caroline in the lead, we walked to the front door. "If Gunner saw them riding on the trail near the Lazy L, it eliminates all the ranches in Cottonwood and south. There are only three ranches in Clarkdale and along the river until you get close to Sedona."

Jill looked at me. "I think we need to look at the horses on those ranches."

I shook Caroline's hand and she held it. "I haven't had many good experiences with men, but you seem…okay." She turned to Jill and held her cigarette aside as they hugged. "You're something special, honey. Gunner doesn't trust many people enough to talk to them, and you nearly had him in a conversation."

Jill released her hug. "You've got your hands full with Gunner."

"Naw, he entertains himself by riding all day. Everyone in town knows him and looks out for him. That's part of the wonder of a small town like Cottonwood; your neighbors watch your back and your kids."

"We'll get some hay shipped over for Gunner's horse, Mojo."

"You don't need to do that. The deal was you'd give him hay when he guided you."

Smiling, Jill said, "He's already guided us for two days. I figure we owe him about fifty bales of hay."

There was a hint of a tear in Caroline's eyes when we turned away. "Where are you going to buy hay?" I asked.

"I'm sure Megan can tell me who sells and delivers hay."

Jill was on the phone to Megan before I had the truck started. After that conversation, Jill punched in another number and had a discussion about a hay delivery. "Will you take a charge card over the phone?" Jill nodded as she listened. "That's fair. Deliver the minimum one hundred bales to Gunner...I don't know his last name."

Jill listened again as I whispered, "A hundred bales?"

She waved off my question. "Great. You know Gunner and where they live." She ended the call and put the phone in her pocket. "River Bend Ranch sells hay, but he'll only deliver a full load if I use my charge card."

"I thought fifty bales was a lot."

"Think about their house and how little they had, then consider our situation. Caroline's probably buying a pickup load of hay on payday, then hoping there's enough money left to buy gas and food."

"She said they won't take charity."

"The hay will be under their lean-to before she gets home. She doesn't know our phone numbers, nor will she know who delivered it. There's nothing she'll be able to do except accept it graciously."

I blew out a breath. "She knows our pickup. I hope we don't wake up in the morning to a load of hay stacked in the pickup bed."

My concern was dismissed with a wave of Jill's hand.

I drove to a café on the outskirts of old Cottonwood and parked in the lot that was half-full of pickups, with a few beat-up older

Fords and Chevys. "This looks like a good place. It seems like the locals eat here."

I shut off the engine and my phone trilled. Jill looked at me. "Aren't you going to answer that?"

"I can't. It's under your seat."

"What? Why is your phone under my seat?"

"I threw it after the conversation with my mother."

Jill hopped out of the pickup and reached under the seat. The ringing ended before she found the phone. "Here, you can listen to the message while we wait for our food."

Jill was deep in thought as we walked into the restaurant. "There probably aren't many ranches with both a sorrel horse with one white sock and a spotted gray pack horse."

After reading the menu options, I checked my phone for messages. "I doubt it was my mother. I told her to call you."

Jill's eyes went wide. "Oh God, I forgot about Mom. How is she?"

"They're doing surgery to repair her broken wrist this morning."

Jill dug the phone out of her pocket and was punching in numbers when my message app opened. Jill was in a panicked discussion with my mother when Matt's message played. "What's happening? I haven't heard from you in two days."

After erasing Matt's message, I pulled up his number from my contacts list and called him. I ordered a Greek Omelet as Matt answered.

"What's going on over there?" Matt asked.

"We've been to half a dozen wine tasting rooms and sampled some really good wines. I can ship a case to you…"

"Okay, smartass. What's happening with the case?"

"Oh, that. We've narrowed the possible murderers from everyone in Arizona, to maybe a dozen men who live on ranches north of here. We have a description of the probable murderer's horses, and we've just ordered breakfast."

"That sounds like you've made a lot of progress."

"We met a guy who had a rodeo head injury. He rides his horse around town all day, just watching people and things. The rodeo injury has affected his ability to function as an adult, but he's sharp and notices a lot of things."

"Will he make a good witness?"

"No. We'll have to use his information to collect the evidence required to arrest someone, but he's pointed us in the right direction." I paused. "And Jill just bought him a hundred bales of hay that'll show up on her expense voucher."

"What?"

"We hired him as our guide and we're paying him with a shipment of hay. The minimum quantity is one hundred bales."

"I hope you're pulling my leg."

"I guess you'll know when her expense voucher shows up for approval."

"You're killing me. Is there some way to have the bill say guide services instead of hay?"

"I doubt it."

I could almost picture Matt shaking his head. "How much are we talking about?"

"One hundred bales."

"I know that smartass. How much does a hundred bales cost?"

"I don't know. I was driving when Jill gave the guy her charge card number."

"OMG! If she put that on her government charge card, I might be getting calls this afternoon."

"I don't know which card she used."

"Ask her."

"What's the magic word?"

"You're killing me, and you want me to say, please?"

I put my hand over the phone as our meals arrived. "Matt wants to know how much the hay cost and if you charged it on your government charge card."

I passed her my phone. "The hay was eight hundred dollars, including delivery and unloading. Yes, I used my government charge card."

She passed the phone back before Matt replied. "I think the threshold to flag an individual purchase is a grand. We may have time to explain before the shit hits the fan."

"My breakfast is getting cold. I'll talk to you later."

"Wait…"

I ended the call and returned the phone to my pocket.

Jill put a dab of butter on her oatmeal before stirring in raisins and brown sugar. "I assume charging hay is going to raise some questions."

I shrugged. "We'll reimburse it if we have to." Jill's mind was elsewhere. "What did you find out about Molly?"

"The surgery went well. They're still unsure of what caused her fall. I guess she may have had a TIA, a mini-stroke, or she may have just fallen and hit her head, which may have caused her to blank out the incident. Ronnie was a little obtuse and not up on the medical jargon the doctor used, but she said the doctor wasn't at all concerned about Mom's long-term recovery."

I mopped up tzatziki sauce with my whole wheat toast. "My mom thinks we need to move back to Spearfish to take care of your dad."

"She mentioned that. She also said she and Chet may move over to our house while my mom recovers. She made it clear that would be an inconvenience and a second choice to us taking proper responsibility for the care of my parents."

"I think she got the order of those options reversed. She likes to care for people, and I make a terrible nurse."

"You don't want to fly back to South Dakota."

"You and I are investigating a murder, dear. And we promised to be in Flagstaff for a baptism."

Jill pulled her napkin off her lap, wadded it up, and threw it on the table. "Oh, crap. I'm losing my mind. I forgot about my mother's wrist injury and now I've forgotten about our commitment to Liz and Jamie."

Spreading jam on my last slice of toast, I smiled. "Welcome to law enforcement. You get caught up in a case and the rest of the world goes away."

While contemplating that, Jill picked up her napkin and ate more oatmeal. "Is that what happened to you and Sherry?"

"That was part of it."

"And the other part was…?

"We grew apart. She became a left-leaning student with all the answers to the world's problems, and I became the 'Nazi with a badge'."

"You never told me that."

"It's a scab that doesn't need to be scratched off."

Jill stirred the last of her oatmeal as the waitress refilled our coffee and set our bill on the table. "What are we going to do next?"

"Let's visit Robyn Tedeschi. Maybe she'll give us a stable tour and we'll see a sorrel horse with one sock and a spotted gray horse."

"Or maybe she'll meet us at the door and tell us to get the hell off her property."

"That's what you said about Gunner's mom. You seem to be hung up on people confronting you with shotguns."

"That incident is etched in my memory."

"They didn't shoot the shotgun at us."

Jill looked around to make sure no one was listening. "We didn't get shot, but that woman's shotgun was pointed in my direction when it went off."

"She missed you by a mile."

Jill rolled her eyes. "Yes, but only because I assaulted her with the only weapon I had."

"You made a nice throw with that shovel."

"Damn it, Fletcher, can you be serious for one minute? I was traumatized by that experience, and you keep minimizing it. We almost died that day!"

I pushed my plate aside and leaned forward. "You can't let the past get in the way of what you need to do. Yes, that was a scary moment, but it will probably never be repeated. If I peed my pants every time I pulled over a speeder who looked suspicious, I would've…washed my pants frequently. We have to be prudent and prepared, but we can't walk into every situation with our knees knocking."

"What were your seven 'P's?"

"Proper prior planning prevents piss poor performance."

"So, if we stick with the seven P plan, we'll be okay?"

"Every plan needs to adapt to the changing situation, like the Mickey Mouse incident. But, making a plan gives you a chance to think through the risks and be prepared to deal with them."

"How do we approach Robyn Tedeschi?"

"We stand on opposite sides of the door so we're not both killed by the shotgun blast."

Jill's napkin barely missed my head. "Like I asked, can you be serious for just one minute?"

"I am being serious. That's the worst-case scenario. But it's a good starting point."

"Now I'm paranoid."

"Listen, the Lazy L is a dude ranch with customers. No one is going to meet us at the front door with a shotgun. That kind of reception would drive away all their business."

Jill stood, pondering that statement while I pulled money out to pay the bill and leave a tip. "Their customers don't show up in a Park Service pickup with a light bar on top."

"I doubt Robyn Tedeschi peeks through the drapes before she opens the door. Besides, we're not in uniform."

"Fine, but if you're killed, I'm not the one who's going to call your mother with the news."

"Good plan. Give Ronnie's number to Matt. Warn him Mom's first question will be about you, not me."

Chapter 15

The two-lane road through old Cottonwood was slow moving. Each corner had a pedestrian crossing with warning signs about the penalties for failing to yield to people crossing the road. I chuckled while waiting for a woman to help her elderly mother across the street.

"Why are you laughing? That could be you and Ronnie in a few years."

"I wasn't laughing at them. I remembered a call I took when I was a St. Paul cop. A jaywalker was clipped by a city bus. When I arrived, the bus driver and jaywalker were nose to nose screaming at each other. The bus driver was running late and thought the jaywalker would wait for him to pass. The jaywalker claimed he had the right-of-way because he'd made eye contact with the bus driver."

"What did you do?"

"Since the jaywalker's injuries amounted to a dirty spot on his Michael Jordan jersey, I gave them both a stern talking to and sent them off."

"Shouldn't you have ticketed one of them, or something?"

"If I'd ticketed one or both of them, I'd have to show up in court to testify. It'd cost me at least three hours of time and the judge would roll his eyes and fine them a dollar plus court costs. It didn't make any sense."

"If the jaywalker had been injured, what would you have done?"

"I would've called an ambulance and written a report that would've gone to the city attorney and the bus line. The bus driver would probably have been disciplined and the jay walker could've tried to sue the city."

Two young women dashed across the street after the older pair, and I eased ahead slowly after they cleared the crosswalk.

Past the last restaurant, the speed limit increased, and the scenery went from city to desert in one block. A few miles down the road was a sign for a 55+ community overlooking the river. The houses ranged from brick mansions to tired clapboard houses, built decades earlier. A sign for the Lazy L Ranch turnoff was on the outskirts of Clarkdale, just after the Verde Canyon Railway station. We drove past a hundred tourists who were lined up for a two-hour train ride along the Verde River.

I'd only driven a quarter mile when I spotted Gunner and Mojo standing on the edge of the road. I stopped and Jill rolled down her window. "Is everything okay, Gunner?"

"I thought I'd guide you to see something."

"We're in the pickup. Can it wait until tomorrow?"

Gunner mounted Mojo and we followed Gunner down the road. "I guess he's guiding us."

Jill watched Gunner. "I hope he's not planning to lead us across a ford in the river or on any of the horse trails."

Gunner turned off the single-lane road to the Lazy L and onto a rutted path that cut uphill. I activated the pickup's four-wheel-drive and followed. His ride was smooth, with Mojo stepping around the ruts and potholes. In contrast, Jill and I were jerked around the inside of the pickup like rag dolls.

Gunner dismounted at the top of the ridge we'd been following. I put the pickup in park, and we got out. "What have you got to show us, Gunner?"

He squatted down next to a well-used horse trail. "This is the main trail the Lazy L uses to take people into the hills."

Jill knelt next to him. "Okay. What's the significance of this trail?"

Gunner pointed to a hoof print in the dusty soil. "Barred horseshoe prints here. Just like the ones on the marsh trail." As soon as he'd said his piece, he walked away.

Jill stood. "I think he wants us to follow him."

A few yards down the trail, Gunner squatted down again. "That horse has been back and forth across here a bunch of times. A bunch."

The trail was dusty and wide enough for horses to ride side-by-side. There were horseshoe prints everywhere. It took me a beat longer than Jill to start picking out the prints made by the barred horseshoes. Once I recognized one of them, I realized there were dozens of tracks, and they'd been back and forth repeatedly.

Jill patted Gunner on the shoulder. "Thanks."

Gunner shied away from Jill's touch as if he'd been burned. He touched his shoulder where she'd patted it, and looked at her, puzzled. "Mom says I'm not supposed to touch girls. It's a rule."

I nodded. "That's a good rule. What else can you tell us about these prints?"

"The ranch has a sorrel with a white stocking. The bar shoe prints are here after that horse goes past. I checked."

Jill smiled and put out her hand. "Can you shake a girl's hand?"

"There's no rule about that."

They shook gingerly and Gunner let go quickly. "You earned your guide fee for today."

Gunner nodded, mounted Mojo, and rode down the hill. He was out of sight by the time I got the pickup turned around.

"What do you think?" Jill asked.

"We'll keep that nugget in our back pocket for the time being. At some later point in the investigation, someone might be very unhappy that we know about that."

* * *

Taking a slower downhill drive mitigated some of our bouncing around, making it more of a rolling ride than our uphill bucking bronco trek. Gunner was gone when we reached the bottom, so I followed the trail back to the Lazy L Ranch road. A cattle guard stretched across the driveway next to the mailbox.

"Fake cattle guard for the tourists," Jill said as we bounced across the metal slats.

"How do you know it's fake?"

"There's no fence on either side. The cattle can walk around it."

With a nod, I agreed. "I wonder if any tourist ever noticed that?"

Jill glanced at me. "I imagine they're all city slickers, like you."

The ranch had a number of out-buildings beyond what was apparently the original ranch house. The structure had been added onto numerous times, the most recent two-story addition dwarfing the original structure.

Jill unbuckled her seatbelt but didn't open the door. "Do you want to bet on whether that addition showed up before or after Robyn's arrival?"

I opened my door. "I'm betting after."

A covered porch wrapped around the house, its collection of rocking chairs shifting gently in the mild breeze. As Jill knocked, I made a point of stepping to the hinge side of the door. Jill saw me move and she nearly jumped to the other side of the door as it swung open.

Stunning in her western-cut shirt, form-fitting jeans, and snakeskin boots, the redhead who opened the door seemed surprised to see us standing on either side of the door. She smiled, revealing pearly white, perfectly aligned teeth. "Can I help you?"

The badge on Jill's belt caught her eye, then she looked at our guns. "Mrs. Tedeschi?" Jill asked.

"Um, yes." She stepped back and held the door. "Please come in out of the heat."

"I'm Jill Fletcher, and this is my husband, Doug."

The entryway atrium was two stories high, topped with windows that surrounded the base of a wrought-iron chandelier. The woodwork, from floor to ceiling, was knotty pine coated with glistening urethane. A stairway rose on the room's right side, its railing made from pine branches rough with knots and burls. To the left, was a living room with floor to ceiling windows facing the hills. A massive fieldstone fireplace covering one wall was accented with mounted elk and deer heads.

"This is spectacular," Jill said, looking at the woodwork.

My eyes were drawn to western paintings on the walls and Frederick Remington bronze castings in tiny alcoves. "I love your art."

"Thank you. I commissioned local artists to paint the Sedona red rocks and the views of the Verde River."

"They're very talented. I've always thought a Remington sculpture would look nice on my bookcase."

Jill smiled. "I think it would look great in the Spearfish ranch house."

Robyn's look of surprise was genuine. "You're from Spearfish, South Dakota?"

"I grew up there. We're currently stationed in Texas, but our retirement plan is to move to the Black Hills." Jill smiled at me, knowing I wouldn't argue our retirement plans in front of Robyn.

Robyn gestured for us to follow her down a hallway. The art changed from paintings to movie posters featuring Hopalong Cassidy, Gene Autry, Roy Rogers, and The Cisco Kid. "I feel like I've fallen into a time warp. These are the movies I remember from my childhood."

Robyn led us into a huge kitchen lined with stainless steel commercial appliances and a center island with a grill. She gestured to stools facing the island. "We have a DVD library of westerns that we show our guests. Most of the children, and many of their parents, have never heard of Gabby Hayes or Roy Rogers. I personally like to show the films made in this area. It's fun when the guests recognize rock features from Sedona. My personal favorite is *Virginia City* with Errol Flynn and Humphrey Bogart. We always show *The Angel and the Badman* because it features the Cottonwood Hotel, where John Wayne courts Gail Russell." Robyn sat on a stool across the corner from Jill. "Can I get you a cup of coffee or a soda?"

I put up my hand. "Thanks, we just ate in Cottonwood."

"What can I do for the Park Service?"

"We're investigating your husband's death," I said.

The smile slid from Robyn's face, and she sighed. "I see. What can I tell you that I haven't already told Rob Henderson?" She paused. "You *have* spoken with Rob, haven't you?"

"We're assisting Rob with the investigation," I said. "He's spread a little thin and since Al's body was found on Tuzigoot National Monument property, we were dispatched to aid with the investigation."

"I'm having Diet Pepsi. Are you sure I can't get you something?" Robyn stood and walked to the giant refrigerator, the inside stocked with neat rows of canned beverages, ranging from soft drinks to wine coolers and beer. "Al was found at the park, but Rob Henderson thought he'd been shot somewhere else."

"Yes," I said as she popped the tab on her soda and sat down. "The coroner says he was..." I paused. "I don't want to get into painful and morbid details. Al was apparently dead when he was left in the park."

"I'm confused. Why are park rangers investigating?"

"We're actually Park Service Investigators," Jill explained. "We're dispatched to investigate deaths or major crimes committed on Park Service property. Even though your husband wasn't killed where his body was found, it's a federal crime to move or deposit a body on any federal property."

"I see."

Jill leaned on the counter, looking very non-confrontational. "Your husband wasn't living on the ranch prior to his death. Is that correct?"

"Al was..." Robyn looked out the window. "He was staying with his girlfriend in Cottonwood. He sometimes came to the ranch to get clothing or gear, but he didn't reside here."

"How long have you been estranged?"

"I don't know that we were estranged as much as not sharing a bedroom anymore."

"But he was..."

"He wasn't honoring his marriage vows," Robyn said. "Does that have some bearing on your investigation?"

"It might if someone were particularly angry about Al's activities."

"If you're asking if I hated him enough to kill him, the answer is no. I was disappointed with his life choices, but we were married and..." Robyn sighed. "I'm Catholic and we weren't going to divorce. He was acting like a schoolboy in heat. I wasn't happy about that, but he was still my husband."

"Are there others who would like to see your husband dead?"

The corner of Robyn's mouth twitched, but she suppressed her smile. "Only about a dozen jealous husbands and boyfriends."

"That's a big suspect pool. Could you narrow it down a bit?"'

"I'd start with his latest bimbo's boyfriend and work back through the list until you find a husband who was angry enough to shoot Al."

"Can you think of anyone else who would have a reason to kill your husband?"

Robyn closed her eyes, considering Jill's question. "He's had some shady business deals over the years. Most of them weren't that big of a deal and they got sorted out."

"How about your employees? Did any of them have a particular problem with your husband?"

I caught a faint flicker in Robyn's eyes when Jill mentioned the employees.

"No. I deal almost exclusively with the staff myself. I don't recall Al having anything to do with the Lazy L staff in the past few years."

"Was there someone he fired who might've held a smoldering grudge?"

Robyn shook her head. "Our staff is mostly transitory, particularly the cowboys who handle the stock. There's a lot of turnover. They get angry, go into town, get drunk, and blow off some steam. Then they move to another ranch. It's really a rinse and repeat kind of world for the cowpokes."

"How about the other staff?"

"There's Anna, who's been with us since before we started the dude ranch. Harrison's been managing the stock for a couple years. I hired Butch as the ranch manager after Al moved out." Robyn paused. "Oh, and Rose has been the groom working with the horses since she graduated from high school."

"You don't think any of them would have a grudge against your husband?"

"I don't know why they would. Like I said, Al hasn't had anything to do with the ranch operation for years."

Cathedral-like chimes sounded. "I'm sorry to cut this short, but we have guests arriving this afternoon. We need to get them oriented and set up in their accommodations."

We followed Robyn out of the kitchen and Jill stopped her in the hallway. "I have just one more quick question."

Robyn wasn't pleased but composed herself. "What would that be?"

"Who inherits the ranch?"

Robyn looked shocked. "I'm Al's wife. I inherit everything."

"There's a rumor that Carlton gets to keep the winery and vineyard."

"I'll allow him to continue the business, but I own the property."

"And Theresa?" Jill asked.

Robyn's veneer started to crack with the question. "I don't see how that's any of your business." Robyn closed her eyes and drew a breath as if she was counting to ten. "Theresa will continue supervising the dude ranch. Carlton and Theresa each get a nice inheritance, but the ranch is mine."

"Thanks for your patience," Jill said, smiling.

I stopped, blocking the door. "Is there any chance we could get a tour?"

"Not while we're entertaining guests." Robyn reached past me for the doorknob. "If you'll excuse me, I have to greet our new arrivals."

The family on the porch looked like they were fresh out of some major city. The husband wore a shirt with a golf course logo and cargo shorts. The wife wore a white outfit that looked like she'd just stepped off a tennis court. The three children appeared to be in their early teens, each with earbuds and some sort of electronic device in their hands. Their shorts were worn, and their t-shirts had logos for bands or places I didn't recognize. The oldest was a boy with his cap worn backwards. The next was a son who had a cap worn slightly askew, like a rapper. The girl's outfit was black, as was her lipstick.

A hulking man, who could've been on the cover of the brochure for the dude ranch, stood behind the family. With a two-day growth of beard, he wore jeans and a western-cut shirt. His vest had a Lazy L brand burned into the leather. His outfit was complete, right down to the gun belt and revolver on his hip. I looked at the cartridges in the belt loops and determined they were real .45 Colts, not blanks.

A young woman joined the group on the porch. "Ah, here's Rose. She takes care of the horses." Her shirt matched Butch's, with the Lazy L logo and her name embroidered over the left pocket. I assumed there was a shop somewhere on the ranch that sold shirts, vests, and caps with the ranch logo.

Robyn smiled and spread her arms. "Welcome to the Lazy L Ranch. I'm Robyn and I assure you that everyone here will do everything within their power to make your stay here an enjoyable experience."

The parents beamed, but the oldest boy rolled his eyes.

"Butch will show you to your rooms in the bunkhouse so you can unpack and freshen up. Once you're settled in, we'll give you a tour of the ranch. After supper, Rose will introduce you to your horses, and we'll go on a sunset ride."

The girl perked up at the mention of horses. "Do you have an Appaloosa for me?"

Robyn looked at Rose. "I think Blossom would be a good fit for this young lady."

Rose smiled. "Blossom would be perfect."

Butch led the group off the porch toward a building that looked like a bunkhouse. I noted the air conditioner at the end of the building. "I see that you provide a western experience, but not without some of the hotel amenities.”

Robyn nodded. “Our guests want to rough it, but not to the point where they’re uncomfortable. We walk a thin line between providing a ranch experience and being a hotel.”

“The cartridges on Butch’s belt were real.”

Robyn nodded. “He sometimes has to shoot a javelina or snake. We have a target range behind the barn where we let guests shoot at silhouettes of bad guys. Butch loads those cartridges with primers and wax plugs. The shots sound real, but the wax won’t penetrate the plywood behind the silhouettes.”

Jill offered her hand. “Thanks for your hospitality.”

Robyn’s smile seemed forced, but she shook our hands. “I hope you find my husband’s killer.”

I smiled back at her. “We have some strong leads, so I think we might make an arrest in the next few days.”

That news momentarily shook Robyn, who was speechless. “Um, so soon?”

“Most murders are solved within 48 hours. We’re well past that, but we’ve uncovered new evidence in the past couple days.”

Robyn jammed her hands in her pockets. “Wow. I somehow thought...” She paused. "Which bimbo's boyfriend are you looking at?"

"We're not at liberty to discuss the details of our ongoing investigation. We'll let you know when an arrest has been made."

Robyn regained her composure. "Thank you. I look forward to hearing that you've brought someone to justice."

We walked to the pickup in silence and waved to Robyn as we drove away. Jill looked at me. "You caught the comment about the wax shooting range?"

Jill nodded. "I assume the coroner will be able to match that wax to the residue the pathologist found in Al's wound."

"So, who took the fatal shot? Butch or Robyn?"

I considered the question. "It's unusual for a wife to shoot her husband unless they're in the heat of an abusive situation. My bet is on Butch. Gunner said the person he saw riding back to the ranch the morning Al was killed was wearing a vest."

"Robyn is an ice-cold bitch. I think she's capable of pulling the trigger without feeling remorse."

I chuckled. "I defer to your assessment of bitchiness. I'm out of my depth on that topic."

"Bullshit. You were married to the woman whose picture is next to the definition of bitch in the dictionary."

"I think that's supposed to be my line."

Our conversation was interrupted when Jill's phone trilled. Jill's conversation was mostly limited to "I see" and "Uh huh." I recognized my mother's voice and the cadence of her monologue.

Jill ended the call and returned the phone to her pocket. "They're releasing Mom from the hospital. They still don't know why she fell, but Mom's sure she just stepped wrong and took a tumble. The EEG didn't show any evidence of a stroke or TIA."

"That's all good news."

"Ronnie says she and Chet are planning to stay with my folks for a couple days until Mom's off pain meds and able to cook."

"Is she still disappointed that we're not on a plane to Rapid City?"

"She conceded that she may have overreacted by demanding that we immediately quit our jobs and move to the Black Hills. She still wants that to happen, but she understands that we need to complete this investigation first."

"That's big of her. We can finish our investigation before we quit and move there."

Jill looked at me. "Your sarcasm is not your most endearing quality."

"Do you prefer my cynicism?"

"I'd say they're the same thing. The sarcasm is a verbal expression of your cynicism."

"You do realize that you're becoming cynical, too."

Jill sighed. "A bit, but you've mastered the craft. I bow to you, the mayor of Cynical City."

"Cynicalopolis."

With an eye roll, Jill said, "You're past that. You're up to Cynicaltopia."

Approaching old Cottonwood, we laughed. Distracted by our discussion, I didn't see the red and blue flashing lights behind me until the siren whooped. I glanced in the rearview mirror, then looked at the speedometer that showed I was going 40-mph as I passed the 25-mph speed limit sign on the city outskirts.

I pulled into the lot of the first restaurant and parked. The unmarked sheriff's car pulled alongside me. Shaking his head, Rob Henderson got out of the unmarked car and walked to my window. "Is the speedometer broken, or do you think I wouldn't ticket a ranger?"

"We were distracted."

Nodding toward the restaurant, Rob said, "Let's have a Coke and talk about your visit to the Lazy L Ranch."

"You're not going to ticket me?" I asked as I locked the truck.

"Nah, I think a stern verbal warning is sufficient. Besides, I don't even have a citation book."

We shared our discussion with Rob, adding the bits supplied by Gunner. Rob nodded, then asked, "So, how do we nail them? It could've been any of the people on the ranch, but the prime suspects are Robyn and Butch."

"I think we can lean on them separately, and they'll turn on each other," I said.

Jill shook her head. "I think it'll be easier than that. Let's ride to the ranch tomorrow."

"What will that do?" Rob asked.

"If we show up unannounced and start asking questions..." Jill hesitated. "Then salt in some of the tidbits we know, I think one of them will break."

Rob shook his head. "Criminals are too smart to fall for that."

"I disagree," Jill replied. "Butch and Robyn aren't hardened criminals. Robyn is polished, but she's prone to angry outbursts, and Butch doesn't seem like the brightest bulb in the chandelier. If we push them a little, either Butch will break down or Robyn will blow up. Either way, we'll get a confession."

Rob wrinkled his nose. "There's no harm in giving Jill's approach a try. If it doesn't work, we can always go to plan B and put them in separate interview rooms and see if one will flip on the other."

Chapter 16

After our hotel breakfast the next day, Jill drove the Park Service pickup to Hoofbeats riding school. Having grown up on a ranch, she was comfortable driving the unpaved road, dodging potholes and sharp rocks like a skier on a slalom course. We crossed a cattle guard where she carefully steered slightly to the side of it.

"Why did you steer to the right when we crossed the cattle guard?"

"They welded the tie rods to the top of the crossmembers. If you hit the ends of the rods, you can puncture a tire."

"Why don't they weld them to the bottom of the rails?"

Jill grinned. "I suppose tire repair provides a steady tourist income for the local garages."

I sighed. "Ranch knowledge."

"Common sense."

"Only if you live on a ranch."

She turned her head and smiled. "City kids have different senses."

Megan met us at the hitching post with Weed and Lash already saddled. "Where are you going today?"

"North," I replied, not wanting to reveal our plans.

"The boys will treat you well."

I patted Weed's neck. "Yeah, Weed and I are BFFs now."

Megan looked at me, then Jill. "All right, Jill. Who's taken over Doug's body?"

"Hey, I'm getting into riding," I protested.

Shaking her head, Jill sighed. "He's delusional today."

Megan smiled. "Did you find someone to deliver hay?"

"Yes, thanks for the suggestion."

* * *

I spotted the orange football helmet through the trees as we passed Dead Horse Ranch State Park. Gunner crossed the river and rode up to us.

"Where are we going today?" he asked.

Jill reined Lash to a stop. "I'm afraid it might be dangerous today. Can you wait here for us?"

Gunner looked disappointed but nodded. "I can help if you get scared."

Jill smiled at him. "I'll find you if I get scared. Okay?"

Gunner nodded.

* * *

Wood smoke rose from the Lazy L cook shack and drifted lazily into the windless sky. The pleasant aromas of burning pine and fried bacon hung in the air.

"We ate only two hours ago, and the smell of bacon already makes my mouth water," I said as Jill rode to the barn.

Rose and Anna were tightening cinches and adjusting stirrups on a string of horses while the tourist family we'd seen the day before, watched from the porch of the cook shack. Butch loaded saddlebags on a pair of pack horses. I tied Weed's reins to a hitching post and followed Jill to the horses. She patted the neck of a spotted gray horse with a buck-pack frame on his back. The horse turned its head, and I'd swear he was smiling at her. His gaze turned to me and went from happy to evil. He stuck out his tongue as if he was mocking me.

"Yeah," I said, "I feel the same about you."

Jill walked among the horses, patting them and making reassuring noises while she looked at the hoofprints they'd made in the dry soil. Butch eyed her with suspicion but drifted away, apparently disinterested in our presence. She stopped when she got to Anna who was tightening the saddle cinch on a sorrel with a white front leg. "You've got bar shoes on him."

"Jess has soft heels, so the farrier chose straight bar shoes for him."

"All the other horses have regular shoes."

Anna nodded. "Yep, just Jess needs bar shoes."

Jess snorted and Rose patted his neck. "He's a good horse who knows the trails. I'm sure he could find his way back to the barn from anywhere in the county."

Jill raised her eyebrows. "In the dark?"

"Daylight or night, I'm sure he could navigate his way home."

Butch drifted farther away and seemed very interested in the Appaloosa farthest from us while Rose checked the saddles and bridles of the other horses.

I approached Anna, who stepped back after checking the last cinch. "I assume you and Butch have access to the horses all day and night."

"We keep the barn locked to keep the guests out. Only Rose, Theresa, Butch, Robyn, and I have keys."

"I assume you weren't out riding Monday night."

Anna laughed. "I'm always in bed by eight because I have to be back here before five to light the wood stove, make pancake batter, and fry bacon."

Rose joined us, patting Jess's neck.

"Where were you Monday night, Rose?"

"Theresa and I went to a movie in town."

Jill nodded at me, gesturing for me to step away from Rose and Anna. "So, it was either Butch or Robyn who rode Jess out to Tuzigoot."

I walked back to the two women and asked, "Could you tell if someone had the horses out Monday night?"

Rose glanced at Butch who was suddenly interested in the length of the stirrups on a saddle. "I wondered about that. Jess and Wesley were dusty on Tuesday morning, and I'd brushed them down after our Monday evening trail ride."

Jill looked over Jess's saddle. "Butch, did you take a couple horses out Monday night?"

Butch was on the horse before Jill finished the question. He spurred the Appaloosa and slapped its hindquarters with the reins. The horse reared back, then was off like a rocket.

The commotion made the other horses nervous, and they danced around. Anna handed Jess's reins to Jill. "Here. Jess is faster."

Jill stepped into the stirrups and was in the saddle before I could protest. Looking back, she spurred Jess. "Grab a horse, Doug."

Anna let loose with a string of profanity as she tried to calm the other horses, making the watching teens laugh. "Doug, take Lightning," she said, handing me a black horse's reins.

I hesitated. "I don't think Lightning would be a good choice for me. Do you have a docile, old horse? Maybe one named Slowpoke?"

"Damn it, get your ass in the saddle. Jill can't handle Butch alone."

I was struggling to get my boot into Lightning's stirrup when Anna slapped my butt like she was urging on a hesitant horse.

I swatted her hand. "Stop that!"

She put her shoulder against my butt and pushed upward. "Damned city kids can't get their butts into a saddle. Get up there!"

I threw my leg across the saddle and was still trying to get my right toe into the stirrup when I heard Anna smack Lightning's rear. I grabbed the saddle horn to keep myself upright as Lightning took off after Jill at a gallop. "Geez, I haven't even got my boots in the stirrups!"

Lightning was apparently chasing Jill without further encouragement from me. With the reins in my right hand and the saddle horn in my left, we galloped across the open desert. Within moments, my new cowboy hat blew off. I didn't look back. I recalled Jill's encouragement from our trail rides on the South Dakota ranch and tried to get in rhythm with Lightning's motion. At some point, the adrenaline eased, and I stopped fighting Lightning, and *rode* him. I looked up and saw Jill far ahead of me, Jess kicking up dust about thirty yards behind Butch and Blossom. We'd crossed open desert, apparently headed for the Verde River and the cottonwood trees lining its banks.

As a bush slapped my knee and calf, I heard a ripping sound and felt a searing pain. Lightning didn't slow, but I looked down and saw that my pants' leg was shredded, with blood dripping from the strips of denim. "Shit. Was that cat's claw or Spanish sword?" I asked Lightning, who ignored me. "I suppose that's why cowboys wear chaps."

We thundered ahead, the cottonwood trees getting closer. Butch slowed and turned his horse into a gap through the trees. Jill closed to within a few yards of him before disappearing behind the cottonwood leaves. Lightning went on at a full gallop despite me tugging on his reins. "Whoa! Whoa!" I screamed as we approached the tree line.

Lightning slowed a bit before turning onto a trail through the branches. Being focused on staying in the saddle, I didn't see the low branch that slapped my forehead. I reeled in the saddle, bending back and feeling my boots strain against the stirrups. I was suddenly struck by fear that I'd fall off with one foot tangled in a stirrup, then be dragged along as Lightning galloped down the riverbed.

Apparently sensing my dilemma, Lightning slowed, and I regained my control of the reins and kept my seat in the saddle. At that moment, I felt like I'd cheated death. My celebration was short-lived when I heard a gunshot, followed by two more. They weren't the crisp barks of Jill's 9mm Glock, but more a roar of some larger caliber gun. I spurred Lightning. "C'mon, Butch is shooting."

At something less than a gallop, Lightning followed a trail along the river, doing a slalom around the cottonwoods. I caught glimpses of Butch and Jill through the trees where the river turned. The two of them were about fifty yards ahead of me, and it appeared Jill was only a horse length or two behind Butch.

Another shot rang out and my stomach clenched. I'd seen enough old westerns to believe it was incredibly hard to shoot from a horse, and even harder to hit someone behind you who was also on a horse, but that was based on Roy Rogers, who *never* got shot as he chased bad guys who were shooting over their shoulders.

"It's the lucky shot that gets you," I said to Lightning as we crossed a shallow portion of river, then rode up the other bank and onto a parallel trail. We came out of the cottonwoods and were back into the desert. I tried to rein Lightning back to the river trail, but he bounded ahead, determined to take his own route. I tried to discern what he was thinking, which immediately seemed stupid until I realized Lightning was cutting across a finger of land that shortened our route to Jill and Butch's path.

Another gunshot rang out, giving me hope that Jill was unharmed and still in pursuit. *Butch's old six-shooter has got to be about empty*, I thought as we slowed to take a trail leading back to the river.

I was focused on the trees we were passing. Something buzzed through the leaves above my head a fraction of a second before I heard the report of Butch's pistol. A second later, four quick shots rang out from Jill's pistol, probably in rhythm with Jess' gallop. I looked up and realized I was ahead of Butch and Jill.

Seeing me, Butch reined Blossom in and tried to urge him up the bank. His gun was pointed at me. I was close enough to hear the click as his hammer fell on a spent cartridge. A split second later, Blossom reared. With Butch aiming his shot at me, he was twisted, off balance, and unprepared for the horse's reaction. He flew out of the saddle, his arms and legs windmilling as he tumbled to the ground. Jill was a second behind, pulling on Jess' reins, trying to stop short of Butch, who slid headfirst down the muddy riverbank.

Butch yelled out in pain before I registered the sound of the rattlesnake. Jill was off Jess without effort, her Glock in her hand. She approached Butch with the gun extended, then stopped and fired five quick shots.

A dark rope seemed to fly into the air. Butch was crab-walking backwards. When he grabbed his arm I thought, *Jill shot him*.

"Don't shoot!" I yelled. "He's down! Hold your fire!"

Jill aimed toward Butch, then fired two more shots as Lightning and I crossed the river.

Lowering her gun, Jill put her hand up, "Stay back, Doug. I think I killed the rattlesnake. Give me a second to make sure it's dead and there's not another one."

Butch was writhing in the muddy river bottom, holding his forearm. "Dammit, I'm snake bit! Get me out of here!"

Lightning danced nervously in the shallow river as I tried to stay in the saddle and determine where the snake was. Seeing Butch's gun near his hand, I pulled my feet free of the stirrups, intending to nimbly hop from the saddle and kick the gun out of his reach. Lightning took one step to the side as I slid down, pushing me off my feet. Stumbling, I flopped backwards into the river, the green water flowing around me as I flailed.

Standing at Butch's feet with her gun at her side, Jill kicked the dead rattlesnake. "Doug, quit fooling around and dial 911. Butch needs an ambulance." The rattlesnake had several bullet holes in its six-foot length. Hitting a writhing rattlesnake multiple times was an amazing feat, reflecting Jill's superb marksmanship.

Shaking the water from my hands, I stepped onto the riverbank. "I'm not fooling around. It was that damned horse." After satisfying myself that the snake next to Butch was still dead, I pulled the cell phone out of my pocket, dialed 911, and told the dispatcher we needed an ambulance.

"Where are you located?"

A bit dazed from the head knock and my tumble into the river, I looked around. "Where are we?"

"We're nearly back to Tuzigoot." Looking closely at me for the first time, Jill paused. "What happened to your forehead?"

I touched it and felt sticky blood, bark particles…and pain. "Umm, there was a low hanging branch."

Butch moaned. "I'm snake bit and you're worried about his bumped forehead?"

Seeing a rise ahead of us, I replied to the dispatcher, "We're in the riverbed next to the Tuzigoot access road."

* * *

With his left hand clamped on his right forearm, Butch leaned on his elbow, then sat up. "Damn, my heart is pounding, and I can feel the venom going up my arm. Cut the snake bite and let me suck the venom out."

Jill holstered her Glock and knelt down, looking at Butch's forearm. "They've learned that sucking out venom isn't effective."

"So, you're just going to stand there and let me die?"

"There's an ambulance coming out of Cottonwood," I said, leading Lightning toward them, then tying his reins to a branch.

Edging closer to Butch, Jill nodded toward his arm. "Roll up your shirt sleeve and let me look at the snake bite."

Butch released his grip on his arm, unbuttoned his cuff, and rolled up the sleeve. From behind him, I could see the two marks made by the rattlesnake's fangs and the tiny trickle of blood from each hole. "Your arm looks bad, Butch."

With a look of terror, Butch's eyes went wide. He missed Jill's glare at me and her headshake. "Am I going to make it?" he asked.

"It's hard to say. I hope Cottonwood has a hospital with antivenom. Otherwise, they'll have to airlift you to Phoenix or Flagstaff. *If it's not too late…*"

Butch's face lost its color, and he studied the bite mark. "Sonofabitch! All this because of that stupid kid and his grapes."

I knelt. "What about the grapes?"

I heard pounding hoofbeats and saw an orange helmet approaching on the riverbank.

Oblivious to Gunner's approach, Butch said, "Robyn's kid has all kinds of big ideas about making the ranch into the next Napa Valley. Carlton wants more, or all of, the water rights to irrigate his damned grape vines. Theresa is willing to go along with him because the vineyard is more profitable than the damned ranch. Besides, he does all the work in the vineyard, and Theresa wouldn't have to operate the dude ranch if they converted everything to vineyard. She could just collect vineyard profits and party."

Gunner and Mojo crashed through the cottonwoods and stopped next to Jill. Gunner looked at us, then fixed on Jill. "You okay, ma'am?"

Jill nodded and patted Mojo. "I'm fine."

Gunner dismounted and stood next to Jill. "I heard shooting. I thought someone got hit." He looked at Butch, who was clutching his snake bite. "Did you shoot his arm?"

"No, I shot the rattlesnake that bit Butch."

Gunner nodded as a siren stopped on the Tuzigoot access road, about a hundred yards away. Rob Henderson stepped out of his unmarked car, the red and blue lights still pulsing.

"Is that the ambulance?" Butch asked, looking over his shoulder.

"That's a county cop. I imagine it takes a while for volunteer firemen to reach the station and fire up the ambulance." I paused, then knelt next to Butch. "What's the big deal if the kid uses more water on the grape vines?"

"Robyn has barely enough water for hay and pasture as it is. Al had a lawyer draw up a new will that leaves Robyn the house but splits the ranch and water rights between the two kids."

"Again, so what?"

Rob Henderson trotted down to the river bottom, his cowboy boots slipping on the muddy riverbank. Holding up his arm, Butch looked at him. "Where's the damned ambulance? I'm dying of a snake bite."

Putting up my hand, I cut off Henderson, who was probably going to reassure Butch that rattlesnake bites weren't usually fatal. "So what?"

"Everything goes to Robyn if Al dies before that revised will is recorded. With Al dead, Robyn owns the entire ranch and water and she's talking to a guy from Phoenix who wants to develop the ranch land. He's willing to pay her millions."

"But the two kids own the ranch and water rights," I said.

"Robyn never signed the new deed. She gets everything now that Al's dead."

Henderson covered his face with his hand, hiding his smile. Our discussion with Butch was marginally legal. He wasn't under arrest, so I hadn't Mirandized him. But Butch's supposition about impending death made our "interview" somewhat questionable. Deathbed confessions are solid gold in a court, but Butch's life *probably* wasn't in danger.

"Al had to die before she was forced to sign the new deed. This way, she's the sole beneficiary of his estate." Butch gasped and looked at the snakebite again as a distant siren wailed. "Where's the ambulance? Is it close?"

"What did Robyn plan to do with the millions she was going to get from the ranch sale?"

"We were moving to Panama. Robyn did some online research and found a community of Americans there. With three million dollars in the bank, we could afford a palace with servants. We'd be in hog heaven."

"You and Robyn were going to Panama?"

"Yeah, but you two screwed that up by nosing around the horses. That damned bar horseshoe was it." Butch looked up at Jill. "If you hadn't tied that to Jess, Robyn would've sold the ranch, and we would've been in Panama before anyone knew what had happened."

Henderson continued to watch without intervention as more sirens neared the river. I picked up Butch's Colt pistol and opened the cylinder. There were traces of red wax on the cylinder. "We found traces of red wax in Al's wound. I assume it's the same red wax you use to entertain the guests at the ranch shooting gallery. You let the guests shoot your Colt .45 using primers and wax bullets. There was wax residue from your gun on the bullet that killed Al."

"Aw shit. The vultures were supposed to pick Al's body clean. No one was ever supposed to find him on the Marsh Trail. I mean, who the hell walks three miles to take a picture of cattails? Right?"

I heard the sirens die as the ambulance parked behind Henderson's car. Handcuffs jangled behind me, then Henderson stepped forward. "Butch Compton, I'm arresting you for the murder of Al Tedeschi. You have the right to remain silent…"

"Hey, I'm dying here! You can't arrest me. I have to get a snake bite antidote."

"You'll get that at the hospital, but you'll be handcuffed to the bed, and we'll put you in jail when the doctor releases you."

Butch was frantic. "NO! Those rangers said I was going to die. They tricked me."

I shook my head. "*You* said you were going to die. I didn't dispute that opinion."

Jill and Henderson helped Butch to his feet and Henderson handcuffed him as he recited the rest of the Miranda warning.

Chapter 17

Rob Henderson took a deep swallow of beer, then smiled. He looked at me as we sat in the 45-70 saloon. "It's going to be hard to wear your new Stetson with those butterfly strips on your forehead."

Reflexively, I touched the cut the doctor had cleaned and closed in the emergency room. "Yeah, I won't be wearing a hat or cap for a while."

Jill leaned close to Henderson and added, "We had to buy some 'relaxed fit' jeans, too. His other pants were too snug over the stitches in his thigh."

"Yeah, I figured anything that would rip open his jeans wasn't going to leave the skin underneath unscathed." Rob glanced at my leg. "That's why cowboys wear chaps. There are plants and cacti in the desert that'll rip you to shreds."

I lifted my Diet Coke to him. "I'll keep that in mind the next time I go galloping across the desert."

Rob chuckled and shook his head. "You two are quite a pair. Jill, you're smart, and Doug's…got street smarts and experience."

I slid my glass closer to me and frowned. "I'm smart, too."

Henderson smiled. "Jill, why do you put up with him?"

She laughed. "He's good in bed."

Henderson was halfway through a swallow of beer. He choked, then covered his mouth with a napkin as he coughed. When he caught his breath, he pointed his finger at Jill. "I've never heard a woman say that."

Smiling, Jill took a sip of beer. "He also cooks and cleans."

Henderson slapped his hand on the table, then shook his head. "And you're just taking all this, Fletcher?"

I shrugged. "It's hard to argue with the truth."

Jill leaned close and made sure no one was listening. "What's the deal with the ranch deeds? Does Robyn really own it all because she hasn't signed the new deed?"

Rob shook his head. "Her name was never on the ranch deed. I went to the county recorder and the ranch was deeded to Al by his father. Robyn's name was never added to the deed after they married. Al didn't need her signature when he transferred the ranch to Theresa and Carlton."

"She didn't know that?" I asked.

"Apparently not. Al filed the revised property deed that makes the two kids co-owners of the ranch and water rights. Al's will grants Robyn half his remaining estate *except* that a murderer can't benefit from the death of the person she killed. So, she can't inherit anything and any life insurance policies naming her as the beneficiary are void."

Jill blew out a breath. "It could take years for Robyn's trial and appeals to work their way through the courts. Are the estate and insurance in limbo until her last appeal is exhausted?"

Henderson smiled. "There's a workaround. Robyn doesn't have to be convicted to be excluded from the estate. A judge can determine that she was the killer based on a simple preponderance of evidence. That's a much lower standard than is required to convict her in criminal court. Once that ruling is made, the kids split the estate."

Nodding, Jill smiled. "I like that result."

"Win, lose, or draw, Robyn isn't going to enjoy the ranch or fancy house. Even if she's acquitted in the criminal case, all she gets are her clothes, car, and jewelry."

I smiled. "Al was smarter than we realized."

"By the way, the Sedona newspaper interviewed the sheriff, and that led to calls from Phoenix and beyond. The story is going to break tomorrow, so you should let your bosses know what's coming."

"What did he tell the newspaper?"

Henderson shook his head. "He's political, so he told them his department solved the murder, then arrested Butch and the victim's wife. He did mention the Park Service investigators who assisted with the investigation."

I held up my Diet Coke and touched the glass to the rim of Henderson's beer mug. "Perfect. We should be able to make a clean getaway without facing any cameras."

Jill shook her head. "It's just as well, I don't know how Doug could've worn the Smokey Bear hat and uniform pants over his stitches."

"Yeah, about that; the Yavapai County Attorney would like to talk to you about Butch's confession. Butch's attorney is arguing he was interviewed under duress, with Butch believing he was coerced and under the assumption he was dying."

"There are three witnesses who heard him offer it voluntarily."

Henderson nodded. "I expect Butch's attorney will be able to negotiate a deal that keeps him off death row in return for his testimony against Robyn Tedeschi. Arizona hasn't executed a woman in a century, but she might be on death row a long time while all her appeals are exhausted."

"What happens to the ranch? Are Theresa and Carlton planning to continue to operate the dude ranch and winery?" Jill asked.

"They decided it would make a great boutique ranch with wine and trail rides. The ranch operation will be smaller, but they'll expand the vineyard using the ranch water rights and quadruple their weekly guest charge. They'll get a whole new clientele who are willing to pay for a combination vineyard, wine tasting, and cowboy experience." After a second of thought, Henderson added, "You might've contributed to the prosperity of the local vineyards, too."

"How so?" Jill asked.

"Theresa said she had a call from Jerry and Paulette about forming a cooperative to explore ways to secure more water for the vineyards. There's a woman flying in from Texas who's going to talk to a group of the winemakers about some sort of computer thing she does to manage water rights."

Shaking her head, Jill took a sip of beer. "You've got to love an entrepreneur."

"Are you talking about the winemakers or Geraldine Holland?" I asked.

"Maybe both." Jill's phone trilled and she looked at the screen. She mouthed, "Liz," then stepped outside.

"You guys really pulled a rabbit out of a hat with this investigation," Henderson said. "I suspected Robyn was behind the murder, but I had no leads. If not for you and Jill, it'd be a cold case."

"You're welcome."

"And you're okay with the sheriff only citing your assistance?"

"I never want to stand in front of a news camera again. My bosses know what we did. That's all I need."

Jill walked back inside and set her phone on the table. "Liz says our godson is being baptized Sunday. She expects us to be there, wearing decent clothes and smiles."

I nodded. "Sounds like a plan."

"They're taking pictures after the baptism. "You'll have to suck in your gut and make sure your zipper is up."

Henderson laughed and lifted his glass to me. "You must be really good in bed."

Jill squeezed my hand. "He's a keeper."

Chapter 18

We drove to Flagstaff Sunday morning, meeting Jamie and Liz at the church. Jill took Noah from Liz. Jamie and I stepped outside.

Jamie stared at the distant mountains. "It sounds like you made a solid arrest in Cottonwood."

"A lot of pieces came together at the last second."

"I talked to Rob Henderson," Jamie said, smiling.

"What did Rob tell you?"

Jamie looked into the distance. "I guess you'll have to figure out how to keep your butt in a saddle."

"The horse ran under a low branch."

Jamie studied the butterfly dressings holding the cut on my forehead closed. "Most people know enough to duck when that happens."

"I was distracted."

Cocking his head, he stared at my forehead. "The butterfly bandages will be interesting in the baptism pictures." He paused. "Jill said you're wearing jeans because your dress pants won't fit over the stitches in your leg."

I decided to change the topic. "You're unusually chatty today."

"Sometimes I don't have anything to say. Today I have ammo to needle you."

"Are you nervous?"

"This whole parenting thing is new to me. So yes, I'm nervous."

"Jill is sad we won't have children."

"Last night I was ready to send Noah home with you. He's got his days and nights mixed up. None of us are getting enough sleep."

We watched the last few people walk into the church. "I think it's time to go in."

The ushers led us to the front row. Noah slept through much of the early service, waking when a hymn was sung, and happy about the music. He was still smiling when the minister called us to the altar and baptismal font. After a short introduction, Liz handed the baby to the minister. Noah liked the minister's soft voice, right up to the point when the baptismal water was dabbed on his forehead. He started crying and was quickly handed back to Liz after he was blessed.

* * *

We had lunch with Liz, Jamie, and Noah at the Stagecoach restaurant. Noah was quiet through most of the meal. We answered questions about the investigation, and I got kidded about my horsemanship, or lack thereof, my bandaged forehead, and limp. After lunch, we stood awkwardly on the sidewalk. Jill cuddled Noah and kissed his forehead.

"I guess we have to go back to Phoenix and catch a flight," I said, shaking Jamie's hand.

Liz's eyes were tear-filled. "I don't know when we'll see you again."

Jill hugged her, then hugged Jamie. "We'll be back for Noah's first birthday party."

I raised my eyebrows. "We will?"

Jill smiled and I knew there was no point in arguing.

We were barely out of Flagstaff when Jill leaned across the seat and picked up my hand. "I feel bad that we'll never have a child, but…kids are a lot of work."

I squeezed her hand. "I love you, kids or not."

Jill's phone trilled and she looked at the caller ID. "Besides, we have our parents and Chet to take care of." She touched the phone and held it to her ear. "Hi, Ronnie. How are things in South Dakota?"

Chapter 19

After opening two beers, Matt led me onto their patio. He closed the sliding door and motioned for me to sit in a chaise lounge by a small table. "We need to talk."

"Uh oh," I replied. "That's about as ominous an opening line as, 'I love you but…'"

"I got a call from the head of the Park Service after we spoke this afternoon. He's uncomfortable having you and Jill on my payroll as law enforcement rangers when you're getting investigative assignments all over the western U.S. He's going to reassign you to the Park Service Investigative Bureau."

I nodded. "I figured that was coming. Where's our new assignment and is the Park Service paying for our relocation?"

"I argued that it really doesn't matter where you are located as long as you have access to an airport and a computer."

Shaking my head, I asked, "What happens if we decline?"

Matt looked at me earnestly. "Why decline? You're doing what you like to do.

You can stay in Port Aransas if you want to. You've got a great reputation and support from the highest levels of the Park Service. The only change is that your salaries and travel expenses won't come out of my budget." Matt paused to make sure Jill wasn't listening. "I signed the expense voucher for the hay purchase, but the auditors may kick that back."

"We could've listed it as payment for a guide service."

Matt pinched the bridge of his nose. "No, falsifying a voucher is grounds for termination. Just be aware that you may have to write a check for the hay." Mulling his words, Matt sipped his beer. "I've enjoyed being your boss. You've brought an element of excitement to my sometimes-mundane work regimen...even if I cringe when I sign your expense vouchers."

"You're more than my boss, Matt. You and Mandy are our closest friends."

Matt looked away, trying to hide his misty eyes. "That won't change no matter what happens. Jill is like Mandy's tomboy sister. She's never been closer to anyone and sometimes I think she likes Jill better than me." Matt glanced at the patio door. "Jill should be storming out as soon as Mandy breaks the news to her."

The patio door slid open and thumped hard against the stops. Jill marched up to Matt's chair with a margarita in hand, spilling a little liquid with her abrupt stop. "Matt Mattson, what's this bullshit about us not working for you anymore?"

Explaining the details, Matt cushioned the blow as he had with me. "It's only a budgetary thing. Nothing else changes."

Jill sat on the edge of a chair and leaned her elbows on her thighs. "This isn't your idea?"

"The inspector general audited human resources. The auditor looked at your investigator titles and asked why you were assigned to Padre Island as law enforcement rangers. The question rose quickly through the bureaucracy, and someone realized you are the only investigators not assigned to the NPS Investigative Bureau. Now you are."

I wrapped my arm around Jill's slender waist. "Matt says we can stay in Texas as long as we have computer and airport access."

Looking down at her margarita, Jill contemplated that option. "If we're not assigned as rangers, what are we supposed to do between assignments?"

"I spoke with Jack Pardee, the director of the NPSIB. He's got dozens of open cases that could benefit from a fresh look. A lot of them are disappearances that are categorized as lost hikers. Others are unsolved assaults and various other major crimes. He wants you to comb through the case files to see if your fresh perspective will catch something missed in the original investigations.”

Trying to sound upbeat, I said, “That sounds interesting.”

Jill wrinkled her nose. “Hell, I thought I would hit the law enforcement ranger mandatory retirement age, then switch over to being an interpretive ranger. I’ve always enjoyed touring school groups around. Grade school kids are like little sponges.”

Matt reached out and took Jill’s hand. “Jill, you can still do that. I’ll hire you in a second.”

Mandy announced that supper was ready, and we all walked into the dining room as Mandy set a smoked brisket dripping with barbecue sauce on the table. “Matt, be a dear and make sure everyone’s got something to drink while I fetch the cornbread,” she drawled with a voice as sweet as honey.

Jill looked tired as she sat. With supper on the table, Mandy abandoned her kitchen duties and switched to counselor mode. “It’ll be okay, Jill. You just won’t have to drive the pickup down the beach or yell at people smoking marijuana in the campground anymore.”

“I thought we’d be able to slip under the human resources radar a few more years. I like things the way they are. We’re stationed here, and the investigative assignments were like mini vacations. From now on, we'll probably be on the road more than we're here."

Matt topped off Jill's margarita and handed me another beer. "The major parks have law enforcement rangers who are capable of handling most of their crimes. The National Park Service Investigative Bureau people only get called out when a park can't handle the investigation. That's either because they don't have the resources, or when the investigation drags on and the in-park rangers hit a dead end."

Mandy passed a platter of cornbread squares. "Let's talk about something more upbeat. Tell me about your godson."

Jill bragged about Noah for half an hour and explained that we'd be splitting our vacations between South Dakota and Flagstaff.

When Jill paused, Mandy jumped up and ducked into the other room. "I almost forgot," she said, handing Jill a sheet of paper. "There's a house around the corner that just went up for sale. Are you still thinking about buying something here?"

After reading the realtor's brochure, Jill handed it to me. "We've talked about a number of options including finding a place with a few acres for horses."

I read the listing, then handed it back to Jill. "I think we should look at this place. Having horses may not be a good fit if we're going to be rushing off on investigations. Besides, we already know we like our neighbors."

Jill's mood didn't brighten despite Mandy's efforts and a couple margaritas. On the drive home she turned to me and said, "Let's look at the house next to Mandy and Matt. If it's as pretty as the brochure makes it sound. We could paint, move in immediately, then retire."

Her comment caught me off guard. "I'm all for looking at the house, but let's give this new arrangement some time. We may like it."

"You're a cop and being called to investigate tough cases is right up your alley. I feel like your sidekick, and frankly that's not as much fun. The thought of reviewing cold cases sounds as interesting as reading the dictionary. Besides, I find our jobs downright scary way too often."

"And I have a hard time seeing myself doing the crossword puzzle and sitting on the porch in a rocking chair."

"We could move to South Dakota."

"Do you really believe I'd be happy riding a horse across the Black Hills in blizzards?"

For the first time that evening, Jill smiled. "You can't see yourself riding a horse across the prairie any time soon?"

"Your dad said something about a 4-wheel ATV. If we ever move to Spearfish, I'd feel more comfortable with a motor under my butt than an unpredictable stallion."

"We don't own any stallions, and horses don't run out of gas in the middle of nowhere."

I reached over and squeezed her hand. "You're a smart investigator and a good interrogator. We're a good team. And, you've become a bit of an adrenaline junkie."

"You left out the part about me being a good shot."

"Does that mean you'll hang in there for a few months and give this arrangement a chance?"

"As long as we don't spend every week living out of a suitcase."

"It sounds like there are a bunch of open cold cases. It'll be fun to read the files and dig around. Technology is changing rapidly, and we may be able to solve some of them without leaving Texas."

"Like the DNA analysis in Florida."

"Yes, using forensic genealogy and searching the internet for people who were thought to be lost or missing, but really just made themselves disappear."

Jill shrugged. "It might be interesting."

"It's always interesting to dig into someone's old cases. Like Matt said, a fresh set of eyes can sometimes pick up on things the original investigator missed."

Chuckling, Jill said, "Like you looking for the ketchup in the refrigerator. You don't look at the obvious location, in the door."

Feeling the change in Jill's mood, I added, "Not being a cynical cop, your perspective might bring a different light to the investigation."

"Six months."

"What about six months?" I asked.

"We do this for six months, then we'll have a discussion about retirement or other options." Jill paused, then added. "If we're not scheduled to fill in as park law enforcement rangers, we'll be able to attend Noah's first birthday, and be in Spearfish with our parents for holidays."

"Oh boy," I said a little too sarcastically.

"A moment ago, you were trying to sell me on this new assignment. Now it's you who's not excited about the opportunities it offers."

"Let's talk about the house next to Matt and Mandy. I'd like to look at it."

Jill reached out and squeezed my hand. "I'd really like living close to Mandy. She offered to help me pick out artwork for the walls."

"What!" I said with feigned anger. "You and Mandy are already decorating the house?"

"You don't care how we decorate, do you?"

"I don't want any pink or purple rooms."

"I understand. Purple is so…dark. Maybe lilac or mauve would be better." She paused to check my reaction, which was close to nausea. "I'm kidding. But remember, pastels are *in* down here."

Sighing, I said, "Fine. Blues, yellows, and greens are acceptable. But not pink."

"Maybe I can decorate while you peruse the cold case files. You can call when you find something interesting or promising."

I nodded and smiled. Having worked cold cases in St. Paul, I knew they were addictive. There's no way Jill would be able to walk away after six months. And I was sure a house in Port Aransas would anchor us and delay discussion about retirement in the Black Hills for years.

The End

Other Dean Hovey mysteries from BWL Publishing Inc.

Doug Fletcher mysteries
Stolen Past
Washed Away
Devils Fall
Prairie Menace
Down River
Burnt Evidence
Gator Bait
Dead End Trail
(Coming in 2023) The Last Rodeo

Pine County Mysteries
Killer Secrets
Deadly Mixture
Fatal Business

Whistling Pines cozies
Whistling up a Ghost
Whistling Pirates
Whistling Bake Off

Dean Hovey is the award-winning and best-selling author of three mystery series. He uses his scientific background, extensive research, and a number of consultants to add reality and depth to his stories. One reader said his characters are like people he'd like to invite over for a beer and discussion.

Hovey's Fletcher mysteries follow U.S. National Park Service investigators Doug and Jill Fletcher as they solve crimes in a series of parks and monuments, sometimes with a bit of humor and often with their evolving relationship. The Whistling Pines mysteries are humorous cozies set in a northern Minnesota senior residence, following Peter Rogers, the Whistling Pines recreation director, as he stumbles through the investigation of murders in his small town. The Pine County mystery series follows sheriff's deputies Pam Ryan and C.J. Jensen as they investigate murders in east-central Minnesota, dealing with crimes, criminals and their own personal dilemmas.

Dean and his wife split their year between northern Minnesota and Arizona.